WITHOUT MERIT

WITHOUT MERIT

A Novel

COLLEEN HOOVER

THORNDIKE PRESS
A part of Gale, a Cengage Company

Copyright © 2017 by Colleen Hoover.
Thorndike Press, a part of Gale, a Cengage Company.

Thorndike Press® Large Print Softcover Romance and Women's Fiction.
The text of this Large Print edition is unabridged.
Other aspects of the book may vary from the original edition.
Set in 16 pt. Plantin.

LIBRARY OF CONGRESS CIP DATA ON FILE.
CATALOGUING IN PUBLICATION FOR THIS BOOK
IS AVAILABLE FROM THE LIBRARY OF CONGRESS.

ISBN-13: 978-1-4328-9980-6 (softcover alk. paper)

Published in 2022 by arrangement with Atria Books, a Division of Simon & Schuster, Inc.

Printed in the United States of America
2 3 4 5 6   26 25 24 23 22

This book is for Cale Hoover. Because I'm your mother and I love you, I sometimes have an overwhelming urge to wrap you in a bubble and protect you from the world. But I also have an overwhelming urge to wrap the world in a bubble and protect it from you. Because you're going to turn it on its head someday.

I can't freaking wait.

CHAPTER ONE

I have an impressive collection of trophies that I did not win.

Most of them I purchased from thrift stores or garage sales. Two of them I got from my father for my seventeenth birthday. Only one of them I stole.

My stolen trophy is probably my least favorite one. I took it from Drew Waldrup's bedroom right after he broke up with me. We had been dating two months and it was the first time I allowed him to put his hand all the way up my shirt. I was thinking about how nice it felt, when he looked down at me and said, "I don't think I want to date you anymore, Merit."

There I was, enjoying his hand on my boob, and all the while he was thinking of how he never wanted his hand on my boob again. I stoically slid out from under him and stood up. After straightening out my shirt, I walked over to his bookshelf and snatched the biggest trophy he had. He never said a word. I figured if he dumped me with his hand up my shirt, I should at least get a trophy for it.

That district championship football trophy was actually the start of my collection. From there, I'd pick up random trophies from garage sales or thrift shops any time something shitty happened.

Fail my driving test? First place in shot put.

Don't get asked to junior prom? All-star cast in one-act play.

My father proposes to his mistress? Little league team champions.

It's been two years since I stole that first trophy. I have twelve trophies now, although far more than twelve shitty things have happened to me since Drew Waldrup broke up with me. But it's surprisingly difficult to find unwanted trophies. Which is why I'm here at a local antiques shop, eyeing the seventh place pageant trophy I've been wanting since I first saw it six months ago. It's about a foot and a half tall and it's from a 1972 Dallas pageant called Boots and Beauties.

I like it because of the ridiculous pageant title, but I love it because of the gold-plated woman on top of the trophy. She's wearing a ball gown, a tiara, and a pair of boots with spurs. Everything about it is absurd. Especially the eighty-five-dollar price tag. But I've been saving up for it since I first laid eyes on it and I finally have enough money to purchase it.

I grab the trophy and turn to walk toward the register when I notice a guy on the second floor of the antiques store. He's leaning over the railing, staring at me. His chin is resting casually in one of his hands like he's been in that position for a while. He smiles as soon as we make eye contact.

I smile back, which is a bit out of character for me. I'm not the type to flirt and I'm definitely not the type to know how to reciprocate when someone flirts with me. But his smile is pleasant and he isn't even on the same floor as me, so I don't feel threatened by potential embarrassment.

"What are you doing?" he calls out.

Naturally, I look over my shoulder to see if he's directing his comment at me. Maybe the guy isn't looking at me and he's talking to someone behind me. But other than a mother who braved the antiques store with her little boy, there isn't anyone else in my vicinity. And the woman and her child are both facing the opposite direction, so he must be referring to me.

I look back up at him and he's still looking down at me with that same smile. "I'm buying a trophy!"

I think I might like his smile, but he's a little too far away for me to tell if I'd be attracted to him. His confidence is attractive in itself. He has dark hair and it's a bit choppy and spastic but I'm not judging because I don't think I've brushed my own hair since yesterday morning. He's wearing a gray hoodie with the sleeves shoved above his elbows. Tattoos cover the arm his chin is resting on, but I can't make them out from down here. From here, he looks a little too young and a little too tattooed to be browsing for antiques on a random weekday morning, but who am I to judge? I should be in school right now.

I turn around and pretend to shop, but I'm aware that he's watching me. I try to ignore it, but every now and then I'll glance back up at him to make sure he's still there. He is.

Maybe he works here and that's why he's lingering, but it wouldn't explain why he won't stop staring at me. If this is his idea of flirting, it's a strange way to flirt. But sadly, I'm attracted to unconventional and strange. So the entire time I browse the store I force myself to seem unaffected, when in reality, I'm very affected. I can feel his stare with every step I take. Stares shouldn't have weight, but knowing his eyes are on me makes my steps feel heavier. It even makes my stomach feel heavier.

I've already looked at everything in the store, but I don't want to check out yet and leave because I'm enjoying this game too much.

I attend a very small public school in a very small town. And when I say small, I'm being generous. There is an average of twenty kids in each grade. Not class. *Grade.*

My entire senior class consists of twenty-two students. Twelve girls and ten guys. Eight of those ten guys have been in class with me since I was five. That narrows the dating field quite a bit. It's hard to find someone attractive that you've spent almost every day of your life with since you were five years old.

But I have no idea who this guy is that's made me the center of his attention. Which means I'm already more attracted to him than any person in my entire school, simply because I don't know him.

I pause on an aisle that's clearly visible from where he's standing and I pretend to be interested in one of the signs displayed on the shelf. It's an old white sign with the

11

word SHAFT written on it and an arrow pointing to the right. It makes me laugh. Next to it is an old sign that looks to be from a gas station. It says LUBRICANT. It makes me wonder if someone placed the sexually suggestive signs together or if it was random. If I had enough money, I'd buy them and start a sexually suggestive sign collection for my bedroom. But my trophy habit is expensive enough.

The little boy who has been browsing the store with his mother is standing a couple of feet away from me now. He looks to be about four or five years old. The same age as my little brother, Moby. His mother has told him no less than ten times not to touch anything, but he picks up the glass pig sitting on the shelf in front of us. Why are kids so drawn to fragile things? His eyes are bright as he inspects it. I appreciate that his curiosity is more important to him than following his mother's orders. "Mom, can I have this?"

His mother is an aisle over digging through a rack of old magazines. She doesn't even turn around to look at what he's holding. She just says, "No."

The boy's eyes dim immediately and he frowns as he goes to set the pig back on the shelf. But his little hands fumble when he tries to set it down and the pig slips from his grasp, shattering at his feet.

"Don't move," I say to him, reaching him before his mother does. I bend down and start picking up the pieces.

His mother plucks him up and sets him a few feet away so that he's out of reach of the glass. "I told you not to touch anything, Nate!"

I glance over at the little boy and he's staring at the broken glass like he just lost his best friend. His mother presses her hand to her forehead like she's exhausted and frustrated, and then bends down and starts helping me pick up the pieces.

"He didn't do it," I say to her. "I'm the one who broke it."

The woman looks back at her little boy and her little boy looks at me like he doesn't know if this is a test. I wink at him before she turns back around and I say, "I didn't see him standing there. I bumped into him and dropped it."

She looks surprised, and maybe even a bit guilty for assuming her son did it. "Oh," she says. She continues to help me pick up the larger shards of glass. The man who was standing at the register when I walked in appears out of nowhere with a broom and a dustpan.

"I'll take it from here," he says. But then he points to a sign on the wall that reads YOU BREAK IT, YOU BUY IT.

The woman takes her little boy's hand and walks away. The little boy glances over his shoulder and smiles at me and it makes taking the blame so worth it. I return my attention to the man with the broom. "How much was it?"

"Forty-nine dollars. I'll only charge you thirty, though."

I sigh. I'm not so sure that little boy's smile is worth thirty dollars. I walk my pageant trophy back to its home and pluck a much cheaper, much less appealing trophy from the shelf. I take it to the register and pay for the shattered pig and my first place bowling trophy. When the man hands me the sack and my change, I head toward the door. Right when I go to push it open, I remember the guy who was watching me from the second-floor railing. I glance up before I walk out the door but he's no longer there. Somehow this makes me feel even heavier.

I walk out of the store and cross the street, heading for one of the tables near the fountain. I've lived in Hopkins County my whole life, but I rarely make it down to the square. I don't know why, because my love

14

for it was solidified when they put up the strange crosswalk signs. The signs display a picture of a man crossing the street, but his leg is lifted high in the air and it's exaggerated to the point that it could pass as a silly walk out of a Monty Python show.

There are also two bathrooms the city had installed a few years back. They're two glass structures that look like a tall cube of mirrors from the outside, but when you're inside the bathrooms you can see out. It's disturbing that a person can be sitting on the toilet doing their business while watching cars drive by. But I'm drawn to unusual things, so I'm one of the few who probably take pride in the strange bathrooms.

"Who's the trophy for?"

Speaking of being drawn to unusual things.

The guy from the antiques store is standing next to me now and I can say with complete certainty that he is most definitely attractive. His eyes are a unique shade of light blue, so they're the first thing to stand out. They seem out of sync with his olive skin and severely dark hair. I stare at his hair a moment. I'm not sure I've ever seen hair that color of black on someone with eyes that color of blue. It's a bit jarring. For me, anyway.

He's still smiling at me just like he was from the railing in the antiques store. It makes me wonder if he smiles all the time. I hope not. I like the thought that maybe he's smiling at me because he can't help it. He nudges his head toward the sack in my hand and I suddenly remember he asked me a question about the trophy.

"Oh. It's for me."

He tilts his head in amusement or wonder. I don't really know which one he's feeling, but I'm fine with either. "You collect trophies you didn't win?"

I nod and it makes him laugh a little, but it's a silent laugh. Almost like he wants to keep it to himself. He slides his hands in his back pockets. "Why aren't you in school right now?"

I didn't realize it was that obvious that I'm still in high school. I drop my sack on the table next to us and slip off my sandals. "It's a nice day. I didn't want to be locked in a classroom." I walk over to the concrete fountain that really isn't a fountain at all. It's a section of concrete, flat on the ground in the shape of a star. The water comes out of holes around the star and spits toward the center. I press my foot over one of the holes and wait for the water to reach me.

It's the last week of October, so it's too

cold for kids to be playing in the water like they usually are in the summer. But it isn't too cold to get my feet a little wet. I like it when the water hits the bottom of my feet. And since I can't afford to get a pedicure, it's the next best thing.

The guy watches me for a moment but honestly, I'm getting used to it. He's starting to feel like my own personal, slightly more attractive shadow. I don't look directly at him as he casually slips off his shoes. He stands next to me and presses one of his feet over the holes.

I glance at his arm now to get a closer look at the tattoos. I was right — they're only on his left arm. His right arm doesn't have a single visible tattoo on it. But the tattoos on his left arm aren't what I expected. They're random and unrelated and none of them connect. One of them is a tiny toaster with one slice of bread sticking out of it. It's on the outside of his wrist. I can see a safety pin near his elbow. The words, "Your turn, Doctor," are sprawled across his forearm. I drag my eyes up his arm and he's looking down at his feet now. I'm about to ask him his name when the water hits my foot unexpectedly. I laugh and step back and we both watch the spout of water shoot toward the center.

The water hits his foot next but he doesn't react to it. He just stares down at his feet until the water stops and moves on to the hole next to him. He lifts his eyes but when he looks at me this time, he isn't smiling. Something about the seriousness in his expression makes everything tighten inside my chest. When he opens his mouth to speak, I hang on to every word.

"Out of all the places we could be, we're right here. At the same time." His voice is laced with amusement, but his expression verges on bewildered. He shakes his head and steps closer to me. He reaches his tattooed arm up and slides his fingers down a strand of my hair that's come loose. The gesture is intimate and unexpected, kind of like this whole moment, but I'm more than okay with it. I want him to do it again, but his arm falls back to his side.

I can't think of a single instance where I've ever been looked at like he's looking at me right now. Like I fascinate him. I know we don't know each other at all and whatever this connection is between us will probably be ruined the moment we have our first real conversation. He'll probably be a douchebag or he'll think I'm weird and then it'll get awkward and we'll be more than happy to go our separate ways. That's how my interactions with guys usually go. But right now in this moment, knowing nothing about him other than the intensity in his expression, it allows me to imagine he's perfect. I pretend he's smart and respectful and funny and artistic. Because he would be all those things if he were the perfect guy. I'm content with imagining he possesses these qualities for as long as he's going to stand here in front of me.

He takes a step closer to me and it suddenly feels like I've swallowed his heart because I have all these extra beats in my chest. His eyes drop to my mouth and I'm certain he's about to kiss me. I hope he is. Which is odd because I've literally only spoken a couple of sentences to him but I want him to kiss me while I'm imagining him to be perfect, because that means his kiss would probably be perfect, too.

His fingers feather up my wrist but it feels more like he has both fists clasped tightly around my lungs. My chills chase his fingers up my arm until his hand is resting against my neck.

I don't know how I'm still standing with the unreliable legs I seem to have right now. My head is tilted back and his mouth is inches from mine, as if he's hesitating. He smiles and whispers, "You bury me."

I have no idea what those words mean, but I like them. And I like how his lips connect softly with mine right after he finishes saying whatever it was he just said. And I was right. It's perfect. So perfect, it feels like the old days in the movies when the male lead would press his hand against the woman's back and she would curve her body backward against the pressure of his kiss like the letter *C* while he pulls her against him. It's just like that.

He's pulling me to him when his tongue slides across my lips. And just like in the movies, my arms are dangling at my sides until I realize how much I want to be in this with him and finally begin to kiss him back. He tastes like mint ice cream and it's perfect because this moment ranks high on my scale of favorites, right up there with dessert. This is almost comical — this stranger, kissing me as if it were the last thing left on his bucket list. It makes me wonder what compelled him to do this.

Both of his hands move to hold my face now, like we have nowhere else to be today. He's not in a hurry with his kiss and he definitely doesn't care who sees this because we're in the middle of the town square and two people have already honked at us.

I wrap one of my arms around his neck

and decide I'll just let him continue for as long as he wants because I don't have anywhere to be right now. Even if I did, I'd cancel my plans in exchange for this.

Right when one of his hands slides through my hair, the water splashes beneath my feet. I squeal a little because it's unexpected. He laughs, but he doesn't stop kissing me. Now we're being soaked because my foot isn't covering the spout all the way, but neither of us cares. It just adds to the ridiculousness of this kiss.

The ringtone on his phone adds even more ridiculousness to the moment because of course we'd be interrupted right now. Of course. It was way too perfect.

He pulls back and the look in his eye is somehow satiated and starving at the same time. He pulls his phone out of his pocket and looks down at it. "Did you lose your phone or is this a joke?"

I shrug because I have no idea which part of this he thinks might be a joke. Me allowing him to kiss me? Someone calling him in the middle of said kiss? He laughs a little as he presses the phone against his ear. "Hello?"

The smile leaves his expression and now he just looks confused. "Who is this?" He waits a couple of seconds and then pulls the phone away from his ear and looks down at it. Then he looks up at me. "Seriously. Is this a prank?"

I don't know if he's talking to me or the person on the phone, so I shrug again. He puts the phone to his ear and takes a step away from me. "Who is this?" he repeats. He laughs nervously and grips the back of his neck. "But . . . you're standing right in front of me."

I can feel the color drain from my face at that sentence. All the color in my body — in this ridiculous moment with this random guy — pools at my feet, leaving me feeling like the second-rate carbon copy of Honor Voss. My twin sister. The girl who is obviously on the other end of that phone call.

I cover my face with my hand and turn around, grabbing my shoes and my sack. I hope I can put as much distance between us as possible before he figures out that the girl he just kissed isn't Honor.

I can't believe this is happening. I just kissed my sister's boyfriend.

I didn't do it on purpose, obviously. I had a feeling she had just recently started seeing someone because she's been gone a lot, but out of all the guys in the world, how was I supposed to know this particular guy was him? I continue to rush away but I can't get far enough before I hear him running after me. "Hey!" he calls out.

This is why he was watching me in the store. He thought I was her. It's why he asked why I wasn't in school, because if he knows Honor well enough to kiss her, he knows Honor would never skip school.

It all makes sense now. This wasn't some random connection between two strangers. This was him mistaking me for his girlfriend and me being a complete fool for not immediately realizing what was happening.

I feel his hand grip my elbow. I have no choice but to turn and face him because I need to make it clear that Honor can never find out about this. When our eyes meet, he's no longer looking at me like I fascinate him. He's staring at his phone and then me and then his phone and then, "I am so sorry," he says. "I thought you were . . ."

"You thought wrong," I snap, even though it was an honest mistake.

Honor and I are identical but if he knew my twin sister at all, he should know she would never be caught dead in public looking like I look right now. I'm not wearing makeup, my hair is a mess, and my clothes are left over from yesterday.

He slides his phone back in his pocket but it begins to ring again. When he pulls it out,

I can see Honor's name flashing across the screen. I grab his phone and swipe my finger across the screen. "Hey."

"Merit?" Honor laughs. "What's going on? Why are you with Sagan?"

Sagan? Even his name is perfect.

"I'm not. I just . . . bumped into him. He thought I was you but then you called and . . . let's just say he was confused." I say all this while staring directly at Sagan. He keeps his eyes locked on mine and doesn't even try to take the phone away from me.

Honor laughs again. "That's funny. I wish I could have seen his face."

"It was priceless," I deadpan. "But you should know to warn your boyfriend that you have an identical twin." I hand the phone back to Sagan. I back away a few steps and he's holding the phone in his hand, unable to take his eyes off me. "Do not repeat what just happened to her," I whisper. "To anyone. Ever."

He nods, albeit hesitantly. As soon as I have confirmation that he won't repeat this to Honor, I turn and walk away. Nothing could ever top this level of embarrassment. Nothing.

CHAPTER TWO

I am such a fool.

But God, it was so beautifully unexpected. His intensity caught me off guard but the second he kissed me I was a goner. He tasted like mint and he was so warm, and then the water was splashing us and it was a sensory overload that I wanted to be an overdose. I wanted it all. I wanted to feel everything. That unexpected kiss made me feel alive for the first time in . . . actually, I'm not sure I've ever felt that way.

Which is exactly why I didn't come to the realization that he thought he was kissing Honor. While that random kiss meant a lot to me, it was nothing new to him. He probably kisses Honor like that all the time.

Which is confusing, because he seemed to be . . . healthy. Not Honor's type, normally.

Speaking of Honor.

I turn on my blinker and reach for my phone on the second ring. It's odd that she's calling me. We never call each other. When I come to the stop sign, I answer it with a lazy, "Hey."

"Are you still with Sagan?" Honor asks.

I close my eyes and release a tiny bit of air. I don't have much to spare after that kiss back there. "No."

She sighs. "Weird. He's not answering his phone now. I'll try calling him back."

"Okay."

I'm about to hang up when she says, "Hey. Why aren't you in school right now?"

I sigh. "Wasn't feeling well so I left."

"Oh. Okay. See you tonight."

"Honor, wait," I say before she ends the call. "What's . . . is something wrong with Sagan?"

"What do you mean?"

"You know. Are you with him because . . . is he dying?"

It's quiet for a moment. But then I can hear the irritation in her voice when she says, "Jesus, Merit. Of course not. You can be a real bitch sometimes." The line goes dead. I look down at the phone.

I wasn't trying to insult her. I'm genuinely curious if that's why she's dating him. She hasn't had a single boyfriend with an average life span since she started dating Kirk at thirteen. She's still heartbroken over the

26

way that relationship left her feeling like she was choking on scar tissue.

Kirk was a nice farm boy. He drove a tractor, baled hay, knew how to flip an electrical breaker, and once fixed the transmission of a car that my father couldn't even fix himself.

About a month before we turned fifteen and two weeks after Honor lost her virginity to Kirk, his father found Kirk lying on the ground in the middle of their pasture, semiconscious and bleeding. Kirk had fallen off the tractor, which ran over him, injuring his right arm. Although the injury wasn't life-threatening, while receiving treatment for the injury, the erudite doctor sought answers as to why Kirk might have fallen off the tractor to begin with. Turns out, Kirk had suffered a seizure as the result of a tumor that had been growing in his brain.

"Possibly since infancy," said the doctor.

Kirk lived three more months. The entire three months he lived, my sister rarely left his side. Honor was the first and last girl he loved, and the last person Kirk saw before taking his final breath.

Honor developed an unhealthy affliction as a result of her first love dying from a tumor that had been growing in his brain, possibly since infancy. Honor found it almost impossible to love any boy after who was of average health and normal life span. She spends most days and nights in online chat rooms for the terminally ill, falling madly in love with boys who have an average life expectancy of six months or less. Although our town is a bit too small to provide Honor with an ample supply of ailing suitors, Dallas is less than a two-hour drive away. With the number of hospitals devoted to terminal illnesses, at least two boys have been within driving distance to Honor. During their last few weeks on earth, Honor spent their remaining days by their sides, determined to be the last person they saw and the last girl they loved before taking their final breaths.

Because of her obsession with being loved eternally by the terminally ill, I'm curious what has drawn her to this Sagan guy. Based on her relationship history, I think it's fair of me to have assumed he was terminally ill, but apparently, that assumption makes me a bitch.

I pull into my driveway, relieved I'm the only one here. If you don't count the permanent resident in the basement. I grab my sack with the trophy in it. Had I known at the antiques store that I was about to experience the most humiliating event in all my seventeen years, I would have bought every trophy they had. I would have had to use Dad's emergency credit card, but it would have been well worth it.

I glance at the marquee as I make my way across the yard. A day hasn't passed since we moved in that my brother, Utah, hasn't updated the marquee with the same promptness and precision that he gives to every other aspect of his life.

He wakes at approximately 6:20 a.m. every day, showers at 6:30 a.m., makes two green smoothies, one for him and one for Honor at 6:55 every morning. (If she doesn't have them made, first.) By 7:10 he's dressed and headed to the marquee to update the daily message. At approximately 7:30 every morning, he gives our little brother an annoying pep talk and then he leaves for school, or, if it's a weekend, he heads to the gym to work out where he walks for forty-five minutes at a level five on the treadmill, followed by one-hundred push-ups and two-hundred sit-ups.

Utah doesn't like spontaneity. Despite the common phrase, Utah does not expect the unexpected. He expects only the expected. He does not like the unexpected.

He didn't like it when our parents divorced several years ago. He didn't like it

29

when our father remarried. And he especially didn't like it when we were told our new stepmother was pregnant.

But he does, in fact, like our half brother that came as a result of said pregnancy. Moby Voss is hard not to like. Not because of his personality, per se, but because he's four. Four-year-old children are fairly liked across the board.

Today the message on the marquee reads "You can't hum while holding your nose closed."

It's true. I tried it when I read it this morning and I even try it again as I walk toward the double cedar front doors of our house.

I can say with certainty that we live in the most unusual house in this whole town. I say *house* because it is certainly not a home. And inside this house are seven of the most unusual occupants. No one would be able to determine from the outside of our house that our family of seven includes an atheist, a home wrecker, an ex-wife suffering from a severe case of agoraphobia, and a teenage girl whose weird obsession borders on necrophilia.

No one would be able to determine any of that from *inside* our house, either. We're good at keeping secrets in this family.

30

Our house is located just off an oil top county road in a microscopic Northeast Texas town. The building we live in was once the highest attended church in our tiny town, but it's been our house since my father, Barnaby Voss, purchased the fledgling church and closed its doors to the patrons indefinitely. Which explains why we have a marquee in our front yard.

My father is an atheist, although that isn't at all why he chose to purchase the foreclosed house of worship and rip it from the hands of the people. No, God had no say in that matter.

He bought the church and closed the doors simply because he absolutely, vehemently, without doubt, hated Pastor Brian's dog, and subsequently, Pastor Brian.

Wolfgang was a massive black Lab who was impressive in size and bark, but lacked a great deal of common sense. If dogs were classified into high school cliques, Wolfgang would most definitely be head of the jocks. A loud, obnoxious dog that spent at least seven of the eight precious hours of sleep my father needed each night barking incessantly.

Years ago, we had the unfortunate distinction of being Wolfgang's neighbor when we lived in the house behind the church. My parent's bedroom window overlooked the back property of the church, which also doubled as Wolfgang's stomping grounds, in which he stomped quite regularly, mostly during the hours my father would rather Wolfgang have been sleeping. But Wolfgang didn't like to be told what to do or when to sleep. In fact, he did the exact opposite of what anyone wanted him to do.

Pastor Brian had purchased Wolfgang when he was just a pup, not a week after a group of local teens broke into his church and stole the week's tithe. Pastor Brian felt that a dog on the premises would deter future robberies. However, Pastor Brian knew very little in the way of training a dog, much less a dog with the intellect of a high school football jock. So for the first year of Wolfgang's existence, the dog had very little interaction with humans outside of his master. Being that Wolfgang got the short end of the stick when it came to intellect and interaction, all of his boundless energy and curiosity were placed solely on the unsuspecting, and possibly undeserving, victim who occupied the property directly behind the church. My father, Barnaby Voss.

My father had not been a fan of Wolfgang's since the moment they became acquainted. He prohibited me and my siblings from interacting with the dog, and it was not uncommon for us to overhear my father threatening to murder Wolfgang under his breath. And at the top of his lungs.

My father may not be a believer in the Lord, but he is an avid believer in karma. As much as he fantasized about murdering Wolfgang, he did not want the murder of an animal hanging over his head. Even if that animal was the worst he'd ever encountered.

Wolfgang's feelings were mutual, or so it was assumed by the way Wolfgang spent the better part of his life barking and growling at my father, inconsiderate to whether it was day or night or weeknight or weekend, only occasionally distracted by a rogue squirrel.

Dad tried everything over the years to put an end to the incessant harassment, from earplugs, to cease and desist warnings, to barking right back at Wolfgang for three hours straight after a Friday evening of consuming three glasses more than his usual evening glass of wine. He attempted all of these things to no avail. In fact, my father was so desperate for a peaceful night's sleep, he once spent an entire summer attempting to befriend Wolfgang in hopes that the barking would eventually cease.

It didn't.

Nothing worked, and from the looks of it,

nothing would ever work, because Pastor Brian cared for Wolfgang a significant deal more than he cared for his neighbor, Barnaby Voss. Unfortunately for Pastor Brian, his fledgling church was at an all-time financial low while my father's used car lot and thirst for revenge were at an all-time high.

My father made a bid the bank couldn't refuse and one Pastor Brian could not himself raise the funds to match. It helped that my father also threw in quite a deal on a used Volvo for the loan officer in charge of the church's foreclosure.

When Pastor Brian announced to his congregation that he'd lost a bidding war to my father, and that my father would be closing the doors to the public and moving our entire family into the church, our family became fodder for gossip. And it hasn't subsided since.

After signing the closing papers almost five years ago, my father gave Pastor Brian and Wolfgang two days to vacate the premises. It took them three. But on the fourth night, after our family moved into the church, my father slept thirteen hours straight.

Pastor Brian was forced to relocate his Sunday sermons, but with divine intervention on his side, it took no more than just one day to find an alternate venue. He reopened a week later in an upscale barn that was used by a deacon to house his collection of tractors. For the first three months, the parishioners sat on bales of hay while Pastor Brian preached his sermon from a makeshift platform constructed out of plywood and pallets.

For six solid months, Pastor Brian made it his personal mission to publicly pray for my father and his wayward soul every Sunday before dismissing church. "May he see the error of his ways," Pastor Brian and the parishioners would pray, "And return to us our house of worship . . . at an affordable price."

This news of being at the top of Pastor Brian's prayer list was unsettling to my father, for he did not feel he had a soul, much less a wayward soul. He certainly did not want the churchgoers praying for said soul.

Approximately seven months after we turned that old church into our family dwelling, Pastor Brian was seen driving a brand-new-to-him Cadillac convertible. The following Sunday, Barnaby Voss was coincidentally no longer a subject in Pastor Brian's passive-aggressive closing prayer.

I was at the car lot the day my father and Pastor Brian worked out the deal. I was significantly younger than I am now, but I remember the deal as if it were yesterday. "You stop praying for my nonexistent soul and I'll knock two grand off that cherry red Cadillac."

It's been several years since any of us have had to listen to Wolfgang bark at night, and several years since my father has greeted a morning in a foul mood. Our family has done a great deal of remodeling inside the church, but there are still three elements that prevent the dwelling from feeling unlike the house of worship it once was.

1) The stained-glass windows.
2) The eight-foot-tall statue of Jesus Christ hanging on the east wall.
3) The church marquee on the front lawn.

The same marquee that remains out front all these years later, long after my father changed the name atop the marquee from, "Crossroads Lutheran Church," to "Dollar Voss."

He chose to name the house *Dollar Voss* because the church is divided into four quarters. And our last name is Voss. I wish there were a more intelligent explanation.

I open the front doors and walk into Quarter One. It consists of the old-chapel-turned-living-area and a rather large kitchen, both remodeled to reflect their new uses, save the eight-foot-tall statue of Jesus Christ on a cross still hanging on the east wall of the living room. Utah and my father worked tirelessly one summer to dismount the eight-foot-tall statue, to no avail. It appeared, after days of failed attempts to remove Him from the living room wall, that Jesus Christ's cross was an actual part of the structure of the building and could not be removed without also removing the studs and the entire east wall of the house.

My father didn't like the idea of losing an entire wall. He enjoys the outdoors, but he is a big believer that the indoors and the outdoors should remain segregated. Instead, he made the decision that the eight-foot-tall Jesus Christ would have to remain. "It gives Quarter One a little character," he said.

He is an atheist, which means the wall hanging is just that and nothing more to him. A wall hanging where an eight-foot-tall Jesus is the focal point. Nonetheless, I make it a point to ensure Jesus Christ is dressed to reflect the appropriate holiday. Which is why the eight-foot-tall statue of Jesus Christ is currently covered in a white bedsheet. He's dressed as a ghost.

Quarter Two, which at one time consisted of three Sunday school classrooms, has since had walls added and is now divided into six rather small bedrooms, large enough to contain one child, one twin-sized bed, and one dresser. My three siblings and I occupy four of the six bedrooms. The fifth bedroom is a guest room and the sixth bedroom is used as my father's office. Which I've never actually once seen him use.

Quarter Three is the old dining hall turned master bedroom. It's where my father sleeps soundly for at least eight hours every night with Victoria Finney-Voss. Victoria has lived in Dollar Voss for approximately four years and two months. Three months prior to the finalization of my father's divorce from my mother and six months prior to the birth of my father's fourth and hopefully final child, Moby.

The last quarter of Dollar Voss, Quarter Four, is the most secluded and controversial of the four quarters.

The basement.

It is set up much like an efficiency apartment, consisting of a bathroom with a standing shower, a very mini-kitchen, and a small living area containing one couch, one television, and one full-sized bed.

My mother, Victoria Voss, not to be confused with my father's current wife of the same name, occupies Quarter Four. It is unfortunate that my father divorced one Victoria, only to immediately marry another, but not nearly as unfortunate as the fact that both Victorias still live in Dollar Voss.

My father's love for the current Victoria Voss was not so much a rebound relationship, but rather more of an overlap, which is the major source of contention remaining among the three adults.

It's rare that my mother, Vicky, ascends from her dwellings in Quarter Four, but her presence is felt by all. Although none are quite as sensitive to the current living arrangement as my father's current wife, Victoria. She hasn't been happy about my mother's occupancy of Quarter Four since the day she moved in to Dollar Voss.

I'm sure it's difficult having to live in a house with your husband and his ex-wife. But probably not nearly as difficult as it was for my cancer-ridden mother to find out my father was sleeping with her oncology nurse.

But that was several years ago and my siblings and I have long since moved past the wrongs our father committed against our mother.

Actually, we haven't. Not even slightly.

Regardless, it's taken all of the last several years for Dollar Voss to be remodeled and revamped to appropriately house the entire Voss family, but my father is patient, if anything.

Despite what is true, we, the Voss family, look very much like a normal family, and Dollar Voss looks very much like a normal house, save the stained-glass windows, the statue on our wall, and the church marquee.

Pastor Brian faithfully updated the marquee every Saturday with clever phrases such as DON'T BE SO OPEN-MINDED THAT YOUR BRAINS FALL OUT and THIS WEEK'S SERMON: FIFTY SHADES OF PRAY.

Sometimes I wonder what the townspeople think when they drive by and read Utah's daily facts and quotes. Like yesterday, when the marquee read THE FACE OF THE NOBEL PEACE PRIZE MEDAL IS A DEPICTION OF THREE NAKED MEN.

I occasionally think it's funny, but I'm mostly just embarrassed. Most of the residents of our small town already feel we're out of place here, living in this old church. Our actions only prove to reinforce those feelings. I think my father actually tried to make an effort to fit in last year and make our house look more like a home than a church. He spent two weeks putting up a cute white picket fence around our entire yard.

The white picket fence didn't do much to make it look more like a home. Now it just looks like we live in an old church surrounded by an out of place white picket fence. A-plus for effort, though.

I go to my bedroom and close the door. I toss my sack on the floor by my bed and plop down onto my mattress. It's almost three in the afternoon, which means Moby and Victoria will be back soon. Then Honor and Utah. Then my father. Then family dinner. Joy.

Today has already been too much. I'm not sure I can take much more.

I go to the bathroom and search the drawers for some sleep medicine. I don't normally take it unless I'm sick, but the only thing I can think of that will get me through tonight without obsessing over my kiss with Honor's boyfriend is a few sips of NyQuil. Which is precisely what I find under the sink.

I take a dose and then text my father when I'm back in my room and under the covers.

41

I'm not feeling well. Left school early and going to bed. Will probably miss dinner.

I turn the sound off on my phone and slide it under my pillow. I close my eyes, but it doesn't help me to stop seeing Sagan in front of me. Honor and I aren't as close as we used to be so it's not unusual that I didn't know about her new fling. I have noticed she's been gone more than usual but I haven't asked her why. As far as I know, she's never brought him to our house, so I had no idea who he was when I saw him today.

If only I had seen his face prior to the incident on the town square, that whole embarrassment could have been avoided. I would have known who he was immediately. If he has even one decent bone in his body, he'll break it off with her and never step foot inside this house. It's not like they're in love. They barely know each other; it's only been a couple of weeks. Anyone in their right mind wouldn't want to come between sisters. Especially twins.

But then again, I doubt he has any intentions to pursue me at all. It was an honest mistake. He thought I was Honor. If he had known I was her sister, he never would have said sickeningly sweet and confusing things like "You bury me" right before sticking his tongue down my throat. He's probably laughing about the mix-up. Hell, he probably ended up telling Honor what happened and they're both laughing about it.

Laughing about poor, pathetic Merit who thought the cute guy was actually into her.

I hate that I'm so embarrassed by it. I should have slapped him when he kissed me. Had I done that, I would be laughing about it with him. But instead, I threw myself at him and consumed as much of that kiss and him as I possibly could. It's a feeling I want to experience again. And that's what has me the most upset. The last thing I want is for there to be something of my sister's that I'm envious of. Just thinking about Sagan kissing her like he kissed me today makes me so jealous, I would bleed green if someone stabbed me.

I've always feared something like this would happen. That someone would assume I was her and I would embarrass myself somehow. Really the only thing that sets us apart is that she wears contacts and I don't. It doesn't matter that I've done all I can to differentiate myself from Honor, including cutting and dyeing my hair, starving myself, and overeating, but we always seem to weigh the same, look the same, sound the same.

But we are not the same.

I am nothing like my identical twin sister, who prefers cadaver hearts to fully functioning ones.

I am nothing like my father, Barnaby, who has turned our entire lives upside down, simply out of spite for a canine.

I am certainly nothing like my brother Utah who spends every waking moment living an externally precise, perfect, and punctual present to make up for all the internal imperfections that live in his past.

And I am absolutely, without a doubt, a far cry from my mother, Vicky, who spends her days and nights in Quarter Four watching Netflix, licking the salt off potato chips, living off disability, refusing to vacate the house where her ex-husband and newer wife, Victoria, continue to live their lives upstairs, primarily in Quarters One and Three.

The NyQuil begins to kick in as soon as I hear the front door open. Moby's voice carries down the hallway and Victoria's voice soon follows as she calls after him to go wash his hands before he eats a snack.

I reach to my nightstand and grab my headphones. I'd much rather fall asleep listening to Seafret than to the sound of my family right now.

CHAPTER THREE

I was hoping I'd never see Sagan again. I was hoping they'd break it off before she brought him around the family for introductions. That hope lasted twenty-four hours until it was diminished. And it's been diminished for almost two weeks now.

In that two weeks, Sagan has been at our house more times than I can count. He's here for dinner every night, for breakfast every morning, and most hours in between.

I haven't spoken a single word to him since the morning he showed up at our house for the first time, a mere twenty-four hours after his tongue was down my throat. I walked out of my bedroom, still in my pajamas, and saw him sitting at the table. As soon as we made eye contact, I spun around and opened the refrigerator. It felt like my heart was a pinball bouncing around inside my chest.

I managed to make it through breakfast

that morning without uttering a single word. Once everyone started to gather their things and leave, I breathed a small sigh of relief until I realized he was still in the kitchen and didn't look like he was leaving like everyone else. I heard Honor tell him goodbye. I wasn't facing them, so it made me wonder if they kissed goodbye. I didn't wonder enough to turn around and witness it, though. I was curious why he wasn't walking out with her. It was a bit odd that he'd linger in a house he wasn't acquainted with after his girlfriend left for school, but that's exactly what he did.

Once everyone was gone but him, I grabbed a rag to wipe down the counter. It didn't need cleaning but I didn't know what else to do with my hands or my eyes. He stood up and picked up the three glasses left behind on the table. He walked them into the kitchen and stood next to me while he poured the contents in the sink.

There was such a heavy silence in the room. It made the moment between us seem much more dramatic than it should have been.

"Do you want to talk about what happened?" he said. He opened the dishwasher like he had the right to be doing dishes in this house. He put the three glasses on the top shelf and then closed it. He dried his hands on a towel and dropped it on the counter while he waited for a response from me. I merely shook my head, uninterested in bringing it up again.

He sighed and then said, "Merit." I made eye contact with him, which was a terrible idea because he dipped his head and looked at me apologetically, which made it impossible to hold on to any form of undeserved anger I held toward him. "I'm really sorry. I just . . . I thought you were her. I never would have kissed you had I known otherwise."

He appeared to be genuine in his apology but as much as I tried to grasp the sincerity, I couldn't help but analyze that last part. "I never would have kissed you had I known otherwise."

Somehow, that felt more like an insult than an apology. And I knew the whole thing was stupid and it really was an honest mistake. Honor didn't know it happened so I should have just been able to laugh it off. But I couldn't. It was hard to laugh off something that affected me like it did. But I did my best to fake it.

"It's fine," I said with a shrug. "Really. It was such an awkward kiss, anyway. I'm glad it was an accident because I was about two seconds away from slapping you."

Something in his expression faltered. I forced a smile as I turned and walked to my bedroom without looking back at him.

That was the last time we spoke.

We don't speak at breakfast, we don't speak at dinner, we don't speak when he's lingering in our living room, watching TV.

But just because we don't speak doesn't mean I don't feel it every time he looks at me. I'm constantly trying to rein in my pulse because it makes me feel guilty that I'm even attracted to him. I don't like being envious of Honor. I try to tell myself that it isn't him I'm attracted to. It was the thought of a stranger desiring me enough to kiss me with as much passion as he kissed me that day. That's what I'm envious of. The idea of it all. It has nothing to do with Sagan or who he is as a person. I don't even know him enough to know if I would like him as a person. And I don't want to know that, which is precisely why I avoid him.

But I do know that he doesn't seem to be Honor's type. And there's absolutely no chemistry between them. Or maybe that's just wishful thinking on my part.

I've been doing my very best to tolerate the entire situation, but it's making me miserable. However, I have a feeling my tolerance won't be as intolerable now, because misery loves company and the thing I am looking at is most definitely miserable.

Despite it being after midnight, I'm holding open the front door, staring down into the frightened eyes of Wolfgang. The very dog that terrorized my father through many of my childhood years.

What a delightful surprise.

My father hasn't noticed, but I haven't been back to school for a while now and my days and nights have been mixed up. I woke up a few minutes ago after everyone else had fallen asleep. I made my way to Quarter One in search of food but before I got to the kitchen, I heard what sounded like scratching against our double front doors. Since we have no animals of the four-legged variety, one would think my first instinct would have been to notify my father of a possible intruder. Instead, I immediately opened the door to investigate the matter myself. If my life were a scary movie, I'd be the first to die.

Wolfgang is whimpering at my feet, covered in mud, shivering from the rain, and from the looks of it, terribly lost. There were several loud claps of thunder that shook the house and woke me up a few times when the storm began to roll through earlier tonight. He probably got spooked and started running until he ended up at the only other place he knows.

I've never actually touched the dog before, since we were ordered to stay away from him as children. I reach my hand out, but I do so with hesitancy. Our father once told us he witnessed Wolfgang eat an entire Girl Scout. I realize now that it was a lie, of course, but with Wolfgang's visit tonight and the ominousness of the moment being heightened by the dark, I'm a bit nervous Wolfgang might assume I'm hiding Thin Mints in my pocket.

But Wolfgang doesn't eat me, not even partially. Quite the contrary, in fact.

He licks me.

It's a quick swipe of his tongue that catches my pinky and then releases it, as if it's more of a peace offering than an appetizer. I open the door a little wider and Wolfgang recognizes it as the welcoming gesture it is and he scurries inside, immediately walks through Quarter One and goes straight for the back door. He then proceeds to paw at the back door as if he wants access to the backyard.

I've always assumed Wolfgang was an ignorant dog, so it surprises me he found his way back to his old stomping grounds. But it surprises me even more that he'd rather be outside in the backyard than here inside where it's dry. I would ask him why he's making such a poor choice, but he's a dog.

I open the back door and Wolfgang whimpers once more and then pushes against the screen door until it opens, as if he's on a mission. I flip on the light to the backyard and watch as Wolfgang descends the steps and rushes through the rain to the doghouse that hasn't been moved or used since he was evicted by my father years ago.

I want to warn Wolfgang that there could be spiders or other occupants who have since taken over his old residence, but he doesn't seem to mind. He disappears inside the old doghouse and I watch for a moment to see if he comes running back out, but he doesn't.

I close the screen door and then the back door and lock the deadbolt. I'll return him to Pastor Brian in the morning. That is if he doesn't figure out how to scale the backyard fence and get home on his own.

I make myself a sandwich and turn on the TV but by the time I'm done eating I still haven't found anything interesting to watch. I slept so long tonight I feel completely energized and I'm hardly even thinking about Honor and her boyfriend. I decide to use my unusual burst of energy to clean my room.

I pop in my headphones and start to clean, but it's surprising how many songs talk about forbidden love or kissing someone. I change the song every time my mind goes there in hopes it will spark an unrelated memory. I skip songs until I get to Ocean and then I grab an old T-shirt to wipe down all my trophies. Every time I buy a new one I dust them and rear-range them. The new bowling trophy I bought a couple weeks ago will go front and center. I reach to the back of my shelf and grab the football trophy I stole from Drew Waldrup. I set it aside for when I change Jesus Christ's outfit later tonight.

I spend the next several hours enjoying a house of solitude while everyone sleeps. I take an uninterrupted shower. I watch the first ten minutes of eight different shows on Netflix. I might have an issue with my attention span because I can never make it through an entire show without getting bored. I do one and a half crossword puzzles before I get stumped on a four-letter word for *word*. When I notice the first tease of sun shining through one of the stained-glass windows, I decide to change Jesus Christ's clothes before anyone wakes up.

I gather all the stuff I need. Once I have the ladder set up in the living room, I climb it with my stolen football trophy in hand. I slide the roll of tape off my wrist and place the trophy in Jesus's right hand, then secure it there with the tape. I readjust the cheese-hat on top of His crown of thorns. When I finish, I descend the ladder and stand back to admire my creation.

I normally give Jesus a temporary nickname, depending on the theme of his outfit. Last month, He was referred to as "Holy Ghost" for obvious reasons. And now, considering He is currently dressed as a Packers fan, complete with a home-team jersey, a Wisconsin cheese hat, and now Drew Waldrup's missing trophy, I think I shall deem Him Cheesus Christ.

"Dad and Victoria are going to be pissed when they see that."

I turn around and a freshly showered and dressed Honor is staring up at Cheesus. I smile, because that's precisely why I went through all this effort. My father is a huge Cowboys fan and he's been talking about tonight's game between Dallas and Green Bay incessantly. He's only going to be mad that I dressed Him as a Packers fan.

Victoria, on the other hand, will be mad that I dressed Him at all. Unlike my father,

Victoria believes in God. And Jesus. And the sanctity of religion. She hates it when I dress up Jesus. She says it's sacrilegious and disrespectful.

I disagree. It would be disrespectful if the actual Jesus Christ were in our living room and I forced Him to change clothes all the time. But this Jesus is fake, made out of wood and plastic. I tried to explain that to Victoria. I told her one of the Ten Commandments is not to worship false idols. Dressing this idol of Jesus up for fun, rather than worshipping it, is actually following the commandment.

She didn't see it that way. But her opposition obviously hasn't persuaded me to stop.

I grab the ladder and take it back to the garage. Dad should be waking up any minute now, so I get rid of the evidence, even though it's a given that I'm the only one in the house who makes an effort to dress Jesus Christ anymore. Honor hasn't seemed to care about eternal life since she became obsessed with the terminally ill a few years ago.

Honor and I may look identical, sound identical, and share identical mannerisms, but we couldn't be more opposite. Most identical twins finish each other's sentences, know what each other is thinking, and share common interests. But Honor and I confuse the hell out of each other. We tried our best to live up to the identical twin standard, but once we hit puberty, we just kind of gave up.

Then when she started dating Kirk, his death put an even bigger wedge between us because up until that point, we had experienced almost everything together. But after Kirk died, she had experienced things I hadn't. Being in love, losing her virginity, experiencing grief. We no longer felt like we were on the same level after that. Or at least she felt she was on a different level than me. And the more time that passes, the more we drift apart.

I walk back into the kitchen from the garage and my steps falter at the sight of Sagan.

His back is to me as he sits at our kitchen table. In our house. At a highly inappropriate time of day. Who visits their girlfriend at seven in the morning? He's becoming a constant fixture in Dollar Voss, which makes me feel less and less envious of my sister every time he chooses to be here. Who in their right mind would willingly return to this house? Has he not met my family? Is he that blinded by his unrequited love for Honor?

He's hunched over, focused intently on

his sketch pad in front of him. When I realized he actually was an artist, I laughed at my luck. I had hoped he was an artist right before he kissed me, but it's only fitting that the more I'm around him, the more perfect he seems. It's karma for being attracted to my twin sister's boyfriend.

Moby walks into the kitchen and shuffles over to the table. Moby is quite possibly the only part of this family that brings me joy, but four-year-olds are fairly liked across the board. There's still plenty of time for Moby to disappoint me.

"Morning, buddy." Sagan ruffles Moby's hair, but Moby is not a morning person, despite his age. He shifts his head away and climbs into the seat next to him. Sagan tears off a sheet of blank paper from the sketchbook he's been hunched over. He slides the piece of paper in front of Moby and plucks a crayon out of a basket in front of him, winning Moby over instantly. There isn't a four-year-old on earth who doesn't love a crayon and a sheet of paper. Moby is always trying to copy the things Honor's boyfriend sketches. Which is humorous considering the morbid themes her boyfriend is always sketching. Just yesterday I found a picture he sketched of Honor. She was sitting in an empty grave, putting on lipstick. On the back, he had written "Till death do us part."

I never know what any of his drawings mean, but they fascinate me. I just don't want him to know that. I also don't want him to know that every time he draws a sketch for Honor and she leaves it lying around like it doesn't even mean anything to her, I steal it. I have several of his drawings now, wrapped in a bathrobe and stuffed in the bottom of my dresser drawer. Sometimes I look at them and pretend they're pictures of me and not Honor.

I'm sure the one he's sketching now will end up at the bottom of my drawer as well because Honor doesn't appreciate the artistic side of him.

Moby glances at me and covers his mouth with his hand, mumbling something intended for only me to hear. He always puts his hand flat over his mouth when he's telling someone a secret, rather than cupping his hand around his mouth. It's so adorable, we don't have the heart to tell him we can never understand a word he's saying. But I don't have to understand him because I know exactly what he's asking for.

I wink at him and grab the box of donuts from the top of the refrigerator. There are two left in the box, so I put one in my mouth and walk the other one to Moby. He takes the donut from my hand and immediately crawls under the table to eat it. I don't even have to tell him to go hide from his mother. He already knows that anything that tastes good to him is off-limits to Victoria.

"You realize you're teaching him to hoard junk food, right?" Utah enters the kitchen in his usual holier-than-thou mood. "If he grows up to be morbidly obese, it's your fault."

I disagree with his theory, but I don't say anything to defend my actions. It would ruin my three-day streak of not speaking. But despite my lack of a rebuttal, Utah is wrong. If Moby grows up to be morbidly obese, that's all on Victoria. She's eliminated entire food groups from his diet. She doesn't allow him to have sugar, carbs, gluten, or any ingredient that ends in *ose.* The poor kid eats steel-cut oatmeal for breakfast every day. Without butter or sugar. That can't be good for him.

At least I sneak him sweets in moderation.

Utah walks past me, heading for his smoothie. He takes it from Honor's hand and leans in to give her a quick thank you kiss on top of her head. He knows not to come near me with his cheerful sibling affection.

If the proof weren't in our DNA, I would say that Utah and Honor seem more like identical twins than she and I do. They're the ones who finish each other's sentences, share inside jokes, and spend the most time together.

Utah and I have nothing in common, other than being the only two people in the Voss family to know its deepest, darkest secret. But since it's something we've never once discussed since the day it happened, it's barely a common thread between us now.

And we look nothing alike. Honor and I look more like our mother. Or at least like she did when she was younger. Her hair used to be a more vibrant blonde, much like ours is now. But she hasn't seen the sun in so long, I've noticed that the color has dulled. Utah looks like our father, with sandy brown hair and pale skin. Honor and I also have a paler shade of skin, but it's not to the degree of Utah's. He has to wear sunscreen if he's going to be outside for more than half an hour or he'll burn. I guess Honor and I lucked out, because we tan fairly easily in the summer.

Moby is just a mix of all of us. Sometimes he looks like our father, sometimes he looks like Victoria. But most of the time he reminds me of this bird off a Dawn dish soap commercial I saw last year. It's not a bad resemblance. It was a cute bird.

Utah takes a seat and bends down to look under the table. "Morning, buddy. You excited about today?"

Moby wipes sticky glaze from his mouth with his shirtsleeve and nods. "Yes!"

"How excited?" Utah says.

"So excited!" Moby says, grinning from ear to ear.

"How excited?"

"The *most* excited!" Moby yells.

There's nothing significant about today worth being excited about. This exchange is a daily occurrence between Utah and Moby. Utah says it's important to get kids pumped up for their day, even if there's nothing significant about it. He says it helps foster a positive neurological environment, whatever that's supposed to mean.

Utah wants to be a teacher and already has his entire college schedule planned out. As soon as he graduates high school in six months, he has a two-day weekend and then begins classes at the local university the following Monday. Honor also signed up to start classes two days after graduation.

Me? I'm still debating on going to class

today, much less college six months from now.

It's unusual to have three siblings who are all seniors in high school at the same time. My mother gave birth to Utah in August and then got pregnant with Honor and me one month later. Apparently it's just a rumor that breastfeeding prevents a woman from ovulating.

When it was time for Utah to start school, she and my father decided to hold him back a year so they could have us all in the same grade at the same time. No sense dealing with different schedules when you can have one schedule for all three of your children.

I don't think they thought far enough in advance to consider having to pay for three college tuitions at the same time. Not that it would matter. My parents don't have the kind of money to pay one college tuition, let alone three. Once we start college, it'll be student loans or nothing for me. Honor and Utah won't have to worry about tuition because as it stands, they're several points ahead of anyone else in the class when it comes to vying for valedictorian and salutatorian. There's no question a Voss sibling will be in the top two spots in the class and will land the coveted scholarships that accompany the awards. It's merely a question of which one of them will come out the most victorious. My vote is on Utah, simply because he runs less of a risk of becoming preoccupied with the terminally ill between now and graduation.

I'm not a competitive person by nature, so grades have never meant as much to me as they do to the two of them. I used to fall somewhere in the middle of the class when it comes to grade point average, but I'm sure my GPA has taken quite a hit in the past two weeks. I haven't been back to school since the day I left early and went to the town square. I might go back but I'm more leaning toward not.

Utah is moving out in a month or two, but it probably won't affect his GPA. Utah isn't the type to party and let his grades slip. Besides, he'll probably still be here most of the time since he isn't going far. He's redoing the floors in our old house — the one located directly behind this one. As soon as he finishes them, he's moving over there. If anything, the peace and quiet will give him even more time to study. And clean. And iron his clothes. He has to be the most impeccably dressed high school senior I've ever encountered at a public school with no required uniform. Honestly, I'll be glad when he moves into our old house. There's been a lot of tension between us for a while now.

I pour myself a cup of juice and sit at the table across from Sagan. He doesn't acknowledge me but he does shield whatever he's drawing with his sporadically tattooed arm. I take note of a few new tattoos I haven't noticed yet. There's some sort of shield, a tiny lizard with one eye. Or maybe it's winking. I would ask him what they mean, but I'd have to speak to him. I just keep my mouth shut and try to sneak a peek at whatever it is he's drawing. I lean forward and try to get a better look. His eyes dart up and meet mine. I ignore the flutter of energy his eye contact gives me and force an unwavering expression. He arches an eyebrow and picks up his sketchbook as he leans back against his chair. He's still looking at me as he gives his head a slow shake to let me know I'm not getting the privilege of watching him sketch.

I don't want to see it anyway.

His phone vibrates and he practically lunges for it. He flips it over and looks at the screen but his face falls flat. He silences the call and flips his phone over. Now I'm curious who makes him so anxious to answer his phone if Honor is sitting right here. Sagan glances up at Honor and she's staring at him. There's a silent exchange between them and knowing they probably have inside secrets burns a hole in my stomach.

I move my attention to Moby, who is still hiding under the table. He's managed to get more of the donut on his face than inside his mouth. "One more?" he mutters with a mouthful. I shake my head. Moderation. Also, we don't have any more.

Victoria enters the kitchen in a rush. "Moby, come get your oatmeal!" She yells this loud enough to spread across all quarters of the house, but if she'd pay closer attention to her child instead of her makeup, she'd notice he's already awake, dressed, and fed.

Victoria grabs a knife from the drawer and a banana. She wipes the blade of the knife across her pink scrubs, judging its cleanliness. Or lack thereof. "Whose day was it to wash dishes yesterday?"

None of us respond to her. We rarely do. Unless our father is in the room, Victoria is of little importance to us.

"Well, whoever unloaded the dishwasher, make sure the dishes are clean before you put them away. These are disgusting." She puts the knife in the sink and pulls another knife out of the drawer. She glances across the kitchen at all her stepchildren sitting around the table. I'm the only one looking at her. She sighs and begins peeling the banana.

I have no idea what my father sees in her. Sure, she's cute for her age, having just turned thirty-five. A good ten years younger than my mother. But that's the extent of Victoria's qualities. She's an overbearing mother to Moby. She takes her job as a nurse way too seriously. Not that being a nurse isn't a reputable career. But the issue with Victoria is she doesn't seem to know how to separate her work life from her home life. She's always in caregiver mode to Moby like he's ill, but he's a very viable four-year-old. And she always wears pink scrubs, even though she's allowed to wear any color or pattern she wants.

I think her pink scrubs annoy me more than anything else about her. I might even be more willing to forgive her for the atrocity she committed against my mother if she'd wear a different color just once.

I remember the day she started wearing pink scrubs. I was twelve, sitting at this very table. She had emerged from Quarter Three, back when Quarter Three was shared by my father and ailing mother. She had been my mother's nurse for about six months and I actually kind of liked her. Until that particular morning, anyway.

My father had been sitting across from me reading the paper when he looked up at her and smiled. "Pink looks really good on you, Victoria."

I know I was young, but even kids can recognize flirting, especially when that flirting only involves one of their two married parents.

Victoria has only worn shades of pink scrubs since that day. I often wonder if their affair began before or after that flirtatious moment in the kitchen. Sometimes the curiosity consumes me so much, I want to ask them the exact hour they began ruining my mother's life. But that would mean we were discussing a secret out in the open, and we don't do that in this family. We keep our secrets buried deeper than the grave Victoria wishes my mother would go ahead and fall in.

They kept the affair quiet for at least a year. Long enough to realize my mother's cancer wasn't going to kill her after all, but not long enough to prevent Victoria from getting pregnant. My father was stuck between a rock and a hard place at that point. It didn't matter which decision he made, he'd still come out the asshole. On the one hand, he could choose not to abandon his wife who had just beaten cancer. But if he chose his wife, that would mean he was abandoning his new pregnant mistress.

It was so long ago, I'm not sure how he came about making the decision he made. I don't have much recollection of any fighting taking place between the adults. I do, however, remember when my mother and father discussed where his new wife and child would live. She suggested he move to our old home behind Dollar Voss and leave her here to manage us children. He refused on the grounds that she wasn't mentally or physically competent enough to manage us children without his help. And sadly, he was right.

My mother had been in a car accident when she was pregnant with my sister and me, and she never fully recovered. To us kids, she's the same person she's always been, considering we didn't know her before the accident. But we know she changed because of how our father references things. He would say, "Before the accident when your mother could . . ." or "Before the accident when we would take vacations . . ." or "Before the accident when she wasn't so ill . . ."

He never said any of those things out of

spite, I don't think. They were just matter-of-fact. There is the Victoria Voss "before the accident" and the Victoria Voss we now have as a mother. If you don't count her bad back, her two-year fight against brain cancer, a slight limp in her step, a severe social anxiety that's kept her in the basement for over two years, a few scars on her right arm, and her inability to make it through an entire day without at least two naps, she's relatively normal.

We used to try to get her to leave the basement and interact with us all the time. The last time she left the basement was to attend Kirk's funeral, and that was only because Honor sobbed and begged her to come. But after that, when the first year of her seclusion came and went and our mother seemed to be functioning just fine with her life in the basement, we had no choice but to accept it. With Utah, Honor, and me, she's checked on daily. My father still buys all her groceries and Honor and I make sure her mini-kitchen is fully stocked. She doesn't have any bills because my father covers utilities on the whole house.

The only issue that has come up in the two years since she's been secluded is her health. Fortunately, my father found a doctor who does house calls if he's ever needed.

And since she refuses to see a psychiatrist for her social phobia, we have no other choice but to accept it. For now. I have a feeling after all three of us kids are out of the house next year, Victoria is going to demand my mother move out. But that's not a battle anyone wants to confront prematurely, especially when my siblings and I will be the first to come to our mother's defense.

Victoria has just resigned to pretending my mother doesn't exist. The same way my siblings and I pretend Victoria doesn't exist. We don't see the point in befriending a woman we despise, simply because she's the mother of our little half brother.

Since the day Victoria entered our lives, our family hasn't been the same. And while we do hold our father accountable for half of our family issues, he is still required to love us. Which makes him harder to blame than Victoria, who doesn't even like us.

Victoria scoops up the bananas and layers them over the top of Moby's bowl of oatmeal. "Moby, come eat your breakfast!"

Moby crawls out from under the table and stands up. "I'm not hungry." He wipes glaze off his mouth with the sleeve of his shirt. There's no hiding that he just inhaled a donut, and there's no sense in trying to hide that I'm the one who gave it to him.

"Moby," Victoria says, taking him in. "What in the world is all over your . . ." Here we go. "Merit! I told you not to give him donuts."

I look at Victoria innocently just as my father walks into the room. She turns her attention to him, waving the knife in the air that she was just using to slice bananas. "Merit gave Moby a donut for breakfast!"

My father gently slides his fingers around her wrist and grabs the knife. He leans in and kisses her on the cheek and then sets the knife on the counter, finding me in his crowd of children. "Merit, we talked about this. Do it again and you're grounded."

I nod, assuming that's the end of it. But Victoria doesn't stop there, because a donut for breakfast is the equivalent to Armageddon and it deserves all the panic.

"You never ground them," she accuses. She grabs the bowl of oatmeal and walks it over to the trash. She angrily scoops the contents of the bowl into the trash. "I've never seen you actually follow through with a single punishment, Barnaby. It's why they act like this."

They being my father's three oldest children. And it's the truth. He's full of empty threats and very little follow-through. It's my favorite thing about him.

"Sweetie, lighten up. Maybe Merit didn't know she wasn't supposed to give him a donut today."

Nothing irks Victoria more than when my father takes our side over hers. "Of course Merit knows not to give him a donut. She doesn't listen to me. None of them do." Victoria chucks the bowl in the sink and bends to pick up Moby. She sets him on the counter near the sink and wets a napkin to wipe donut remnants off his face. "Moby, you cannot eat donuts. They are very bad for you. They make you sleepy, and when you're sleepy, you can't perform well in school."

Never mind the fact that he's four and isn't even in real school yet.

My father sips from his coffee cup and then reaches over to Moby and ruffles his hair. "Listen to your mother, buddy." He carries his coffee and newspaper to the table, taking the seat next to me. He gives me a look that says he's not happy with me. I just stare at him with the hope that he demands I apologize, or asks me why I broke one of Victoria's rules again.

But he doesn't. Which means my no-speaking streak is looking good for day four.

I wonder if anyone will notice my taciturnity. Not that I'm giving anyone the silent treatment. I'm seventeen years old. Hardly a child. But I do feel invisible in this house most of the time and I'm curious how long it will take before someone notices I haven't spoken out loud.

I realize it's a bit passive aggressive, but it's not like I'm doing it to prove a point to them. It's simply to prove a point to myself. I wonder if I can make it an entire week. I once read a quote that said, "Don't make your presence known. Make your absence felt."

No one in this family notices my presence or my absence. They would all notice Honor's. But I was born second, which just makes me a faded copy of the original.

"What's going on the marquee today, Utah?" my father asks.

It's bad enough all the ex-parishioners of this church still hold a grudge against my father for buying this house, but the marquee digs the knife in even deeper. I'm sure the daily quotes that have nothing to do with Christianity get under people's skin. Yesterday's quote said CHARLES DARWIN ATE EVERY ANIMAL HE DISCOVERED.

I had to Google that fact because it sounded too insane to be true. It's true.

"You'll see in five minutes," Utah says. He

72

downs the rest of his shake and pushes away from the table.

"Wait," Honor says. "Maybe you should hold off on updating the marquee today. You know, out of respect."

Utah stares blankly at Honor, which clues her in that none of us knows what she's talking about.

She looks at my father. "Pastor Brian died last night."

I immediately turn my attention to my father at that news. He rarely shows emotion, and I'm not sure what kind of emotion this will bring him. But surely it'll be something. A tear? A smile? He stares stoically at Honor as he absorbs the news.

"He did?"

She nods. "Yeah, I saw it on Facebook this morning. Heart attack."

My father leans back in his chair, gripping his coffee cup. He looks down at the cup. "He's dead?"

Victoria puts a hand on my father's shoulder and says something to him, but I tune her out. Until this moment, I had forgotten all about Wolfgang showing up last night.

I put my hand over my mouth because I suddenly want to tell them all about the dog showing up in the middle of the night, but I feel like I might choke up.

What does it say about me that I didn't have any sort of reaction just now to the news of Pastor Brian's passing, but realizing his dog came back to the only other home he's ever known makes me want to tear up?

Honor called me a sociopath once while we were in the middle of a fight. I'll make it a point to look up that word later. There might be some truth to that.

"I can't believe he's dead," my father says. He stands up and Victoria's hand slides off his shoulder and down his back. "He wasn't that much older than me."

Of course that's what he's focused on. Pastor Brian's age. He's less concerned about the death of a man he's been warring with for years and more concerned that he was close in age to someone who is old enough to fall over dead from a heart attack.

Utah is still paused at the door. He looks like he's in a state of disbelief. "I don't know what to do," he says. "If I don't acknowledge his passing on the marquee, people will accuse us of being insensitive. But if I acknowledge it, people will accuse us of being disingenuous."

What an odd thing to be worried about in this moment.

Honor's boyfriend tears out his drawing

and stares down at it. "Sounds like you're screwed either way, so I'd just go with whatever you feel like going with." He says all this without looking up from his drawing. But his words reach Utah anyway, because after a brief moment of pause, Utah walks out the front door toward the marquee.

I'm confused by two things. One being the constant and repeated presence of Honor's boyfriend at our breakfast table. Two being the fact that everyone seems to know him so well that they're perfectly fine with him joining in on the family conversation. Shouldn't he be too nervous to speak? Especially around my father. He's only been hanging around for a couple of weeks now. Meeting his girlfriend's family seemed to sit really well with him. I hate it. I also hate that he doesn't seem like the type of person who talks a lot, but the few things he does say have more weight than if anyone else were to say them.

Maybe that's part of the reason I've decided to go on a verbal strike. I'm tired of everything I say not having meaning to anyone. I'll just stop talking so that when I do talk, my words will count. Right now it feels like any time I talk, my words circle right back into my mouth like a boomerang and I'm forced to swallow them again.

"What's a heart attack?" Moby asks.

Victoria bends and begins to help Moby put on his jacket. "It's when your heart stops working and your body goes to sleep. But it only happens when you're an old, old man like Pastor Brian."

"His body went to sleep?" Moby asks.

Victoria nods.

"For how long? When is he gonna wake up?"

"Not for a long time."

"Is he gonna get buried?"

"Yes," she says, sounding a bit annoyed with the natural curiosity of her four-year-old. She zips his jacket. "Go get your shoes."

"But what happens when he wakes up? Will he be able to get out of the ground?"

I smile, knowing how much Victoria hates telling Moby the truth. He asks all the normal questions about life and Victoria makes up the most bizarre answers. She'll do anything to protect him from the truth. I once heard him ask her what the word *sex* meant. She told him it was a terrible TV show from the eighties and that he should never watch it.

She places her hands on Moby's cheeks. "Yes, he can get out of the ground when he wakes up. They'll bury Pastor Brian with a cell phone so he can call them when it's time to dig him back up."

Honor sputters laughter and spews juice everywhere. Utah hands her a napkin and whispers, "Does she think this is healthier than telling him the truth?"

We're all watching this conversation with fascination. Victoria can sense it because even though she's failing miserably, she's giving it her best effort to put Moby's questions to rest. "Let's go find your backpack," she says, pulling on his hand. He stops following her right before they make it to the hallway.

"But what if his phone battery dies while his body is sleeping? Will he be stuck in the ground forever?"

My father grabs Moby by the hand, sweeping in to rescue the desperate Victoria. "Come on, buddy. Time to go." Right when they round the corner to the hallway, I hear Moby say, "Isn't it time for your body to sleep, Daddy? It's getting really old, too."

Honor starts laughing, and I think her boyfriend does, too, but his laugh is quiet and I don't want to look at him. I cover my mouth because I'm not sure if laughing out loud counts against my verbal strike, but Victoria's mothering skills are humorous at best.

Victoria is staring at all of us with her

hands on her hips, watching us laugh. Her face turns as pink as her scrubs and she walks swiftly out of the room, headed toward Quarter Three.

I would feel sorry for her if she didn't bring this on herself.

Utah and Honor begin to pack up their things. I walk to the sink and pretend to busy myself, hoping they don't ask me if I'm going to school today. I usually take a different car than the two of them because they both stay after school. Honor for cheerleading practice and Utah for . . . whatever it is Utah does after school. I'm not even sure. I go to my room, mostly to avoid looking at Honor's boyfriend because every time I do I feel a little bit of his mouth on mine from that day on the square.

I wait in my room and listen for the front door to open and close and even then I wait several more minutes. When the house is finally quiet and I'm certain he's gone, I open my bedroom door and slowly walk toward the kitchen to ensure the coast is clear. My mother is downstairs, but the chances of her coming out of the basement to ask why I've skipped school are less than the chances of the Cowboys beating the Packers tonight.

Speaking of. I'm a little disappointed my father or Victoria didn't notice Cheesus before they left.

On my way into the kitchen, the marquee outside the window catches my attention. I squint to read the words Utah selected to display.

THERE ARE MORE FAKE FLAMINGOS IN THE WORLD THAN REAL ONES.

I sigh, a little disappointed in Utah. If it were me, I would have paid my respects to Pastor Brian. Either that, or I wouldn't have updated it at all. But to update it without acknowledging the death of the man who erected that very marquee seems a little . . . I don't know . . . like something people would expect from a Voss. I don't like validating their negative perception of us.

I glance in the living room and then the kitchen, wondering what I'm going to do with myself today. Another crossword puzzle? I'm getting really good at them. I sit down at the table with my half-completed book of crossword puzzles. I flip it to the puzzle I finished on Friday and start on the next one.

I'm on the third question across before the doubt begins to seep in. It's no big deal, this has been happening every day since I stopped going to school. A sense of panic rears its ugly head, making me question my choice.

I'm still not quite certain why I stopped going. There wasn't a single catastrophic or embarrassing incident that influenced my decision. Just a bunch of small ones that continued to pile up until they were hard to ignore. That, coupled with my ability to make choices without giving them a second thought. One minute I was at school and the next minute I decided I'd rather be browsing antiques than learning about how terribly we lost the Battle of the Alamo.

I like spontaneity. Maybe I like it because Utah hates it so much. There's something freeing about refusing to stress over stressful situations. No matter how much thought or time you put into a decision, you're still only going to be wrong or right. Besides, I've accrued more knowledge this week by doing these crossword puzzles than I probably could in my entire senior year attending high school. It's why I only do one puzzle a day. I don't want to get too intellectually ahead of Honor and Utah.

It isn't until I finish the puzzle and close the book that I notice the sketch left on the table. It's placed upside down in front of the spot I was seated at this morning. I reach across the table, slide the sketch toward me and flip it over.

His drawings make no sense. What would

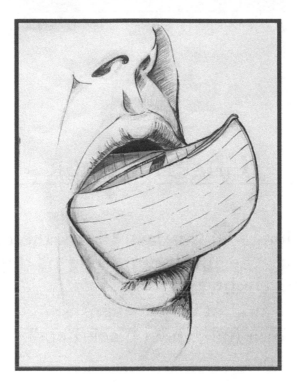

possess him to draw a picture of someone swallowing a boat?

I flip it over and look at the back of it. At the very bottom, it reads, "If silence were a river, your tongue would be the boat."

I flip the drawing back over and stare at it a moment, completely taken aback. Did he draw this of me? Was he the only one in this house to notice I haven't spoken since Friday?

"He actually noticed," I whisper.

And then I immediately slap the drawing on the table and groan. I just ruined my no-speaking streak. "Dammit."

CHAPTER FOUR

"How long will this last?" I ask the cashier, dropping the fifty-pound bag of dog food onto the counter.

"What kind of dog?" she asks.

"It's for a full-grown black Lab."

"Just one?"

I nod.

"Maybe a month. Month and a half."

Oh. I was guessing a week. "I don't think he'll live with us that long." She rings up the total and I pay with my father's debit card. He said to only use it in emergencies. I'm sure food is an emergency to Wolfgang.

"You need help carrying it out?" someone from behind me asks.

"No thanks," I say, taking my receipt. I turn around to face him. "I only got the one bag . . . *what* are you wearing?" I didn't mean to say that out loud but I wasn't expecting to be met with the likes of the guy I'm staring at right now.

Peeking out beneath his hat are sporadic pieces of red hair, too bright to be authentic. So bright, it's almost offensive. His face is decent, a little imperfection here and there. But I didn't give it much notice because my eyes went straight to the kilt he's wearing. I guess the kilt itself isn't tripping me up as much as the clothes he chose to pair it with. He's wearing a basketball jersey and neon green Nikes. Interesting ensemble.

The guy looks down at his outfit. "It's a basketball jersey," he says innocently. "You don't like Blake Griffin?"

I shake my head. "Sports aren't my thing."

He sets what looks like a lifetime supply of beef jerky on the counter. I wrap both arms around the ginormous bag of dog food and head to my car.

The car I drove here isn't specifically mine, but that's because my father never keeps a car long enough for any of us to claim ownership over it. Vehicles have always rotated in our driveway and the only rule is that whichever person leaves the house first each day gets first pick. I think that's the true reason behind Utah's extreme punctuality.

Last month a faded red 1983 Ford EPX appeared in the driveway. It's such a terrible car, they stopped making them almost as quickly as they started. I think my father has been having trouble selling it because it's the longest any vehicle has lasted before it's been sold. And since I rarely leave the house on time, this unfortunate Ford has been driven more by me than the rest of the family put together.

I place the bag of dog food in the trunk and am about to open my front door when kilt-guy appears out of nowhere. He's chewing on a piece of beef jerky, assessing my car like he's about to steal it. He walks toward the front of the car and taps his neon green Nike against the front tire twice.

"Think you can give me a ride?" He looks at me and leans against the car. Despite the kilt, there's no trace of a Scottish accent. There's also no trace of a Texas accent, either. But when he said the word *you* just now, he sounded a tad British.

"What kind of accent is that?" I ask. I open my front door and stand behind it to put a barrier between us. He looks harmless, but I don't like his confidence. I need to shield myself from it. Overly confident people should never be trusted.

He shrugs. "I'm from all over," he says, but he says, *over* with an Australian twang.

"Ovah? Are you Australian?"

"Nevah been there," he says. "What kind of car is this?" He walks to the rear of the car to read the make and model.

"Ford EPX. They're extinct," I tell him. "Where do you need a ride to?"

He's back from the rear of the car, but now he's standing on the same side of the door as me. "My sister's house. It's a few miles east of here."

I give him another once-over. I'm aware of how stupid it is to give a complete stranger a ride. Especially a stranger in a kilt who can't seem to nail his own accent. Everything about him screams unstable, but my spontaneity and refusal to weigh the consequences of my decisions are my two favorite things about me.

"Sure. I'm headed east." I sit in the driver's seat and shut my door. He grins at me through the window and runs around to the passenger side. I have to lean across the seat to unlock the door so that he can open it.

"Give me a second to grab my things." He takes off in a sprint across the parking lot until he reaches a pile of stuff propped next to the front entrance of the store. He grabs the backpack and throws it over his shoulder, then a thirty-gallon black trash bag and a small suitcase on wheels.

I agreed to give him a ride. Not him and

everything he's ever owned.

I pop the trunk and wait for him to finish loading his belongings. When he's back inside the car, he puts on his seat belt and smiles at me. "Ready."

"Are you homeless?"

"Define homeless," he says.

"A person without a home."

His eyes narrow in thought. "Define home."

I shake my head. "You are the strangest person I've ever met." I crank the car and put it in reverse.

"You obviously haven't met very many people. What's your name?"

"Merit."

"I'm Luck."

I shoot him a quick glance before pulling out onto the highway. "Luck? Is that a nickname?"

"Nope." He opens his container of beef jerky and offers me a piece. I shake my head. "You a vegetarian or something?"

"No," I say. "I just don't want any beef jerky."

"I have granola bars in my suitcase."

"I'm not hungry."

"You thirsty?"

"Why? You don't even have a drink to offer me if I am."

"I was going to suggest a drive-thru," Luck says. "*Are* you thirsty?"

"No."

"How old are you?"

I'm starting to regret my spontaneity. "Seventeen."

"Why aren't you in school right now? Is today a holiday?"

"No. I'm finished with high school." It's not a lie. Finished and completed are two different things.

"I'm twenty," he says, moving his attention out his window. His knee is bouncing up and down and he's tapping the fingers of his right hand on his leg. All his fidgeting has me questioning my decision to give him a ride to his sister's house. I make a mental note to look at his pupils if he faces me again. It would be my luck to pick up a random stranger who is coming down from a high.

"How many dogs do you have?" He's still staring out the window as he asks me this.

"None."

He faces me and arches a brow. I use the opportunity to assess his pupils. Normal.

"Why are you buying dog food if you don't have dogs?"

"It's for a dog at my house, but he's not our dog."

"Are you dog sitting?"

"No."

"Did you steal him?"

"No."

"What kind of dog is it?"

"Black Lab."

He grins. "I like black Labs. Where do you live?" I must make a face that indicates what I think of that invasive question, because he immediately responds. "I didn't mean your exact address. I just meant in relation to where I'm going."

"I don't know. I don't know where you're going."

"To my sister's house."

"Where does your sister live?"

He shrugs. "This way," he says, pointing in the direction we're going. He pulls his phone out of his pocket. "I have a picture of her house."

"You don't know her address?"

He shakes his head. "No, but if you can just drop me off somewhere in the general area, I can ask around."

"General area of where?"

"The general area of my sister's house."

I press my hand against my forehead. I've known this guy all of five minutes and I'm already overwhelmed. I have no idea if I like him or if I can't stand him. He's a little bit fascinating, but in a slightly annoying sense. He's probably one of those people that can only be tolerated in spurts. Kind of like a thunderstorm. They're fun if they only appear when you're in the mood for one. But if they show up when they aren't wanted, like at an outdoor wedding, they ruin everything.

"How did you finish school already? Are you one of those people that's better at everything than everyone else? Like Adam Levine? You probably play guitar."

What does that even mean? "No, I don't play guitar. And I'm not better at everything. I'm not as good at asking questions as you."

"You're also not good at answering them."

Is he seriously insulting my conversation skills? "I've answered every question you've asked."

"Not in the way you're supposed to answer questions."

"There's another way to answer questions other than giving the correct answer?"

He nods. "You're giving short answers, like you aren't interested in having a conversation. It should be a two-man sport, like a Ping-Pong match. But with you it feels more like . . . bowling. Just going one way down the lane."

I laugh. "You should learn social cues. If someone is answering your questions like they don't want to answer them, maybe you should stop asking questions."

He stares at me a moment and then opens his container of beef jerky again. "You want a piece yet?"

"No," I say again, growing more agitated with him by the second. "Are you dumb? Like . . . are you a legit stupid person?"

He closes his container and sets it on the floor between his legs. "No, I'm actually very smart."

"What's your issue, then? Are you on drugs?"

He laughs. "Not any illegal ones."

He's smiling at me, taking this entire conversation in stride. This is normal for him? He's completely at ease. It makes me wonder what other kind of people he's encountered in his life for him to think what's happening right now is normal.

I exit the highway and decide the best course of action would be to drop him off at the only gas station in our town.

"You got a boyfriend, Merit?"

I shake my head.

"Girlfriend?"

I shake my head again.

"Well, is there anyone you find intriguing?"

"Are you hitting on me or is this just you asking questions?"

"I'm not actively hitting on you, but that's not to say I wouldn't. You're cute. But right now I'm just making conversation. Ping-Pong."

I blow out a frustrated rush of air.

"You're about to hit a turkey," he says, matter-of-fact.

I slam on my brakes. Why would there be a turkey on this road? I scan the road in front and around us but see nothing. "There's no turkey."

"I meant metaphorically."

What the hell? "Never tell a driver they're about to hit something metaphorically! Jesus Christ!" I let off the brake until the car starts moving again.

"It's a bowling term. Three strikes is a turkey."

"I am so lost."

He sits up straighter and pulls his leg up in his seat so that he can face me. "Conversation should be like Ping-Pong," he repeats. "But conversation with you is like bowling. It's a long, one-way lane. Three strikes in bowling is a turkey. And since you aren't answering my questions, I used turkey as an analogy to describe your lack of . . ."

"Okay!" I say, holding up a hand to shut him up. "I get it. Yes. There's a guy. Anything else you want to know before you start overexplaining metaphorical road kill again?"

I can already sense his excitement that I'm agreeing to participate in his conversation. Even if it is just to shut him up. "Does he know you like him?" he asks.

I shake my head.

"Does he like you?"

I shake my head again.

"Is he out of your league?"

"No," I say immediately. "That's so rude."

But even though his question was rude, it does give me pause. When I first saw Sagan at the antiques store, I had a quiet fear that he was out of my league. But when I found out he was dating Honor, it never even crossed my mind that she was out of his league. I hate that I might have thought she deserved him more than I did.

"Why isn't he your boyfriend?"

I grip the steering wheel. I'm a mile away from the gas station. One more stop sign and I can drop him off.

"Don't hit the metaphorical turkey," he says. "Why aren't you dating this fellow you find intriguing?"

Fellow? He seriously just referred to another guy as a fellow. And his turkey metaphor doesn't even make sense. "You use analogies wrong."

"Don't avoid the question," he says. "Why aren't you and this guy dating?"

I sigh. "He's my sister's boyfriend."

The words are barely out of my mouth before Luck starts laughing. "Your sister? Holy crap, Merit! What a terrible thing to do!"

I give him the side eye. Does he think I don't realize how terrible it is to be attracted to my sister's boyfriend?

"Does your sister know you like him?"

"Of course not. And she never will." I motion toward his phone. "Let me see the picture of your sister's house. I might know where it is." I'm more eager than ever to drop him off now.

Luck scrolls through the pictures on his phone. Right when I get to the stop sign, he hands me his phone.

You've got to be kidding me. I'm being pranked, right? I immediately throw the car in park. I zoom in on the picture of Victoria standing in front of Dollar Voss. The picture looks a couple of years old because the white picket fence my dad put up last year isn't in this picture.

"Looks like it might have been a church at some point," Luck says.

"Victoria is your sister?"

He perks up. "You know her?"

I hand him back his phone and grip the steering wheel. I press my forehead against it. Five seconds later, a car behind us honks. I look in my rearview mirror and the guy behind us holds up his hands in frustration. I put the car in drive. "Yes, I know her."

"You know where she lives?"

"Yep."

Luck faces forward again. "Good," he says. "That's good." He starts tapping his fingers on his leg again. "And you're taking me to her house? Right now?" He seems nervous again.

"Isn't that where you want to go?"

He nods, but even his nod seems unsure.

"Does your sister know you're coming?"

He shrugs his shoulders as he stares out the passenger window. "There's not really a correct answer to that question."

"Actually, there are two potential correct answers. Yes and no."

"She may not be expecting me today. But she can't abandon me without expecting me to show back up at some point."

I had no idea Victoria had a brother. I'm

not so sure my father knows Victoria has a brother. And he's so . . . different. Nothing like Victoria.

I turn onto our road and then pull into our driveway. I put the car in park. Luck is staring at the house, still tapping his leg and bouncing his knee, but not making an effort to get out of the car.

"Why does she live in a church?" He pronounces church without the *r*. Chuch. All of his annoying confidence is gone, replaced by an equally annoying amount of vulnerability. He swallows and then reaches to the floorboard to pick up his container of beef jerky. "Thanks for the ride, Merit." He puts his hand on the door and glances back at me. "We should be friends while I'm in town. You want to exchange numbers?"

I shake my head and open my door. "That won't be necessary." I pop the trunk and get out of the car.

"I can get my own stuff," he says. "You don't have to help."

I open the trunk. "I'm not. I'm getting my dog food." I struggle to pull the bag out from beneath all of Luck's belongings. Once I have a secure grip on it, I head for the front door.

"Why are you taking your dog food to my sister's house?" When I don't stop to answer him, he starts following me. "Merit!" He reaches me just as I stick a key in the front door. When it unlocks, I face him. He's still staring at the key in the door.

"Your sister is married to my father."

I wait for him to absorb that information. When he does, he takes a step back and tilts his head. "You live here? With my sister?"

I nod. "She's my stepmother."

He scratches his chin. "So that makes me . . . your uncle?"

"Step-uncle." I walk through the front door and toss the bag of dog food onto the floor. Luck stands in the doorway as he runs a hand through his hair and then grips the back of his neck. "I already pictured you naked," he mutters.

"Now would be a good time to stop doing that."

Luck glances back to the car and then peeks his head inside the house. "Is my sister home right now?" he whispers.

"She doesn't get back for a couple of hours. Get your stuff and I'll show you where to put it."

While he heads back to the car, I drag the dog food through the kitchen and set the bag next to the back door. I find a couple of old bowls and fill them with water and food, then take them out back. Wolfgang is halfway out of the doghouse, lying on his stomach. His ears perk up when he hears the back door shut, but he doesn't move. His ears go limp again when he sees me. He just watches as I set the bowls down next to his doghouse. He makes no move to devour the food, even though he's been a whole day without it.

I reach out and pet his pathetic head. "Are you sad?" I've never seen a grieving pet before. I didn't even know they could grieve. "Well, you can stay here as long as you need to. I'll try to hide you from my father as long as I can, but you better not bark all night."

As soon as I stand up, Wolfgang lifts himself off the ground, just far enough to reach his food bowl. He sniffs the food and then the water, but he lies back down again and whimpers.

Luck appears next to me. "Has he eaten that brand before?" He's still holding his suitcase, trash bag, and backpack. I look back at the house.

"Why didn't you just leave your stuff inside?"

He looks down at his stuff and shrugs. He nods his head toward the dog. "What's wrong with him? Is he dying?"

"No. His owner died yesterday. He showed

up in the middle of the night last night because he used to live here."

"That's impressive," Luck says, tilting his head. "What's your name, dog?" Wolfgang's eyes scan over Luck, but he doesn't move.

"He can't answer you." I think that goes without saying, but I'm not convinced Luck comprehends how reality works. "His name is Wolfgang."

"What?" Luck grimaces. "That's a terrible name. He should have been named Henry."

"Obviously." I'm being sarcastic, but again, I'm not sure Luck comprehends that level of communication.

"Are you in mourning?" Luck asks Wolfgang.

"Will you stop asking the dog questions?"

Luck looks at me, perplexed. "Are you always this angry?"

"I'm not angry." I turn and walk toward the house.

"Well you aren't *not* angry," he mutters from behind me.

Once we're inside the house, he follows me to Quarter Two. I take him to the spare bedroom across the hall from me. "You can stay in the guest room." I open the door and pause in the doorway. "Or not."

There's stuff all over the guest room. Shoes on the floor, the bed is unmade, there are toiletries on the dresser. Who's staying here? I walk to the closet and open the door to find several of Sagan's shirts hanging up. "You've got to be kidding me."

How could my father allow him to sleep in the same house as her? This is further proof that he doesn't care. He doesn't even care if Honor gets knocked up at seventeen!

Luck slides past me and walks to the wall opposite the door. Several sketches are lying on the dresser. He focuses on a sketch of a man hanging from a ceiling fan by a string of feathers. "Looks like I have a very morbid roommate."

"You don't have a roommate," I say. "He doesn't live here. I don't know why all his stuff is here."

Luck picks up a toothbrush on the nightstand. "You sure he doesn't live here?"

"You can sleep in my father's office." I have Luck follow me to the end of the hallway. "There's a sofa bed in here. When Sagan leaves, you can have the guest bedroom."

"His name is Sagan?" Luck follows me into the room and drops his backpack on the sofa. "I can see why you find him intriguing. His art is . . . interesting."

"I don't find him intriguing."

He laughs. "You said in the car you found

him intriguing. Is Sagan not the guy who's dating your sister?"

I close my eyes and release a frustrated breath. I only told him that because I never thought I'd see him again.

Luck props his suitcase against the desk and looks around the room. "It's not much, but it's already better than where I've been sleeping."

"You better not repeat that," I say to him.

He looks at me like I'm the weird one of the two of us. "That this is better than where I've been sleeping?"

"No. The other thing. I only told you about my sister's boyfriend because I didn't think I'd ever see you again."

Luck smiles. "Relax, Merit. Your love life doesn't interest me enough to repeat it."

I don't know why, but I believe him. "Thanks. You want a tour of the house?"

He nods. "Eventually. I'd like to unpack first."

"Okay."

I turn, expecting him to want privacy, but instead he says, "Why is there a statue of Jesus Christ on the living room wall?" He opens his suitcase and begins pulling out clothes. "Or better yet, why is he dressed like a Packers fan?"

"This used to be a church." I take a seat

on the sofa and watch as he unpacks.

"Is your father a preacher or something?"

"Quite the opposite, actually."

"What's the opposite of a preacher? An atheist mime?"

"My dad doesn't believe in God. But he got a good deal on the church, so he moved us in a few years ago. Right before he started sleeping with my mother's nurse."

He glances over his shoulder. "Your father sounds like an asshole."

I chuckle. "You're being way too kind."

Luck pulls a shirt out of his suitcase and walks it to the closet. "What happened after your mom found out about the affair?"

"He divorced her and married his mistress."

"I guess the mistress would be my sister?"

I nod. "How do you not know any of this? Has it been that long since you last saw Victoria?"

He walks over to the couch and drops down next to me. He falls back against the arm of the couch and props his arms behind his head. "Why don't you live with your mom?"

"I do. She moved to the basement."

I wait for the shock to register on his face, but he just casually raises an eyebrow. "She lives here? In the basement of this house?"

I nod. "Why did you say your sister abandoned you?"

"It's complicated."

"Where are your parents?"

"Mostly dead," he says, matter-of-fact. "I should try to get a nap in before she gets here. It's been a while since I've slept."

He does look tired, but I've never seen him before today, so I have no point of reference. I nod and head for the door. "Good night."

I step out into the hallway and acknowledge what a weird twenty-four hours this has been. Pastor Brian dies, Wolfgang returns, I randomly pick up a hitchhiker in a kilt who turns out to be my step-uncle. This day might call for an addition to my trophy collection by the time it's over.

As I'm making my way through Quarter Two, I pause at the door to the guest room. I glance left and right even though no one is here but Luck and me. And my mother, of course. I open the door and inspect the room Sagan is staying in. I've always been kind of oblivious, but this takes oblivion to a new level. How long has his stuff been here? I just assumed he'd been coming over for breakfast every morning and staying late at night. I'm surprised my father is allowing this, even with how lenient he is sometimes.

I sit down on the guest bed and pull his sketchbook onto my lap. I know I shouldn't be looking through his things, but I feel justified since I was out of the loop that we added a new member to our household. I flip through the sketchbook, but all the pages are blank. All of them except for one. In the very back of the sketchbook, there's a drawing of two girls with their arms around each other.

After closer inspection, I realize there's more to it than that. My hand goes to my mouth when I realize what I'm looking at.

It's a depiction of me and Honor, stabbing each other in the back.

Why would he draw this?

I flip it over, but this one isn't titled like the one from this morning.

"What are you doing?"

I immediately slide the book off my lap. Sagan is standing in the doorway, which marks the second most embarrassing moment of my life. Funny that they both include him.

I don't normally snoop. I don't know how to talk my way out of this. I stand up, painfully aware that I don't know what to do with my hands when I'm this embarrassed. My arms are stiff at my sides. I clench my fists and then unclench them.

"I didn't know you moved in," I mutter.

He steps into the room and his eyes fall to the sketchbook I was just skimming through. His eyes meet mine again. He looks annoyed. "I've lived here for two weeks, Merit."

Two weeks?

Until this moment, I never realized just how much time I spend alone in my room. For two weeks he's been living across the hall from me? And no one thought to tell me?

He stares at me and I stare right back, because I have no idea what else to do.

I hate the way he looks. I hate his hair. I especially hate his mouth. His lips are weird. They don't have grooves in them like most lips have. They're smooth and tight and I hate that every time I look at them, I remember what it was like when they were kissing me.

But what I hate the most about him are his eyes. I hate how I feel when I look at them. Not that his eyes are accusatory, but I always get swallowed up in guilt when he's looking at me. Because no matter how much his individual features annoy me, they complement each other very nicely. I look down at my feet and wish the last five minutes never happened. I shouldn't have walked in here. I shouldn't have looked at the sketch he drew. And I shouldn't have stared so long at him just now. Because I'd give anything for him to look at me the way he looked at me when he thought I was Honor. The fact that I want that embarrasses me more than being caught in his room.

I rush past him, refusing to look at him as I make my way out into the hall. I walk straight to my bedroom door and open it, then slam it shut. I fall onto my bed and I feel the tears as they begin to sting at my eyes. I don't even know why I'm emotional. It's so dumb.

What a weird, shitty day.

I pull my phone out of my pocket to text my father. I rarely ask him for anything, but this is an emergency.

Can you stop by the thrift store on your way here and see if they have any trophies?

I wait a few minutes to see if he responds, but he doesn't. Sadly, I'm not surprised.

I lie down on my bed, pull my blanket over me, and think about the picture Sagan drew of me swallowing a boat this morning. It's such a strange picture. I hate how much I like it. I hate that no matter how hard I try not to, I like him a little more every day. Part of me wonders if it's actually him I like, or if I'm just a jealous person. I've never been jealous of any of Honor's boyfriends before him. But then again, they were all dying.

I'm so angry that he's living here now. I was convinced it would be easy to avoid him, but now he's living in the room across the hall from me. I'm going to be subjected to their relationship and to him kissing her and loving her.

I know my father doesn't believe in God, but luckily, atheism isn't hereditary. I hardly ever pray, but I feel like now is as good of a time as any. I roll onto my back and look up at the ceiling. I clear my throat. "God?"

Not gonna lie. It feels weird talking to the ceiling. Maybe I should kneel like they do in the movies.

I throw the covers off and kneel on the floor against the bed. I lower my head and try it again with my eyes closed.

"Hey, God. I know I don't pray as much as I probably should. And when I do pray, it's always something selfish. I apologize for that. But I really need your help. I'm sure you saw what happened with my sister's boyfriend a few weeks ago. I can't stop thinking about him. I don't like the person it's turning me into. I've been having these irrational thoughts, like maybe he was meant for me and not Honor. Maybe you created him as my soul mate, and because Honor and I are identical, his soul got confused and fell in love with her. Because they're nothing alike. They have nothing in common. She doesn't even like the best parts of him. But even if they were to break up, there's no way it would work out between us. I'd never do that to my sister, and as much as I'm attracted to him, I could never love someone that was once with Honor. It's out of the question. So I'm not coming to You to ask You to show him the error of his ways. I'm coming to You to ask if You would just send me someone else. Someone who will completely take my mind off him. I don't want to have the thoughts I've been having anymore. Or at least I don't want to be having them about my sister's boyfriend. I wouldn't mind having these thoughts about someone else. So . . . yeah. I'm merely asking for an alternative soul mate. Or even just a distraction. I don't even care if it has to do with another person. Any interest that isn't Sagan would be great. Whatever you can spare."

I open my eyes and then crawl back into bed. Praying is so awkward. Maybe I should do it more.

"Oh, yeah. Amen."

CHAPTER FIVE

"Merit, wake up."

I didn't know it was possible to roll my eyes before opening them, but I accomplish this feat. "What," I grumble, pulling the covers over my head.

"You need to wake up," Honor says. She flips on the light to my bedroom. I pull my cell phone out from under my pillow to see what time it is.

"It's six in the morning," I mutter, annoyed. "None of us wake up this early." Not to mention she knows I don't go to school anymore, so what's it matter if I'm awake?

"It's six in the evening, dumb ass. It's your night to take Mom dinner." She slams the door.

It's six in the evening? Which means it's still today. Shitty today.

Joy.

I spoon mashed potatoes onto a plate next

to a piece of blackened chicken. There may not be much about Victoria to like, but her cooking has always been good. I do wonder, though, what it must be like to have to cook extra food every night for your husband's ex-wife who lives in your basement.

I spin around to grab a roll for the plate, but I bump into Sagan, who has appeared behind me. "Sorry." I try to move around him before having to inhale his scent, or God forbid, look at his face. I move left, he moves right. We're still in each other's way. I move right, he moves left. Are you freaking kidding me?

He laughs at our little dance, but that's because he can breathe when he's around me. He only loses his breath around Honor. I finally spin and walk the other direction and go around the bar. Right before I reach the basement door, I glance back in the kitchen. Honor is now standing next to her boyfriend, making her plate. But he's staring at me with a quizzical look.

He must think I'm such a bitch, especially when something as simple as being in his way happens. I'm not able to laugh it off like he does. I get frustrated and go the other direction.

"Merit?"

I'm not even halfway down the stairs and

she can tell it's me. She's somehow memorized the footsteps of everyone in the house. I guess when all you do is watch Netflix and play on Facebook, you get pretty good at listening to footsteps.

"Yeah, it's me."

She's sitting on the couch when I make it down to the basement. She closes her laptop and slides it to the floor. "What's for dinner tonight?"

"Chicken and potatoes again." I hand her the plate and take a seat next to her on the couch. She looks at the plate and sets it down on the table next to her.

"I'm not really that hungry," she says. "I'm trying to lose ten pounds."

"Maybe you should go for a run. The weather is nice."

She frowns. I think I'm the only one who still tries to encourage her to go outside. But at this point, it's not really encouragement. It's more a sarcastic suggestion.

"You haven't been down to see me since last week." She reaches up her hand to brush my hair over my shoulder, but she hesitates before touching me. Her hand falls back to her lap. "Have you been sick?"

Frustrated is a better word. The older I get, the harder it is to understand her phobia. I get not wanting to leave your house, but to hole yourself up in a basement for years while your children continue to live their lives upstairs seems more like the world's longest temper tantrum than a social phobia.

"Yeah, I haven't been feeling well," I say.

"Is that why you've been out of school?"

I narrow my eyes a bit, wondering how she knows I haven't been going to school.

"Your principal called today to check on you."

"Oh. What did you tell him?"

She shrugs. "I didn't answer my cell phone. He left a voice mail."

I let out a quiet sigh of relief. At least the school doesn't know the extent of her social phobia. They still call her before calling our father whenever an issue arises.

My mother tosses the blanket off her lap and stands up. "Can you mail something for me tomorrow?" She walks the length of her living room — all four feet of it — and grabs an empty box from her shelf. "I have some books I promised I'd get to Shelly."

My mother may not leave the basement, but she's got more friends than Honor and I put together. She's obsessed with reading and has joined several online reading groups. If she isn't watching Netflix, she's reading a book or doing video chats with her book friends. I sometimes walk in on her video chats and she'll introduce me and make me talk to her friends. She tries so hard to put on the air of a normal mother leading a normal life. But sometimes when I'm forced to be in one of her videos, I get the urge to scream, "She hasn't left the basement in two years!"

"Shelly said she mailed me a package last week. It should be here tomorrow."

"I'll bring it down when it gets here," I assure her. She writes an address on the box and while she has her back to me, it's the first I've noticed of her outfit. She's wearing a black maxi dress that goes all the way to her feet. "Your dress is cute. Is it new?"

My mother nods, but doesn't reveal how she got it. She must order her clothes online because she hasn't had a visitor other than her children and occasionally my father when they need to discuss a parenting issue. It's a shame, too, because she's gorgeous for her age. It doesn't matter that she hasn't left the basement in forever; she still takes very good care of herself. She applies makeup every morning and her hair is always washed and styled. She probably still shaves her legs every day, which makes no sense because if I decided to never leave the house again, the first thing I would do is stop shaving.

Maybe she's in an online relationship. Normally I wouldn't advocate for those, but I support anything that might give her motivation to leave the basement in the future.

I take the box from her and head toward the stairs. I used to hang out with her for longer periods of time, but it's gotten hard to do that lately. I'm starting to resent her. I used to feel sorry for her and assumed her social phobia wasn't something she could control. But the older I get and the more of my life she misses by choosing to stay in the basement, the angrier at her I am. Sometimes I get so angry when I'm down here, I start shaking and have to leave before I explode on her.

Which is where things will lead if I don't get out of this basement right now.

"See you later, Mom," I say as I head back up the stairs.

"Merit," she says, calling after me.

I let the door to the basement close behind me.

Victoria is in the kitchen, cutting up a chicken breast for Moby. Everyone else is already at the table eating. I grab a plate for myself, just as my father walks through the front door. It's half past six now and his football game starts at seven, so he has his dinner plate made before I do. When I finally walk my food to the table, there's only one empty seat left. Right next to what's-his-face. Honor is on the other side of him, leaning into him and laughing at something he just said. I'm sure it was clever, whatever it was.

I plop down in my chair and scoot it forward. Moby is seated on my other side, to my relief. "You have a good day?" I ask him.

He's shoving a bite of corn in his mouth when he nods. "Tyler got in trouble for saying bastard."

Most of us laugh, but Victoria gasps. "Moby, that's a bad word!"

"Technically, it isn't," my father says.

Victoria glares at my father. "It is when you're only four and you say it at preschool."

"What's a bastard?" Moby asks.

"A kid born to parents who haven't gotten married yet. It's what you almost were," I reply.

You would think I slapped the kid with the way Victoria reacts to my comment. She immediately pushes her chair back and stands up. "Go to your room!"

I laugh because at first I think she's kidding. But then I stop smiling because her anger is authentic. You've got to be kidding

115

me. I look at my father and he's staring at Victoria, his fork paused in front of his mouth. I look back at Victoria. "He asked what a bastard was. Did you want me to lie to him?"

Victoria's eyes are boring into mine. Her nostrils might even be flaring. I've never seen her so mad. I honestly didn't say it out of cruelty. "A bastard is a child born out of wedlock," I say to Victoria. "Isn't that what he almost was?"

Victoria points toward the hallway. "You will not speak that way in front of my child, Merit. Go to your room." She looks to my father for backup. "Barnaby?"

I scoot back and fold my arms over my chest. I'm not backing down. "So you want me to lie to your child?" I look at a wide-eyed Moby. "Since sex is a bad eighties TV show, a bastard is the commercial." I look at Victoria. "Is that better?"

"Merit," Utah says. He says it like I'm the one out of line at this table. I turn my attention to him.

"Are you seriously taking Victoria's side now?"

"Can we please just make it through one meal as a family without a fight breaking out?" Honor says, frustrated.

"Barnaby?" Victoria says, still standing,

still waiting for him to punish me.

My father wraps his hand around Victoria's wrist and tries to get her to sit back down. "I'll deal with her later. Let's just eat, okay?"

Victoria snatches her hand away from my father and grabs her plate. She walks toward the kitchen and tosses her food into the trash can.

"Save the scraps," I call out to her.

"Excuse me?"

I point to the trash. "The scraps. Wolfgang can eat them."

"Wolfgang?" my father says. "Why are you bringing up that bastard dog?"

"And here we go again with that word," Honor mutters.

"Is that why there's a bag of dog food by the back door?" Utah asks.

My father's eyes move to the bag of dog food. He stands up. "Is that dog here?"

I take a bite of my mashed potatoes because I have no idea if I'm about to be sent to my room, but I'm hungry. "He showed up in the middle of the night last night," I say with a mouthful. I swallow and throw my thumb over my shoulder. "He's in the backyard."

"You let him in the backyard!?" my father yells.

117

Victoria throws her hands in the air. "Oh, this is just great. You get angry at her for allowing a dog in the yard but not for calling your son a bastard?"

I hold up my fork. "I said he was *almost* a bastard," I clarify.

"Why do you always do this?" Utah whispers. He's so quiet when he says it, which means he's not directing his question at Victoria on the other side of the kitchen. Surely he isn't talking to me.

"You think this is my fault?"

"It usually is," Honor says. "We can't get through one meal without you doing something to piss her off."

I laugh incredulously. "And that's my fault?" I raise my voice loud enough for Victoria to hear our conversation. "Maybe she gets pissed off because she's an unreasonable person. Just ask the little brother she abandoned."

I make sure to look at Victoria so I can see her face. Sure enough, that last sentence was a shocker.

"What did you just say?" She's looking at me like she either didn't hear me or doesn't want to hear me. I open my mouth to repeat what I said, but my father interrupts me.

"Merit," he says, more defeated than angry. "Go to your room."

Victoria slowly turns her head toward my father. "You told her about Luck?"

He immediately shakes his head. "No, they don't know about Luck. She's pushing your buttons."

Now I'm dying to know what she doesn't want us to know. I take two more quick bites of my potatoes in case I'm forced to carry out my punishment. "I'm not pushing her buttons." I swallow and wipe my mouth and then prepare to explain myself. Not that I should be required to do so.

"Wolfgang showed up here last night. It was raining and I felt bad for him, so I let him in the backyard. Then I found out Pastor Brian died and forgot to tell any of you about the dog. I went to Tractor Supply to get dog food today and this weird guy in a kilt asked me for a ride to his sister's house, which turned out to be this house. His name is Luck, he's Victoria's little brother, and he's asleep in Dad's office, since Sagan apparently lives in the guest room now. And like it or not, the definition of a bastard is a child born out of wedlock. And in case any of you forgot, Victoria got pregnant while Dad was still married to Mom, so Moby was practically a bastard."

When I finish my explanation, everyone is

119

quietly staring at me. I face forward and give my full attention to my food.

"He was wearing a kilt?" Sagan asks. As much as I wish he wasn't talking to me, I appreciate him trying to ease the tension with humor. "What color was it?"

I force myself to look across the table at him. A small smile plays across his lips.

"Green plaid."

He nods appreciatively. "Can't wait to meet him."

"My brother is here?" Victoria says. Her voice is much quieter now. "Luck is here? In this house?"

I start to respond, but I don't have to because Luck is now standing at the end of the hallway. "Technically, it's not a house," he says to her. "It looks more like a misunderstood church."

I'm starting to understand what Luck meant about conversations being a Ping-Pong match, because we're all looking back and forth between Luck and Victoria, waiting for the emotional reunion.

Victoria's hand goes up to her mouth. My father walks up to her and puts his hands on her shoulders, trying to take her attention away from her little brother. "Sweetie," he says soothingly. "Let's go talk it out with him in the bedroom."

Victoria shakes her head and pushes past my father, toward Luck. "You can't just show up unannounced, Luck. You need to leave."

Luck doesn't move. He looks a little surprised by her reaction. "You aren't going to hug me first?"

Victoria takes a step closer to him. "Leave," she says. "And next time you want to show up without apologizing first, try calling. It'll save you money on travel!"

"Victoria," my father says in a whisper. He pulls her in the opposite direction. "Go to the bedroom. I'll be there in a second." She immediately starts trying to hide the fact that she's sniffling a bit when she walks away from Luck, toward their bedroom. My father faces Luck.

Luck smiles and walks toward him with his hand out. "You must be my brother-in-law," Luck says. My father reluctantly shakes his hand.

"Barnaby."

"I honestly thought she'd be over it by now," Luck says. "She's right. Maybe I should have called first."

"Be over what?" Honor asks. Luck swings his gaze to Honor and he gives her a familiar smile, but then his smile disappears when he notices me.

He looks back at Honor, then back at me. Then he points between us. "Which one of you gave me a ride today?"

I lift my hand.

"Thank you for the hospitality, Merit." Luck walks toward the table. He introduces himself to Utah, Honor, and then Sagan. When he gets to Moby, he kneels down in front of him. "You must be my nephew."

"I'm a nephew?" Moby asks. "Merit said I'm a bastard."

"*Almost* a bastard," I correct.

"Luck," my father says, interrupting the introductions. "Can we please sort this out first before you make yourself at home?"

Luck stands up and puts his hands on his hips. "Yeah, sure. But . . . I just woke up from a four-hour nap. Kind of already made myself at home." He laughs, but he's the only one laughing. I have to hand it to him. Luck is cheerful, if anything.

He follows my father to Quarter Three. I'm sad they're moving the conversation out of Quarter One. I was enjoying it.

"Sounds like your day was productive," Honor says to me. "At least you weren't wasting away your *entire* life by sleeping all day."

I can put up with a lot, but Honor's snarky attitude about my decision to stop going to school is my boiling point. I toss my roll back on my plate. "Tell me, Honor. What have I missed this week that's going to miraculously prep me for life beyond high school?"

"An opportunity to graduate, maybe?"

I roll my eyes. "I can get a GED before Christmas."

"Yes, because that's a reasonable alternative to a scholarship," she says.

"You want to talk to me about reasonable?" I challenge. "Does your new boyfriend know how reasonable you've been when it comes to your past relationships?"

Honor's jaw clenches. I've hit a nerve. Good. Maybe she'll back off.

"That's not fair, Merit," Utah says.

"Whatever," I mutter. I tear off a piece of my bread and pop it in my mouth. "Of course you're going to defend her. She's your favorite."

Utah leans back in his chair. "I don't have a favorite sister. I'm defending her because you always get too personal with your attacks."

I nod. "Oh, right. I forgot. We like to sweep things under the rug and pretend Honor doesn't need therapy."

Honor glares at me from across the table. "And you wonder why you have no friends."

"Actually, I don't wonder that at all."

The raised voices coming from Quarter Three interrupt our sibling bonding. It's too muffled to make out what they're saying, but it's clear that Luck and Victoria aren't having the homecoming Luck was hoping for.

"Did anyone else notice how strange his accent was?" Sagan asks.

"Thank you!" I say. "It's so weird! It's like his brain can't decide if he grew up in Australia or London."

"He sounded Irish to me," Utah says.

Sagan shakes his head. "Nah, that was just the kilt playing tricks on you."

I laugh and then glance down at Moby, who is still seated next to me. He's looking down, so I can't see his face. "Moby?"

He doesn't look up, but he sniffles.

"Hey. Why are you crying?"

Moby sniffles some more and then says, "Everyone is fighting."

Ugh. Nothing can make me feel worse than when Moby is upset.

"It's okay," I say. "Sometimes adults fight. It doesn't mean anything."

He wipes his eyes on his shirtsleeve. "Then why do they do it?"

I wish I had an answer for him. "I don't know," I say with a sigh. "Come on, let's wash up and I'll tuck you in." Moby has always been a great sleeper. He's been sleeping in his own bedroom in Quarter Two since he was two. His bedtime has always been seven, but I heard Victoria tell him a few days ago that she would change it to eight in a few weeks.

The rest of us don't really have a bedtime. My father likes us to be at the house on school nights by ten, but once we're in our rooms, he never checks on us. I'm rarely ever in bed before midnight.

I take Moby to the bathroom and help him brush his teeth and wash his hands. His bedroom is right across the hall from where Luck is staying, which, by the sound of the shouting continuing in the other room, might be my father's office again within the hour. Victoria puts Moby to bed most nights, but occasionally he'll ask for Honor, Utah, or me to do it. I enjoy tucking him in at night, but I only do it when Moby specifically asks for me. I don't like to do Victoria any unnecessary favors.

Moby's room is whale-themed, which I hope changes before he starts having sleepovers. It's bad enough he was named after a murderous whale, but for Victoria to actually go so far as to extend the theme to his bedroom is just asking for Moby to get bullied.

Moby likes the whales, though. He also loves that he was named after a whale. *Moby-Dick* is Victoria's favorite book. I also don't trust people who claim for a classic to be their favorite novel. I think they're lying just to sound educated, or they simply haven't read another book beyond high school English requirements.

My favorite book is *God-Shaped Hole.* It's not a classic. It's better than a classic. It's a modern-day tragedy. I've never read *Moby-Dick* but I can almost bet it doesn't leave you feeling like you have less skin than before you opened the book.

I tuck Moby into his bed, pulling the whale-themed blanket up to his chin. "Will you read me a story?" he asks.

It's not entirely inconvenient so I nod and grab a book from his bookshelf. I choose the thinnest one, but Moby protests. "No, read 'The King's Perspective.'"

That's a new one. I glance back at the bookshelf and scan through them but I don't see one with that title. "It's not here. How about *Goodnight Moon*?"

"That's for babies," he says. He picks up a stack of pages from the table beside his bed. "Read this one. Sagan wrote it." He shoves it toward me.

I take the pages from him. They're stapled together in the top left corner. In the center of the front page it reads:

The King's Perspective
By Sagan Kattan

I sit down on the edge of the bed and run my fingers over the top of the page. "Sagan wrote you a story?"

Moby nods. "It's a true story. And it rhymes!"

"When did he give you this?"

Moby shrugs. "Like seven years ago."

I laugh. Moby is the smartest four-year-old I know, but he cannot, for the life of him, grasp the concept of time.

I move to the spot next to Moby and sit against the headboard. I normally don't make myself this comfortable when it comes to tucking him in, but I might be more excited about story time than Moby is tonight. I feel like I'm in on one of Honor's boyfriend's secrets and it makes me way more excited than it should. I pull my knees up and rest the pages on my thighs. "The King's Perspective," I say aloud. I glance down at Moby. "Do you even know what *perspective* means?"

He nods and rolls over onto his side so that he's facing me. "Sagan said it's kind of like putting someone else's eyeballs inside your own head."

"Pretty close," I say. "I'm impressed."

I am impressed. Not so much with Moby, but with Sagan for taking the time to write him a story. And for obviously explaining its meaning.

Moby sits up and flips the page for me. "Read it!"

On the next page is a picture of a bird. It looks like a cardinal.

"Is the story about a bird?" I ask Moby.

"Just read it!" he says.

I flip the page again. "Fine. No spoilers."

The King's Perspective

There's a story of a King
And this story is very true
Some say it's just a rumor
Some say it's just a ruse

They called the man King Flip
But that wasn't really his name
His name was Filipileetus
But that's too hard to say

King Flip had a penchant
For really expensive things
He liked anything shiny
And anything with bling

He had the nicest castle
Out of all the lands
But that didn't stop him
From wanting one even more grand

So he bought a town called Perspective
And made the people build him a castle
At the top of their highest mountain
He didn't care if it was a hassle

When the work was finally done
He decided to go inspect it
But when he arrived in the town of

Perspective
It was exactly as he'd left it

He couldn't find a castle
It wasn't on the mountain
It wasn't on the beach
It wasn't on the mainland

He immediately grew angry
And sought his just revenge
On all those who had fooled him
On the town, his army did descend

When the people were all dead
A red cardinal then appeared
"King Flip, what have you done?
You killed good people, I do fear."

King Flip tried to explain
That the town deserved to die
For his castle was never built
Or he would see it with his own eyes

The bird said, "But king, you merely
    assumed.
You didn't even try
Look from a different perspective.
Don't just look from your own two eyes."

The bird then led him over to where

The castle should surely be
He then moved aside a boulder
And King Flip fell to his knees

For inside the mountain was the castle
The most magnificent one ever built
King Flip couldn't believe his eyes
He quickly became wrecked with guilt

He had killed so many people
People he should have protected
Simply because he couldn't see
The castle from their perspective

"Hide their bodies!" King Flip yelled.
"Hide every last one!
Put them inside the mountain.
And then close those doors for good!"

The king's army hid the bodies
And King Flip fled the land
He went back to his old castle
And never spoke of Perspective again

Some say this story isn't true
Some say the town never existed
But look at any map and you'll see
There is no longer a town called
    Perspective.

I flip back to the first page of the poem, a little in shock by what I just read. This is a children's poem? This is just as morbid, if not more morbid than the art he creates. And the fact that Moby now believes it's a true story!

"You know this is fiction, right?" I look down at Moby but his eyes are closed. I didn't even notice he had fallen asleep while I was reading. I place the story back on his nightstand. I turn off the light before I leave the room and head straight to Quarter One. Sagan is in the kitchen helping Honor wash the dishes. "What is wrong with you?"

They both look up at me, but I'm staring at him.

"Is that an open-ended question?" he asks.

"You slaughtered an entire town of innocent people!"

He nods as registration marks his expression. "Oh, you read to Moby."

"That's disturbing! It's his favorite story now."

"What are you talking about?" Honor asks me.

I flip a hand in her morbid boyfriend's direction. "He wrote a poem for Moby, but it's the worst children's story I've ever read."

"It's not that bad," he says in defense. "It has a good message."

"Does it?" I ask, flabbergasted. "Because the message I got was that a materialistic ruler wasn't happy with the peasants he hired to build his castle, so he slaughtered them all, hid their bodies in a mountain, and went on with his happy life."

Honor makes a face to show how disturbed she is. I make it a point never to make that expression. Seeing it on her lets me know how unappealing it would be on me.

"You completely missed the message, then," he says. "It's a poem about perspective."

"What are we talking about?" Utah asks as he walks into the kitchen.

"The story I wrote for Moby."

Utah laughs as he grabs a soda from the refrigerator. "I loved that story," he says, right before he takes a sip. He wipes his mouth. "I can't listen to this all night," he says, referring to the arguing still coming from Quarter Three. "Want to go swimming?"

"We're in," Honor says, referring to Sagan and herself. "Anything to get out of this house."

They all look at me. No one verbally invites me, but with the way they're all looking at me, I assume this is their way of asking if I'd like to come along.

"I'm good," I say, turning down their non-verbal invite. I've never gone swimming at the hotel with Honor and Utah before. It's gotten to where they don't even invite me, but since I'm standing right in front of them they probably feel pressured. When I turn them down, Honor almost looks relieved.

"Suit yourself," she says, tossing the dish towel on the counter.

Sagan is still looking at me, but with a touch of curiosity in his expression. "You sure you don't want to come?" he asks.

The fact that he looks like he'd appreciate my company makes me want to change my mind. With Honor and Utah, it's obvious they prefer to hang out without me. They don't find my presence an added bonus. To them, my presence is an inconvenience. But the way he's staring at me, it seems he might actually value my presence.

It confuses me. It makes me want to go swimming with my siblings for the first time since they started going the day Utah got his license.

The bedroom door to Quarter Three opens and Luck appears. He walks into the kitchen with his hands shoved in his pockets. My father and Victoria are close behind. My father clears his throat as he addresses all of us.

"Luck will be staying with us for a while. Victoria and I would appreciate it if you would all make him feel welcome."

It's odd, because even though it seems Luck won this argument, his demeanor says otherwise.

"Welcome," Utah says to him. "Feel like going swimming?"

"You have a pool?" Luck asks.

Utah shakes his head. "No, but there's a hotel in town with an indoor heated pool and Honor has connections."

"Nice," Luck says. "Let me grab some shorts." He begins to walk out of the kitchen, but turns to me. "You're coming, too, right?" Luck says this as if it's a plea not to leave him stranded with the rest of my siblings.

I am the only one he's had any interaction with beyond an introduction. I nod. "Yeah, I'll come."

Sagan is just about to round the corner when he hears me accept Luck's invite. He looks over his shoulder at me with a moment of pause, but then continues walking.

"Where's Moby?" Victoria asks.

"I put him to bed already." I let that be the end of our conversation as I head toward my room.

Earlier today I was regretting running into Luck at the store, but now it seems I might finally have a friend in this house. I never go swimming with Utah and Honor because they never seem to want me to, but I'm afraid if I don't go tonight, Luck will bond with the three of them and I'll be odd man out again.

I grab a one-piece and an oversized T-shirt and head back into the hallway. Sagan is walking out of his room and pauses when he sees me. He opens his mouth, but before he says whatever he's about to say, Honor opens her door. His mouth clamps shut.

Now I'll be wondering what he was about to say for the rest of the evening.

They follow Utah and Luck outside. I stop by the bathroom and grab a few towels. Before I reach the front door, I look up at the statue of Cheesus Christ.

I wonder if God answers prayers before they're asked of Him? Is that why Luck is here? Is he the distraction from Sagan that I prayed for earlier?

"Are you responsible for His sacrilegious outfit?"

My father's voice jolts me from my thoughts. He's standing a few feet away, staring at the statue.

"Nope," I lie. "It must have been an im-

136

maculate conception of wardrobe."

I go to close the front door and I hear my father's muffled voice from the other side. "If the Cowboys lose, you're grounded!"

The Cowboys chances of losing are good. The chances of my father actually following through with a threat are not.

CHAPTER SIX

One of the most utilized vehicles in our driveway is the Ford Windstar. It holds seven people, but at the rate our household is growing this month, we'll need an upgrade soon. I was the last one to the van but Honor's boyfriend sat in the back and left one of the middle bucket seats open for me. Luck is in the other one. Honor is in the front passenger seat and Utah is driving.

We live in the middle of nowhere, in a town too small to be significant enough for a hotel with a pool. It's twelve miles to the nearest store and even farther to the hotel we're heading for. This will be at least a fifteen-mile drive. But in a rural area like this, it'll only take thirteen minutes to get there.

"So . . ." Utah says. "You're Victoria's brother?"

"Half brother," he specifies.

I chuckle under my breath because he seems to want to claim Victoria as much as we do.

"Where are you from?"

"Everywhere," Luck says. "Victoria and I have the same father, different mothers. She lived with her mom and I lived with our father and my mother. We moved around a lot until my parents divorced."

"Sorry to hear that," Honor says.

"It's fine. Happens to everyone," he says, matter-of-fact.

No one follows that comment up with a question.

"You didn't tell me you had an identical twin, Merit," Luck says, directing his attention at me.

"You talked the whole time we were in the car," I respond, looking away from him and out the window. "Wasn't much room to fit in my whole life story."

"Not true, because your life story was precisely what I was trying to get out of you," he says with a laugh.

"And you didn't get very far, did you?"

"Far enough to know all about the guy you have a crush on," he says.

My head snaps in his direction. I raise an eyebrow in warning, letting him know he went too far with that comment.

"Wait," Honor says, turning around in her seat. She looks at me. "You have a crush on someone?"

I roll my eyes and look out the window again. "No."

"Who is it?" Honor says, directing her question at Luck.

I scratch at my jeans nervously, hoping he doesn't open his mouth. I don't know him at all. He might get a kick out of embarrassing me.

"I can't remember his name," Luck says. "Ask Merit."

Honor turns back around in her seat. "Merit doesn't tell me things like that." Her voice is accusatory.

I glance at Luck and he's staring at me. "You two have a weird dynamic for identical twins."

"No we don't," I disagree. "There's a false stigma attached to twins."

"Exactly," Honor says in agreement. "Not all twins have things in common beyond their appearance."

"I think you two have more in common than you think," Sagan says from the backseat. Honor glances over her shoulder and glares at him. I'd like to turn around and glare at him, too, but I actually feel things when I look at him, unlike Honor. I don't even know if Honor is attracted to him. She doesn't look at him like I would look at him if he were my boyfriend. And if he were my boyfriend, I'd be sitting in the backseat with him and not in the front seat where Honor is sitting.

I feel bad for him. He's got so much more invested in this relationship than she does. I could tell that simply by the way he kissed me when he thought he was kissing her. He's moved in and committed and she's just waiting around until a less healthy guy comes along.

Luck turns around and faces Honor's boyfriend. "How do you fit into this family?"

"He fits in with me," Honor says from the front seat, answering Luck's question that was actually posed to Sagan.

If he were my boyfriend, I'd let him answer his own questions.

"How did you and Honor meet?" Luck asks him.

I keep staring out the window, but I listen closely. I've never asked either of them this question directly, so I've only heard bits and pieces from eavesdropping.

"I had an allergic reaction to something I ate," Sagan says. "Ended up in the hospital and that's where I met Honor."

Luck faces forward. "Were you in the hospital, too?" he asks Honor.

Honor just shakes her head, but she doesn't elaborate on why she was in the hospital. I have half a mind to tell Luck that Honor was there saying goodbye to yet another boyfriend when she unknowingly set her sights on Sagan, incorrectly assuming he was about to meet his demise.

"Honor was visiting a friend," Sagan says, now answering for Honor.

They can't answer their own freaking questions?

No one speaks for a few minutes, even though I have a million questions for Luck and a million more for Sagan. When we pull into the long driveway of the hotel, Utah finally throws a question over his shoulder.

"Why does your sister hate you so much?"

"Half sister," Luck clarifies. "She's still mad at me for something I did over five years ago."

"What'd you do?" Honor asks, unbuckling her seat belt.

"I killed our father."

My hand pauses on my seat belt. I look up and Luck unbuckles his seat belt and slides open the minivan door. He gets out, but the rest of us are paralyzed by his last comment. Once he's outside the van, he straightens out his kilt and then looks back inside at all of us.

"Oh, come on. I'm kidding."

Honor exhales. "That's not funny," she says, throwing open her door.

When we get inside, Honor walks up to the front desk and rings the bell. A few seconds later, one of Honor's friends from school, Angela Capicci, appears from the back office.

I've never liked Angela. She was a year ahead of us in school, but she and Honor have been casual friends since we were kids. Being as though most of our friends aren't allowed over at our house due to the rumors (founded or not) about our family, the friendships Honor and I form with other people are almost always casual. I keep more to myself than Honor does. I'm not as good at hiding my distaste, and I've always distasted Angela. She's the type of girl who allows the attention from guys to value her worth. And from the way she's eyeing Luck right now, she must be in need of a little valuing. "Hey," she says to him with a flirty grin. "You're new."

Luck nods and returns her flirtatious smile. "Fresh off the boat."

She raises an eyebrow, unsure of how to respond to his comment. She looks back at

143

Honor. "My shift ends at eleven. If you guys are still here, I'll join you."

"We have to be home by ten," Honor says. She holds up the key card. "Thanks for this."

Angela nods, bringing her gaze back to Luck. "Anytime," she says, her voice dripping with invitation. Her eyes remain glued to Luck as we make our way toward the bathrooms to change. Honor and I walk into the girls and she immediately pulls her shirt off and begins changing without walking into one of the stalls. I'm a bit more modest than she is, and the idea of someone walking into the bathroom while I'm squeezing into my bathing suit is enough to force me into the stall to change. I have my jeans and T-shirt off when Honor says the inevitable.

"So who was Luck referring to?"

I pause for a moment, then begin pulling on my swimsuit. "What are you talking about?"

"In the van," she says, clarifying what I already know. "He said you told him you had a crush on a guy. Do I know him?"

I close my eyes and try to imagine the hell that would break loose if I admitted to her that the guy I have a crush on is her boyfriend. It would be the end of what little relationship we have left as sisters. I open the door to the stall, pulling my T-shirt over my head. "He was lying. There's no one. I hardly even leave the house; how would I meet someone?"

Honor looks a little disappointed in my answer. She also looks . . . stunning.

"Is that a new bathing suit?" I ask her. She's in a red bikini with black trim. It covers her as well as a bikini can cover her, but the color and the cut are perfect. I look down at my oversized T-shirt that's covering up my ill-fitted, plain black one-piece, and I frown.

"I've had it a few months," she says, slipping her hands into the top to push her cleavage together. "You just never come swimming with us so you haven't seen it."

"You know I don't like swimming," I mutter.

Honor folds her jeans and sets them on the sink counter. Our eyes meet in the mirror. "Is that the reason?"

Although it would appear otherwise, the question is rhetorical. Honor knows the reason I don't swim with them has nothing to do with how I feel about the water. I don't come because of my strained relationship with her and Utah. The relationship that's been strained for five years now.

She walks out of the bathroom and I give it a moment before I follow her. The last thing I need to witness is her boyfriend's expression when he looks at her in that bathing suit.

I notice I sometimes refer to him in my head as "her boyfriend" instead of Sagan. I wonder if I'll ever stop referring to him as her boyfriend and not by his name. I just really like the name Sagan. It's smart and sexy and I don't want it to fit him, but it does. So well. Which is why I just want to refer to him as his title. Honor's boyfriend. It's less appealing.

Wishful thinking.

I take off my T-shirt as I look in the mirror. I stare at my one-piece and wonder why everything looks better on Honor, even though we're identical. She looks prettier in dresses, better in jeans, taller in heels, sexier in swimsuits. We have the same body, same face, same hair, same external everything, but she pulls off her look with more maturity and sophistication than I ever could.

Maybe it's because she's more experienced than I am. She's got three years on me when it comes to losing her virginity. That could be why she walks with an air of confidence that eludes me. The only guy I've ever made out with is Drew Waldrup and he didn't even get to third base. That whole debacle didn't end with me gaining more confidence. It ended with me being mortified.

At least I got a trophy out of it.

I know I'm being ridiculous. Losing your virginity doesn't make you more of a woman than a virgin. It just means your hymen is broken. Big whoop.

I pull the T-shirt back over my head. I'm not about to swim in front of Honor's boyfriend like this with Honor looking like she does.

The four of them are in the water when I walk into the pool room. I keep my head down, not wanting to make eye contact with anyone as I make my way over. I'm not even sure I want to swim yet, so I sit down on the ledge at the shallow end and let my legs dangle in the water. I watch the four of them swim for a good half hour, ignoring Luck's pleas for me to join them. When I refuse for the third time, he finally swims over to me. He grins and presses his back into the wall, watching as Utah and Sagan race from one end of the pool to the other. Honor is now sitting on the edge of the deep end, waiting to declare a winner.

"You two are identical, right?" Luck says, spinning around in the water so that he's facing me.

"On the outside."

He reaches to me and tugs on the hem of my T-shirt. "Then why are you hiding your bathing suit with this T-shirt?"

"I feel more comfortable covered up."

"Why?"

I roll my eyes. "You never stop with the questions."

He waves toward Honor. "If people can see her, they can see you. It's the same thing."

"We're two different people. She wears a bikini. I don't."

"Is it a religious thing?"

"No." I've known him half a day and he's already ranking up there with Utah and Honor on the irritation scale.

He leans in and brings his voice to a whisper. "Is it because of Sagan? Is he why you feel uncomfortable?"

"I never said I was uncomfortable. I just said I'm more comfortable in a T-shirt."

He tilts his head. "Merit. There is a vast difference between you and your sister's confidence levels. I'm trying to figure out the root of that."

"There's no difference. We're just . . . she's more outgoing."

He pulls himself up out of the water, plop-

148

ping down next to me on the ledge. Utah also gets out, but only because his phone is ringing. He takes the call and walks out of the pool room.

Honor and Sagan are still at the deep end, but he is now helping Honor back float. His hands are under the water, palms pressed against her back. He's laughing as he talks her through the motions. The jealousy scorches my throat as I attempt to swallow it down.

"You make it too obvious," Luck says.

"What?"

He nudges his head toward them. "The way you look at him. You need to stop."

I'm embarrassed that he noticed. I don't acknowledge the truth in his comment, though. Instead, I turn our conversation around on him. "Why does Victoria hate you?"

For the first time, sadness registers in his expression. Or maybe it's remorse. He kicks his right leg up and slings water several feet.

"Our father wasn't that involved in either of our lives and my mother was having trouble controlling me. She thought Victoria might be able to help, so I went to live with her when I was almost fifteen. I wasn't even there for a week before I stole all her jewelry and pawned it."

I wait for him to explain the rest of the story, but he adds nothing else. "That's it? You took some jewelry when you were younger so she kicked you out and has refused to speak to you for five years?"

He leans to the right and then to the left and drags out the word when he says, "Weeeell, it was more than just a little jewelry. Apparently, what I took had been passed down for generations on her mother's side and it meant a lot to her. When she confronted me about it, I was insensitive. I was a punk kid who was supporting a weed habit. We got into a huge fight and I left. Never went back."

"You haven't spoken to her since that happened?"

"No. We were never that close anyway."

"Why did she forgive you tonight?"

"I told her my mother died and that I have nowhere else to go." He pauses. "And I was able to track down one of the rings. I gave it to her and apologized. And it was sincere, because I really do feel bad for what I did. I think an apology is all she's really wanted this whole time."

Funny how Victoria needs apologies from people, but she's never once apologized to any of us for tearing our family apart. "So now what?"

"I guess now I get to know my nieces and nephews."

"Don't call us that. It's so weird."

"Why is it weird?"

I shrug. "I don't know. I just don't think I could ever look at you like an uncle."

"Are you attracted to me?"

I scoff, and maybe even cringe a little. Luck is good-looking, and I would be lying if I said my head wasn't heading in that direction earlier today, before I found out he was Victoria's half brother. But now that I'm aware, there's not an inkling of attraction there. I can't even entertain it long enough to kid around with him. "Don't flatter yourself."

He laughs. "Easier said than done."

I glance over at Honor and her boyfriend again. They're both floating on their backs in the water, holding hands. It makes me wonder if there's a difference between Honor and me when it comes to simple things like holding hands. Would I hold Sagan's hand the same way? Do Honor and I kiss the same way? Would he even be able to differentiate between the two of us? Did he think the kiss with me at the fountain was different than all the other times he's kissed her? Does he ever get us confused?

"Can you tell us apart?" I ask Luck.

He shakes his head. "Not really. But you're both so different, it probably won't take me long to be able to tell who is who."

"How are we different? You've only known us a few hours."

"I can just tell. You both give off different vibes. I don't know, it's hard to explain. You just seem . . . more serious than her."

"You mean she seems more fun than me."

He looks at me pointedly. "Not at all what I said, Merit."

"I know, but that's the consensus. I'm the quiet, angry twin. She's the outgoing, fun one."

"I don't know either of you well enough to make that determination yet."

"Well, it won't take you long to figure it out. And then Honor will be your favorite and you'll hang out with her and Sagan and Utah and the four of you will become best friends."

He nudges me with his shoulder. "Stop that. It's unattractive."

I laugh. "Good. You aren't supposed to be attracted to your niece."

"You keep that self-deprecating attitude up, you'll have nothing to worry about." He looks over at Honor. "You guys have odd names. What's up with that?"

"Says the guy named Luck," I reply.

"What was your mother thinking?" As soon as I say it, I regret it. He's probably still grieving her recent death and here I am bringing her up. "Sorry," I mutter. "That was insensitive."

"No worries. She was a terrible person. I haven't seen her in years."

"I thought you lived with her. And that's why you came here, because she died."

He raises a brow. "No, I told you that's what I told Victoria. But I haven't lived anywhere since Victoria kicked me out. Hopped on a bus to Canada to stay with a friend of mine. A few months and a fake ID later, I got a job on a cruise ship. Been doing that for the last five years."

"You've been working on cruise ships?"

He nods. "I've been to thirty-six different countries so far."

"That explains the sporadic accent."

"Maybe so. I liked reinventing myself on every cruise. The work and routine were monotonous, so I would pretend to be someone different on every sail. I have about fourteen different accents nailed. It went on for so long, I get confused now when I try to talk normal."

I stare at him for a moment, watching him watch the water. "You're . . . interesting."

He straightens his back and slaps his

hands on his knees. "That's one way to put it." He hops out of the pool and stands up. "I'll be back in a little while." He grabs a towel, then walks out of the pool room with no further explanation. I watch until the door closes behind him. When I turn around, Sagan is the only one in the pool and he's swimming toward me. I try to find something else to look at, but I just make myself feel more awkward. I force myself to make eye contact with him and try to ignore the sudden chaotic hammering of my pulse.

"Why aren't you getting in?" he asks.

"I was talking to Luck." I feel exposed not being in the water. I jump into the pool and allow myself to sink to the bottom before coming back up to face him. When I finally do break the surface, I push my hair back and open my eyes. Honor is walking out of the pool room.

"Where's she going?" I ask, turning to him.

"She has to pee." He moves to the shallowest part of the pool and sits. It's only a few feet deep, so his shoulders are still above water. I sit next to him so I don't have to look at him. My chin barely breaks the surface. The room is a stark, silent contrast to what it was just moments ago. The quietness is only making my pulse worse, so I force myself to break up the silence. "What's your story?"

He spins in the water so that he's facing me. There are drops of water on his lips, but they roll off when he smiles. "Can you be more specific?"

I swallow hard. "Why did you move in with us?"

"Does it bother you that I live with you?"

I shrug. "Honor is only seventeen. It's a little soon for her boyfriend to move in."

"I'm not her boyfriend."

He says that like he's okay with the fact that she's keeping her options open. "You aren't dead enough for her to want to make it official?"

He doesn't laugh. I knew he wouldn't. It was a low blow. He moves back to the wall and I'm thankful. Conversations with him are much easier when he's not in my line of sight.

I still can't take the quiet and find myself wishing Utah and Honor would return. I try to bring up a subject that has less of a chance of reminding me that he makes out with Honor on a daily basis. "Why were you named Sagan? Are your parents fans of the astronomer?"

He looks at me with slightly widened eyes.

"I'm impressed you know who Carl Sagan is. And no, I wasn't named after the astronomer, although I wouldn't have minded it much. Sagan was my mother's maiden name."

I lift my arms in front of me and push the water away from me in waves. "I don't know a whole lot about Carl Sagan, but my father used to keep one of his books on our coffee table. *Cosmos.* I would flip through it sometimes as a kid."

"I've read all his books. I think he's fascinating, but I could just be partial because of the name." He disappears beneath the water and then comes back up, smoothing his hair back. "What's your middle name, Merit?"

"I don't have one. Our parents were planning on having one daughter and naming her Honor Merit Voss. But there were two of us, so they just gave us each a first name and didn't even bother with middle names."

Sagan stares at me with a tilt of his head, his expression full of curiosity.

"What is it?"

He smiles a little and then says, "You have a speck of brown in your right eye. Honor doesn't have one."

I'm surprised he noticed. Very few people notice. In fact, I'm not sure anyone has ever pointed that difference out before. He's very observant. Which makes me question the drawing I found in his notebook and what motivated him to draw Honor and me stabbing each other in the back. I dip myself underwater again to ward off chills. When I come back up, I wrap my arms around myself and look at him. I can't think of anything to say, though. Or maybe I have way too much to say and I don't know where to start.

Sagan smiles at me appreciatively for a moment, then lifts his hand and slides away strands of my wet hair that are stuck to my cheek. "That's the most you've spoken to me since we met," he says casually.

His fingers don't linger at all, but the feel of them does. And his stare. And the chills that crept up my arm after he touched my cheek.

I nod, a little embarrassed by his comment. "Yeah. I'm not much of a talker."

"So I've noticed."

I feel two things at once. I feel the weight of my attraction to him. It's so heavy, it feels like an anchor wanting to pull me under the water. But I also feel very defensive of my sister. If I had a boyfriend and he touched Honor's cheek like Sagan just touched mine, I'd find it highly inappropriate.

A person can't help their attraction to another person, but a person can help their actions toward another person. Brushing hair from my cheek while looking at me the way he was looking at me was definitely an action he should have controlled. I know this, because since the moment I found out he was Honor's boyfriend, I've done everything in my power to fight my attraction for him out of respect for my sister. But he doesn't seem to be fighting it very hard because he's looking at me right now like he wants to pull me under water and breathe his air into my lungs.

I glance over my shoulder, back at the door, waiting for one of them to return. Any of them. I'd even take Utah at this point. It's suffocating being the only one in the room with Sagan.

I face forward again and force myself to ask him more questions. Maybe I'll find out something terrible about him that will make me stop feeling this way. "You never said why you moved in with us."

He forces a tight-lipped smile. "It's kind of a depressing story."

"Well, now I'm even more curious."

He narrows his eyes as if he's sizing up my trustworthiness, but then he just gives me a clipped answer. "My family situation is a little complicated right now." He doesn't elaborate.

"You mean they're worse than mine?"

"Your family isn't so bad," he says.

Of course he believes that. He's not the one who's forced to live there. He's there by choice. "Yeah, well, stay in your corner because from my perspective, they aren't much to brag about."

His expression leaves no hint of his thoughts. He just stares at me as calmly as the water has become around us. Our knees touch briefly and it sends a shiver over me. I notice the same chills climbing up his arms when his gaze drops to my mouth. Just like it did the day he mistook me for Honor and created this monster inside of me with his kiss. I need him to back up a few miles. Or lunge for me.

Just like he's lunging for his phone.

Here and then gone.

He hopped out of the pool as soon as his phone started ringing. I've never seen anyone so anxious when their phone rings. I want to find out why he gets like that, but I also hope I never find out because that would mean we'd have to have another conversation.

Sagan answers his phone as he's walking out of the pool room. I'm alone now. It's kind of creepy, so I jump out of the water and grab the last towel. I also grab the key card and my stuff and head to the bathroom to change.

Honor has a fresh face of makeup and she's currently brushing her hair at the sink. She's already changed out of her bathing suit. "Is everyone ready to go?"

"More than ready," I say, closing the stall door behind me.

"I'll be in the van," she says on her way out the door.

I finish changing clothes, but I don't bother brushing my hair or applying makeup like Honor did. I just don't care as much as she does.

When I make it back to the front desk to return the key, Sagan is in the lobby, still on the phone. Honor hands him his dry clothes and he smiles at her and then walks them to the bathroom. Honor and Utah both walk outside and once again . . . I'm all alone. Because the front desk clerk is nowhere to be found.

"Angela," I say, tapping the key card on the counter. I'm not sure if I should just leave it on the counter and go, or if I should wait on her to return to the desk.

"Coming," she says, a little too cheerful. The door to an office opens and she slips

160

out, smiling a little too widely. She combs through her hair with her fingers.

"Just returning this." I slide the key across the counter to her. I'm about to walk toward the exit, but I pause when Luck emerges from the office Angela just came from. He's still wearing the shorts he had on in the pool. I look at Angela, but she darts her eyes away, tucking the back of her work shirt into her skirt. I look back at Luck.

"Is everyone ready?" he asks casually, as if I didn't just interrupt whatever was happening in that office.

I nod, but I don't speak. I just walk away quietly because I'm speechless.

Did that seriously just happen?

Luck was in the middle of a conversation with me a mere fifteen minutes ago when he got up and walked away. How — in the span of fifteen minutes — did he end up having sex with a girl he doesn't even know in the office of a hotel?

I'm angry and I don't even know why. I couldn't care less who Luck has sex with. I don't even know him. I'm angrier about the fact that I wouldn't even know the first thing about having sex, much less a quickie with a guy I've never met before. Sex seems like such a monumental thing. It should take months to lead up to, and he accomplishes it in fifteen minutes.

The door is open when I reach the van. Honor is sitting in one of the two middle seats, so I save the other one for Sagan and take the backseat this time. I'm not sure I want to sit by anyone at this point.

Sagan walks outside and climbs in the front seat.

"Where's Luck?" Honor asks.

"He's getting dressed," Sagan says.

"He got held up," I add. "He was busy screwing Angela in the back office."

Honor spins around in her seat, wide-eyed. "Shut up! Angela is dating Russell!"

I really don't care.

"Is she really?" Utah asks. "Isn't that Shannon's older brother?"

Honor turns around in her seat. "They've been dating for like two years. I can't believe she'd do that to him!" Her words make it appear that she's upset about Angela cheating on her boyfriend, but her voice is way too eager over the possibility of it happening. Honor has always loved gossip. It's one of the many things she and Utah have in common.

Luck finally returns to the van, pulling his shirt over his head as he takes his seat. He closes the door and Honor doesn't waste any time. "Did you really just have sex with

162

Angela?"

Luck turns around in his seat and faces me. "Really, Merit?"

I feel guilty for telling them now. It seems like I came straight out to the van with gossip, but I only told them because I was . . . I don't know. Why did I tell them?

Luck turns back around in his seat. "I don't kiss and tell."

"She has a boyfriend," Honor says.

"That's lovely," Luck says, uninterested.

"You're going to make things even worse for us," Honor says.

"What's that supposed to mean?"

"The Voss family already has a terrible reputation around here, thanks to our father and Victoria. Now we've added you to the mix and you're a man whore."

Luck laughs. "Do people not have sex in this town?"

"They do," I say. "But there's usually more than a one-minute screening process."

"Yeah, well, sex doesn't mean as much to me as it must mean to you guys."

"What if it meant something to Angela?" Honor asks.

Luck rolls his head and looks at Honor. "Believe me. It didn't."

"Says a lot about your performance," I say with a chuckle.

Luck turns around and hugs the seat, looking at me. "Speaking of sex," he says, challenging me with his stare. "Have you ever had sex with that guy you have a crush on? What's his name again?"

I shake my head, silently begging him to shut up, but I can tell I've upset him by starting this whole conversation. He very well might bring Sagan into the fold just to get back at me.

"You look embarrassed," he says, narrowing his eyes. "Are you a virgin, Merit?"

Sadly, I'm probably the only virgin out of this whole group. But I'm not about to discuss that with anyone in this van.

"Are you?" Luck asks again.

"Stop," Sagan says from the front seat. His voice is shockingly authoritative.

Luck raises an eyebrow and then slowly turns back around. Sagan glances in the rearview mirror and finds me. I have no idea what thoughts are going through his head, but they don't seem to be in my favor. He holds eye contact for a few seconds and then looks away. I close my eyes and press my forehead against the back of Luck's seat.

I shouldn't have come tonight. This is why I never hang out with any of them. It never ends on a good note.

Chapter Seven

There are only twenty-four hours in today, just like every other day, but today seems twice as long.

We got back to the house a little after ten from swimming. Sagan took a shower first and then Honor took one. Utah has a shower in his bedroom, so he and Luck took turns using that one. By the time I got a free shower, there was no hot water left. I couldn't even wash my hair, but I honestly don't care. I'll take a shower when everyone is gone tomorrow.

I pulled the drawing Sagan did this morning out of my dresser and hung it on the wall next to my bed. I decided I wanted to look at it all the time. I'm looking at it right now as I sit on the floor next to the wall that separates mine and Honor's bedrooms. She and Sagan just started arguing and I want to hear every word of it. However, I only get bits and pieces because Sagan is too quiet in his rebuttals. Honor is the one raising her voice.

"You knew this when we met!" she yells.

He quietly responds with something inaudible and then she says, "You sound like my father."

He says something else and she completely loses it. "I am not!" she yells. "I knew him before I knew you, so don't you dare make me feel guilty!"

Oh.

That sounds bad.

A few seconds later, the door to Honor's bedroom slams shut. Then the door to Sagan's bedroom slams shut. Then someone knocks on my door.

I jump up because it's probably Honor and the last thing I want her to see is me sitting on the floor next to the wall, eavesdropping on her conversation.

I open the door, but it isn't Honor. It's Luck.

"Oh," I say. "Hey."

"Can I come in?"

I open the door wider and he walks in, assessing my room. I close the door while I assess him. He's wearing a pair of navy blue sweatpants and mismatched socks. He doesn't have a shirt on, but he's wearing a scarf.

"Why are you wearing a scarf?"

"It's cold in my room."

"Why don't you put on a shirt?"

"They're all in the wash."

He's so matter-of-fact, like a scarf without a shirt is completely normal. He walks over to my bed and falls down on it, propping his head up with his hand. "Are you mad at me?" he asks.

"Mad at you?" I sit down on the bed and relax against the headboard. "No. Why?"

He rolls onto his back and sees the drawing I hung up. He reaches out and touches it. "I'm not everyone's cup of tea."

I laugh. "Yeah, well, you're in good company."

He continues tracing the drawing with his finger. "Did Sagan draw this for you?"

"Yeah." I don't know why, but there's a little bit of guilt in my response. Maybe because Sagan shouldn't be drawing pictures for his girlfriend's sister. I know it was innocent for him, but my reaction to his gesture was anything but. It just made me like him even more than I did before he gave me the picture.

"I can see why you like him," Luck says. He rolls back onto his side. "Does he flirt with you?"

"No," I say immediately. "He likes Honor.

167

I doubt he even notices me."

"Are you blind? Were you not in the car earlier when he took up for you?"

"He wasn't taking up for me. He just wanted everyone to stop talking about sex."

Luck shakes his head. "He got defensive when I asked if you were a virgin. I think your feelings might be mutual."

Luck has no clue what he's talking about. He's been here less than a day. "He wasn't defending me."

"Okay," Luck says. "Do you have a shirt I can borrow?"

"Look in my closet."

Luck crawls off the bed and walks over to my closet. He thumbs through the clothes for a bit. "I can see why you're a virgin. Do you own anything other than boring T-shirts?"

I ignore his insult. "Probably not. I like T-shirts."

He pulls one of my favorites off the hanger and pulls it over his head. It's a purple shirt that says, "Ask me about my purple shirt." He leaves the scarf on and then sits back down on the bed, but relaxes against the headboard next to me.

"I never said I was a virgin," I clarify.

He rests his chin on his shoulder and stares at me with a smirk. "You didn't have to. You get uncomfortable every time I say the word."

I roll my eyes. "Are you an expert? How many people have you had sex with?"

"Forty-two."

"I'm being serious, Luck."

"I am, too."

"You've had sex forty-two times?"

He shakes his head. "No, you asked how many people I've had sex with. That answer is forty-two. But I've had sex three hundred and thirty-two times."

I laugh. "You are so full of shit."

"I can prove it."

"Please do."

He hops off the bed and leaves my room. I use his absence to try and imagine how anyone could possibly have sex with that many people, let alone know exactly how many times they've had sex in their life.

He just keeps getting weirder.

Luck returns and closes the door, then sits in the same spot again. He's holding a small, worn notebook. "I keep track." He opens the first page and there's a list of initials on the left-hand side of the page, locations in the middle and a date on the right-hand side. I snatch the notebook from him.

I flip through it and read a few of the lines off.

P.K., crew quarters, November 7, 2013.
A.V., lido deck, November 13, 2013.
A.V., lido deck, November 14, 2013.
B.N., hotel in Cabo, December 1, 2013.

I continue flipping through the notebook, through 2014, 2015, 2016. "Oh my God, Luck. You're sick."

He grabs the notebook from me. "Am not."

I shake my head in disbelief. "Why would you keep track of that?"

He shrugs. "I don't know. I like sex. I figured someday I might break a record, or maybe I'll want to write a book about my adventures. Keeping track of it helps me to remember everything."

I grab the notebook from him and flip straight to the back page. I look at the last entry and sure enough, he's already added Angela and today's date. Although, he only put the letter A.

"I didn't catch her last name," he says.

I reach to my nightstand and grab a pen for him. "It's Capicci."

He smiles and adds the letter C to the entry. "Thanks." He sets the pen and the notebook down on the bed and leans his head back.

"Were you ever in love with any of them?"

He shakes his head. "Not a reciprocated love."

I sigh. "I know how that feels."

We're quiet for a moment, but then he says, "Thanks for the shirt, Merit. I need to get to sleep. Have to look for a job tomorrow."

I was enjoying the company, oddly enough. "Wait."

Luck pauses and waits for me to keep talking, but he can see in my expression that I'm a little hesitant to ask him what I want to ask him. He sits back against the headboard. "What is it?"

I spit it out before I change my mind. "What was your first time like?"

He laughs. "Terrible. For her. Not so terrible for me."

"Did she know it was your first time?"

"No. She didn't even speak English. Her name was Inga. I was the new guy on crew so I was a hot commodity among the ladies. The whole thing lasted about thirty seconds."

"Oh. That's embarrassing."

He shrugs. "It was at the time, but everyone's first time is always the worst. I eventually got better. And I got to make it up to her a couple of years later, so I redeemed myself."

"Why do you think first times are always the worst?"

He looks up in thought. "I don't know, there's just so much expectation. Society puts a lot of weight on losing your virginity, but in my opinion, it's better to just get it over with. Sleep with someone who doesn't mean much to you so it'll be less embarrassing than it already is. Then, when you finally do meet someone you really like, you can be with them without all the awkwardness."

I think about what he's saying and surprisingly, it makes sense. I hate the anticipation of what my first time will be like and who it'll be with and how old I'll be. I hate worrying that it might never happen and I'll grow old never experiencing sex or love or relationships. I'm not like Honor. I don't fall in love easily. I don't even know how to flirt easily. And I'm definitely nothing like Luck. I still can't fathom what happened with Angela earlier. I don't understand how someone can meet a person and within minutes be sharing such an intimate experience with them.

Maybe that's why I can't understand it, because I'm equating intimacy with sex.

"Any more questions?" he asks.

I shake my head. "No, I think that's

enough to keep me awake all night."

Luck laughs and stands up. Before he walks out, he pauses in front of my trophy shelf. He picks up the first place fencing trophy. "Fencing?" He looks at me suspiciously. He replaces it and reads a couple more of the plaques on the other trophies, then he looks at me over his shoulder with an arched brow. "Did you actually win any of these?"

I smile. "Define win."

Luck shakes his head. "I've met a lot of people in my life, Merit. But you might be the strangest of them all."

"Runs in the family."

He closes the door just as my phone vibrates under my pillow. Speaking of strange. It's a text from my mother.

If you're still awake could you bring me a razor? I'm in the shower and mine broke.

I roll my eyes dramatically and drop my phone onto my bed. Why does she even need to shave? No one would ever notice how hairy her legs are. She doesn't interact with anyone!

I grab a disposable razor from the bathroom and run it down to Quarter Four. She's in the shower, so I walk into her tiny bathroom and hand it to her over the shower curtain.

"Thanks, sweetie," she says. "While you're down here, do you mind taking those dishes on the fridge back upstairs?"

"Sure." I close the bathroom door and find a few days' worth of dishes on top of her mini-fridge. They're clean, even though she has no kitchen sink. She must have washed them in the bathroom sink.

You would think she'd be desperate enough for her own kitchen by now. I don't understand why she still lives here. She could move into the house Utah is remodeling. She could lock herself in her bedroom and never leave, just like in the basement. It's been vacant since the last tenants moved out six months ago. It's not healthy for anyone. Especially her.

As I'm walking toward the stairs with her dishes in hand, my eyes fall to a pile of medication on the table next to her couch. She's been on several different medications since as early as I can remember. Medication for her cancer, pain pills for her back, anxiety pills. I look back at the bathroom to make sure the door is shut. I set the plates down on the couch and pick up one of the pill bottles. It's the medication she takes for pain.

My hands begin to shake as I open the lid. They always do this when I come down here and take some of her medicine. I'm always scared she'll catch me, or scared she'll notice some are missing. But with as many teenagers that are living in Dollar Voss now, it'll be impossible to pinpoint who did it.

I empty a few pills into my hand and then shove them in my pocket. I put the bottle back where I found it and I take the plates up to the kitchen. I rush to my room and pull the pills out of my pocket and count them. Eight. I've never stolen that many at once. I like to spread it out so it'll be less noticeable. The bottle was more than half-full so maybe she won't be able to tell that eight are suddenly missing.

I walk to the closet and pull the bottle of pills out of my black boot. I've been hiding them in this boot since I started stealing them. Honor hates these boots, so I don't have to worry about her borrowing them and finding my stash. I open the empty Tylenol bottle, adding the eight to the pile of twenty I've already stolen.

I've never actually taken one. In all honesty, I don't even know why I steal them. I have no desire to become addicted to medication like she is. I think I steal them out of spite. Just like the trophy I took from Drew

Waldrup's bedroom.

I don't normally steal things. The few times I have, it's simply a return for my anger. I stole two sets of Valentine-themed scrubs from Victoria once. I had no intention of wearing them, but knowing *she* couldn't wear them made the theft worth it. I donated the scrubs to Goodwill and pretended I had no idea what she was talking about when she asked all of us if we'd seen her pink scrubs with the hearts on them.

Other than the trophy from Drew Waldrup, the scrubs, and the pills, I've never stolen anything from anyone else. Not that I don't have the urge. I can't stop wondering what it would be like to steal Honor's boyfriend.

I place the boot back in my closet and shut my closet door. On my way back to my bed, my foot meets something that isn't carpet. I look down and notice a sheet of paper on my bedroom floor. I pick it up and turn it over.

I'm assuming the girl in the picture is me, since Sagan slid the picture under my door rather than Honor's. In the picture, I'm sitting at the bottom of a pool. A rope is tied around my waist on one end and the other end is tied to a floating cinder block. I flip it over and read the caption.

"Coming down for air."

I sit down on my bed and continue to stare at it. Coming down for air? What does that even mean? Why would he draw this?

Before I can talk myself out of it, I walk across the hall and knock on his door.

"It's open," he says.

I open the door and he's sitting on his bed with his sketchbook in his lap. When he looks up and sees me, he pulls the sketchbook to his chest.

"What does this mean?" I ask him, holding up the sketch.

He stares at me a moment and then returns his attention to the drawing in his lap. "Sometimes I just get ideas, so I draw them."

"You drew a picture of me drowning! Is that supposed to comfort me?"

"It's not a picture of you drowning."

"Then what is it?"

He sighs and slides his notebook off his lap. He tosses his covers aside and stands up. He's not wearing a shirt and it's the only thing I can focus on, despite the fact that he's walking toward me. I have so many thoughts, but the closer he gets, the more jumbled they become. When he reaches me, he takes the drawing out of my hands but he doesn't break eye contact with me.

"I like that you like my drawings, Merit. I drew this one and thought you might like it. It doesn't mean anything." He sets the drawing down on his dresser and then returns to his spot on the bed. He pulls his sketchbook onto his lap again and gets back to whatever he was doing before I interrupted him.

I swallow my embarrassment. Why is he making it seem like I'm overreacting?

I turn toward the door, but then I spin and walk back to his dresser and grab the drawing. When I walk out of his room, I close his door a little too hard. That only serves to embarrass me more.

I hang the drawing next to the one he drew of me this morning. I don't like that he's drawn two pictures of me today. I would prefer to be ignored by him much more than being the center of his artistic attention.

CHAPTER EIGHT

I didn't even pretend to get ready for school this morning. I heard everyone rushing around in the usual morning Voss chaos, but I stayed in bed the entire time. I'm surprised Honor and Utah haven't told my father about my skipping school for the past two weeks. They hounded me about it for a few days but once they realized I wasn't listening to them, they stopped bringing it up. No one knocked on my door to ask where I was. Not even my father.

I wonder if anyone would even notice if I ran away?

They'd probably notice. They just wouldn't be upset about it.

I reach under my pillow to check the time and notice a text from my father, sent an hour ago.

Cowboys lost last night. I blame you. Please undress Jesus and burn His clothes as soon as you get home from school today.

I know he's trying to be funny, but the fact that he incorrectly assumes I'm at school negates the rest of his text. It's like we don't even have parents. We have a mother living in our basement and a father living in his own world. No one has a clue what's going on with anyone around here.

I check the time and it's just after noon. I get dressed and go scour the kitchen for something to eat. No one is here and I noticed the door to Luck's room is open, so he must be out looking for a job like he mentioned he was going to do last night.

I eat a sandwich and then go to the garage to get the ladder. Thanksgiving is the next holiday, but I'm not really in the mood to dress Him. I take the ladder to the living room and begin pulling off the duct tape that's securing the trophy to his wrist.

The door to the basement opens unexpectedly. I'm hoping my mother is about to walk out, but it's not my mother.

It's my father.

He quietly closes the door and then walks to the kitchen counter where he downs a bottle of water. He tucks in his shirt, grabs his jacket off the back of one of the chairs, and heads for the door. He opens it and is about to shut it when he finally sees me.

It's like we've both seen a ghost.

He glances back to the basement door then looks back up at me.

Why was he in the basement?

Why was he tucking in his shirt?

Why does he look so guilty?

I can't move. I'm holding the football trophy in one hand and the cheese hat in the other. My father is still staring at me, frozen in place. He finally looks down at his feet. He goes to pull the door shut but then opens it again and looks at me. "Merit." His voice is timid and regretful. I don't say a word.

He doesn't follow my name up with anything else. Instead, he hesitates, then shuts the door and leaves me alone with Cheesus Christ.

It takes me a moment to gather my thoughts enough to climb down the ladder. I walk over to the couch and sit down as I stare at the basement door.

Did he just have sex with my mother?

Did my mother just let him?

I can't process what just happened. I can't.

I immediately rush across Quarter One and open the door to Quarter Four. I run down the stairs to the basement and find my mother zipping up her dress. I look at her unmade bed and then look back at her. At her disheveled hair and flushed cheeks.

"Did you just have sex with him?"

When the words leave my mouth, my mother looks just as shocked as my father looked a few minutes ago.

"Excuse me?"

I point up the stairs. "I just saw him walk out of here. He couldn't even look me in the eye."

My mother sits down on the bed, dumbfounded. "Merit. There are some things you're too young to understand."

I laugh. "Age has nothing to do with it, Mother. Are you seriously having sex with him, knowing he sleeps in bed with Victoria every night? Is that why you refuse to move out? Because you think he'll leave her for you?"

She stands up and walks past me, heading for her bathroom. She looks in the mirror and wipes her fingers under her eyes, getting rid of the mascara streaks.

"Is that why you still dress up every day? Because you're trying to steal him back?"

She spins around and takes a step forward. "I'm your mother and you will not disrespect me like this."

Now that makes me laugh. "You call yourself a mother?" I can't even look at her. I turn around and make my way to the stairs. When I get halfway to the top, I spin and walk two steps back down. She's at the base of the stairs looking up at me. "You haven't been a mother to me since I was twelve. You haven't been a mother to any of us! And now I know why. Because Dad is the only thing you've ever cared about!" I run the rest of the way up the stairs. She calls my name but I don't return to the basement. Right before I slam the door, I yell down, "The only thing separating you from crazy is a few cats!"

I go back to my room and slam my door. I fall onto my bed and check my texts again. There are two. One from Dad and one from Honor.

Dad: I'm sorry you saw that. Please let me talk to you about it before you jump to any conclusions.

Delete.

Honor: Do you think you can cover for me tomorrow night?

Oh, great. Another adulterer in the making. The apple didn't fall far from the tree.

Me: Cover for you in what way? From Dad or Sagan?

Honor: Both. I'll text you about my plans later. Have to put my phone away.

I slide my phone back under my pillow. I'm curious what she's hiding from Sagan, but from the sound of their argument last night, it has to do with a guy. I'm sure one of her online friends is near death, so she wants to be there for him in ways that Sagan wouldn't approve of.

I swear to God, this family is the worst. No wonder so many people hate us.

I roll onto my side and face the wall. I stare at the pictures Sagan drew and trace all the lines in them. My fingers are on their third path when someone knocks at my door.

Before I can say it's open, the door swings open and Luck walks in sporting a new head of jet-black hair. He's smiling, which only annoys me further. "Guess what?" he says.

"I can't possibly."

He plops down on the bed next to me. "I got a job."

I roll back over and stare at the wall. "Good. Where?"

"You know where we met?"

185

"You got a job at Tractor Supply?"

"No, it's on the same street as that, though. The coffee store. I'm a barista."

I smile, even though I don't feel like it. But it's actually perfect for him. "When you say coffee store, are you referring to Starbucks?"

"Yeah, Starbucks."

I laugh a little, curious as to how he couldn't possibly remember the name of Starbucks. But it's Luck, so it makes sense. "Is that why your hair is black now? You had an interview today?"

"Nah, I was actually going for green but I think I let the dye stay on for too long. Speaking of black, why is it so dark in here? This lamp is an insult to Thomas Edison." He fingers the string of my lamp, pulling it. It turns off and then he turns it back on.

"I don't have any windows."

"I can see that. But why?"

I roll over onto my back. "My father divided all the rooms into two when we moved in. Honor got the half with the window after the wall was put up."

Luck scrunches up his nose. "That's not fair."

"I didn't want a window."

"Well, then. I guess it worked out well." He scoots down until he's lying next to me.

"Why are you still in bed?"

I wonder if I should tell him about what just happened with my mother and father. I decide against it. I want to talk to my father first. I'm hoping I was wrong. I'm hoping he values his marriage to Victoria more than he valued his marriage to my mother. At least then I could believe he learned something from ripping our family apart. Because right now, it doesn't appear he learned his lesson at all. Sex is more important to him than his wives. Than keeping his family together.

"Is sex really all it's cracked up to be?" I ask Luck. "Why do people risk so much for it?"

"You're asking the wrong person. I don't think I value it as much as most people."

"I hope to God I don't, either." I don't want it to rule my entire life and every decision I make. It seems that way with my father. With Victoria. With my mother. I want sex to be meaningless so it has absolutely no control over me. In fact, it would be great if I could just get it over with.

I roll over onto my side and prop my head up on my hand. "Luck?"

He's staring at me apprehensively. "What?"

I swallow nervously. "Do you think

187

maybe . . . we could . . ."

Luck laughs, but I don't crack a smile. I'm dead serious, even though I can't seem to come out and ask him. When he sees that I'm not smiling, he lifts up onto his elbow. "No. I'm your uncle."

"Step-uncle."

"Not any better."

"It's by marriage."

"You don't even know me."

"I know you better than you knew Angela and you had sex with her."

He narrows his eyes at that response. "You're a virgin, Merit. I'm not having sex with you." He falls onto his back like the conversation is over.

I'm not giving up. "You said yourself that people put too much weight on losing their virginity. I just want to get it over with. Sex doesn't mean anything to you anyway."

He's quiet for a moment. And then, "Why? Why me? Why now?"

I shrug. "I'm not everyone's cup of tea," I say, repeating how he described himself to me yesterday. "I've never really had the opportunity to get it over with until now."

He looks at me and I can see in his eyes that he's contemplating it. I don't know if it's because he wants to help me or if it's because he's a guy and most guys would

188

take me up on this offer without question.

"You don't like me, do you?" he asks.

"In what way?"

"Are you attracted to me?"

I debate lying if it will help him make his decision, but I go with the truth instead. I don't want him to think I like him when I don't. Even if it would help my case right now. "No. Not really. I mean, I think you're a good-looking guy. But I'd be lying if I said I was attracted to you."

He stares at me a moment and then says, "Merit, you better be certain about this. Because sex is just sex to me and this won't mean a damn thing to me."

"I don't want it to mean anything to you. That's the point."

"So it's just a means to an end?"

I nod. "The end of my virginity."

He studies me closely, waiting for me to change my mind. When he sees I'm not going to, he shrugs. "Okay, then. Let me grab a condom." He hops out of the bed and I fall onto my back.

He said *condom* with an accent. He's starting to sound more and more American now. And I can't believe this is where my train of thought is when I just asked a guy to have sex with me. A guy I'm not even attracted to.

189

Is this really happening?

Do I want it to happen?

I do. I want to get it over with. Rip the Band-Aid off. I don't want it to mean anything at all. I want it to be trivial with little effect on my life. I want to be the exact opposite of my parents.

When Luck returns, he closes the door and locks it. "Do you mind if I turn off the lamp?"

"I'd actually prefer it."

He turns off the lamp and climbs into bed. We both crawl under the covers and begin to remove our clothes. "You sure about this, Merit?"

"Yep," I say as I struggle my way out of my jeans. My heart is starting to race and my conscience is fighting to break through the wall I've put up. But I don't stop until all my clothes are off. Once we're both undressed beneath the covers, Luck scoots closer to me. "It probably won't feel good," he warns.

I don't know why, but that comment makes me laugh.

"I'm serious," he says. His hand meets my hip. "It might even hurt."

"It's fine. My expectations aren't that high right now."

He scoots closer and pauses with his hand

still on my hip. "You want me to kiss you?"

I think about his question for a moment. I'm not sure that I even want to kiss him. Is that weird? Of course it is. This whole thing is weird. "I'll leave that up to you."

Luck nods, just as his hand slides up to my waist. It isn't until he reaches my breast that I feel the weight of what's about to happen. I try not to let it weigh too heavily.

It's just sex.

I can do this.

Almost every adult in the world has done this.

I can do this.

He gently rolls me onto my back and then reaches for the condom. As he's putting it on, a good thirty seconds go by that I could use to change my mind. But I don't. Luck then rolls on top of me, holding his weight up with his hands on either side of my head. He brushes my hair back which is an oddly sweet gesture and then he reaches between us and spreads my legs.

I close my eyes. He presses his forehead into the pillow beside my head. "You sure?"

"Yes," I whisper.

I keep my eyes closed and I try not to focus on the fact that I made such a spontaneous decision. But I can't really think of any negative consequences that will come of this. I won't have to worry about never losing my virginity and Luck will get to add another line to his book.

"Last chance to change your mind, Merit."

"How long does it usually last?" I whisper.

Luck laughs in my ear. "You already hate it that much?"

I shake my head. "No, I just . . ." I stop talking. I'm making it even more awkward.

Just when I think I'm no longer going to be a virgin, my phone lights up. "Someone's calling you," Luck says. I glance to my left and fumble for my phone. I try to power it off, but the screen is still lit. Luck is just staring down at me. His face contorts and then he's not on top of me anymore. He falls onto his back.

"I can't do it."

"Seriously?" I ask. "We were two seconds away!"

He nods. "I'm sorry. It's just . . . when your phone lit up . . . you made this face that reminded me of Moby."

I cringe.

"He kind of looks like you and Honor. It's weirding me out."

I pull the covers up over my breasts. "That's gross."

He doesn't disagree. "Are you okay?"

I nod. "Yeah." My voice isn't very reassuring, though.

He turns on the lamp and then sits up. I look the other way as he removes his condom and pulls on his pants. "You aren't mad at me, are you?"

I assume it's safe to look in his direction now. He's holding his shirt, looking pathetically regretful as he stares down at me. "No. I'm sure I can find someone to do it eventually." I'm mostly kidding.

He gives me an apologetic, yet reassuring smile. "Whoever you have sex with, it'll be better than what this would have been. I promise."

I laugh. "Yeah, I'm not sure it can get much worse than what just happened."

Luck flips me off. "I'm normally very impressive and have excellent follow-through. This is a rare exception."

I like that he's still playful. We just experienced one of the most awkward things two people can possibly experience, and from the looks of it, nothing changed between us because of it.

He opens the door with impeccably terrible timing. Sagan is walking by, but he pauses as soon as Luck opens the door.

It's just a two-second glance, but I feel

more in this visual exchange with Sagan than I did during the entire past fifteen minutes with Luck. Sagan's eyes are locked on mine. His eyes move to Luck. His eyes are back on mine. Luck quickly steps out of my bedroom and closes the door, but he's not fast enough to save me from the absolute most horrific part of this entire day.

I pull the covers over my head and try to wish away the last ten seconds. I didn't want anyone to find out about what just happened between me and Luck, but Sagan is the absolute last person I would have wanted to find out about it.

I can feel the tears of embarrassment begin to form as I roll over.

I'm drowning in regret.

"Coming down for air," I whisper.

It's been several hours since I almost lost my virginity. I'm still the same and I have a feeling I'd still feel the same if my hymen were no longer intact. I wouldn't feel sexier, I wouldn't feel more worldly, I wouldn't be miraculously confident. If anything, I'm a bit . . . disappointed. Why do people risk so much for sex?

So far, all it's caused me is mortification. I'm so embarrassed to face Sagan, I haven't even left my room since he walked past it. I can hope he didn't assume the worst, but Luck walked out of my room without a shirt. Sagan saw me in bed, the blanket covering me just enough to make it obvious I wasn't wearing clothes.

I'm not embarrassed that he might have caught me having sex with someone. It shouldn't matter to Sagan if I'm seeing anyone else because Sagan isn't my boyfriend. He's dating my sister.

I'm embarrassed because it was Luck. We share a relative. It's disturbing. And now Sagan probably thinks the worst of me.

Luck came to my room during dinner and asked if I wanted him to bring me something to eat. He thought I was too mortified to come out of my room because of him, but it has nothing to do with Luck. In all honesty, I don't even regret what almost happened. I only regret that Sagan knows about it.

As embarrassed as I am, though, I doubt my feelings even come close to what my father must be feeling. He knows I know that he's still sleeping with Mom. And I'm sure he's terrified I'm going to tell Victoria. Or anyone else in the family for that matter. He's so mortified, he didn't even come to my room to talk to me about it.

All I've heard from him today was in a

stupid text. "I'm sorry you saw that. Please let me talk to you about it before you jump to any conclusions." In other words, he'd appreciate the opportunity to swear me to secrecy before anyone else finds out what's really going on around here.

So many secrets in this house. And yet, the one secret I should have told years ago is the one I've kept the quietest.

Speaking of quiet. I haven't heard anyone moving around in the house for a while, which means everyone is probably in bed now. Not only am I starving, but I would put money on the fact that no one has fed Wolfgang today. I go to the kitchen and open a frozen dinner. After I put it in the microwave, I grab a pitcher from beneath the sink to fill it with dog food.

I'm rinsing it out when my father finally gets the balls to confront me. I heard the door to their bedroom open right after I closed the microwave. I heard him walk into the kitchen when I bent down to grab the pitcher. I felt him hesitate at the counter as I was rinsing out the pitcher.

And now he's standing in the way of me and the back door.

"I have to feed Wolfgang." I say it in such a way that should indicate I don't want to do anything other than feed Wolfgang. Especially have a conversation with him about his infidelity.

"Merit," he says, looking at me pleadingly. "We need to talk about this."

I walk around him to the bag of dog food. "Do we?" I ask as I scoop some into the pitcher. I turn around and face him. "Do you really want to have a conversation with me about it, Dad? Are you finally going to explain why you started cheating on Mom when she needed you the most? Are you finally going to explain why you chose Victoria over the rest of this family? Are you finally going to explain why you were in the basement having sex with Mom today while everyone thought you were at work?"

He takes a quick step toward me and says, "Shh. Please." He looks panicked, like Victoria might overhear this conversation. It makes me laugh. If he doesn't like the thought of getting caught, why does he do things he doesn't want people to find out?

I nod. "Oh, I see. You don't want to discuss why you're a pathetic husband. You just want me to promise I won't tell anyone."

"Merit, that's not fair."

Fair? He's going to talk to me about fair? I've had very little respect for him these past few years, but today has completely diminished what little was left.

"Believe me, Dad. I won't tell anyone. The last thing this family needs is another reason to hate you."

The timer on the microwave goes off. When my dad looks in that direction, I use the break in eye contact to walk out the back door. Thankfully, he doesn't follow me. I walk across the yard to Wolfgang's doghouse. He's just lying there, looking up at me. He's not even excited to eat. Do dogs suffer from depression? I wonder if human Xanax would work on him. If so, I should feed him some of my mother's.

I sit down next to his doghouse and Wolfgang crawls forward a little and lays his head in my lap. He licks my hand and it's honestly the sweetest thing anyone's done for me all day. At least he appreciates me.

"You aren't so bad, you know?" I scratch between his ears and his tail begins to wag a little. Well, wag might be a bit of a stretch. It twitches, almost in a convulsive way, like it's been so long since he's been happy that he forgot how his tail works.

"Let me get you some water." I grab his empty water bowl and walk to the far side of the house and turn on the water faucet. I glance to the left, at Sagan's bedroom window. There's a light on, which means he's probably up drawing. I wonder what he's drawing. Probably a morbid picture of me losing my virginity.

The water bowl overfills and the water spills over onto my shoe. "Shit." I step back and pour some of the water out of the bowl, then drop the hose.

"Merit?"

I spin around, but no one is behind me.

"Over here."

It's Sagan's voice. It's coming from his window. His curtains are pulled back and his arms are folded on the inside of the windowsill. The only thing separating us is the window screen and a few feet.

"What are you doing?"

I reach down and turn off the water. "Feeding Wolfgang." My hands fumble around the faucet, but Sagan's presence has me a nervous wreck now. I don't notice the metal wire holding on the faucet covering until I slide my wrist across it and cut myself. "Ouch," I say, jumping back. I turn my hand over and there's already blood bubbling up out of the cut across my wrist.

"You okay?" He leans closer to the window screen.

"Yeah, I just cut myself. I'm fine, though. It's superficial."

"I'll bring you a Band-Aid." His curtain falls shut and I hear him walking across his bedroom.

Crap. He's coming out here.

I close my eyes and inhale, hoping I can pretend I'm not still completely mortified. I hope he doesn't bring up what he saw today. Surely he won't, it was none of his business.

I wipe my wrist on my T-shirt and then walk the bowl of water to Wolfgang. I return to my spot on the ground, just as the back door opens. It's dark out, but there's a full moon tonight, which means I'll have to make eye contact with him like a normal person.

Wolfgang lifts his head and he starts to growl as Sagan comes closer. I pet him on top of his head. "It's okay, boy." The gesture reassures Wolfgang. He nestles his head in my lap again and sighs.

When Sagan reaches us, he squats down, handing me a Band-Aid. I take it from him and open it. At least he didn't try to apply the Band-Aid himself. He would have seen how bad I'm shaking.

"So this is the infamous Wolfgang, huh?" He reaches out to pet him and Wolfgang allows it. Never mind the fact that Wolfgang's head is in my lap and now Sagan's hand is touching something on my lap and what is oxygen?

"He's a beautiful dog." Sagan moves from a squat to a seat on the ground. He's so close, his knee is touching mine. The contact makes it more difficult to breathe so I do my best to keep it unnoticeable. Sagan's hand is still on Wolfgang's head. "Is he always this subdued?"

I lift a shoulder as I secure the Band-Aid to my wrist. "He didn't used to be. I think he's depressed."

"How old is he?"

I think back to the year the war began between my father and Pastor Brian. I was probably eight or nine. "He's almost ten years old, I think."

My answer makes Sagan sigh. "He may not have much more time in him."

"What do you mean? Dogs live a lot longer than ten years, don't they?"

"Some breeds do. But Labs live an average of about twelve years."

"He's not dying, though. He's just in mourning."

Sagan rubs a hand across Wolfgang's stomach. "Feel this," he says. He grabs one of my hands and slides it over the path his hand just took. "His stomach is swollen. Sometimes that's a sign that they're about to die. And with his lethargic temperament . . ."

Something gets caught in my throat. I make a sound, like a gasp and a cough mixed with disbelief. I quickly cover my mouth, but then the swelling in my throat causes tears in my eyes. Why am I sad? I've spent my whole life hating this dog. Why would I care if he's dying?

"I'll call a vet tomorrow," Sagan says. "It wouldn't hurt to get him checked out."

"Do you think he's in pain?" I ask, my voice just above a whisper. I feel a tear escape my eye and I discreetly wipe it away. Or at least my intention was to be discreet, but Sagan saw it because he's staring way too hard.

A smile tugs at his lips. "Look at that," he says quietly. "Merit has a heart."

I roll my eyes at his comment and use both hands to pet Wolfgang now. "You don't think I have a heart?"

"To be fair, you come off kind of . . . brash."

I wasn't expecting his honesty. It makes me laugh. "Is that your way of calling me a bitch?"

He shakes his head. "I'd never call you that."

Sure, he'd never call me a bitch. But it doesn't mean he's not thinking it. Sagan just doesn't say mean things out loud.

Maybe that's a product of how he was raised. Or maybe he's some kind of saint. Or an angel brought to earth to test my morals.

Wolfgang rolls over and scoots closer to me. My eyes flick up to Sagan's but when I see he's looking at me, I immediately look back down at Wolfgang. I once again do whatever I can to find something about him to dislike.

"What are you allergic to?"

Sagan tilts his head. "Nothing," he says, looking confused. "Why? That's such a random question."

"Last night in the van you said you had an allergic reaction to something you ate. And that you met Honor in the hospital."

He nods a little, then cracks a smile. "Oh. That." He pauses and then says. "I was lying. For Honor."

Of course he was. That's what good boyfriends do for their girlfriends.

"Which one was a lie? That you had an allergic reaction or that you aren't allergic to anything?"

Sagan pulls at a piece of grass and twists it between his fingers. "I met your sister through a friend of mine. I was visiting him in the hospital." He drops the grass. "So was she."

I wait for him to elaborate, but once again he keeps his stories clipped and uninformative. But I take it he lied about why he was in the hospital out of guilt. He doesn't want anyone to know that he met Honor through his dying friend, and that, from the way it appears, they're seeing the same girl. How messed up is that?

I guess that explains the argument in Honor's bedroom the other night. And Honor wanting to keep her visit with Sagan's friend a secret from him.

I don't know why, but this satisfies me. Knowing she's seeing both of them and he's seeing her while still somewhat being flirty with me . . . it makes me feel like the better person out of the three of us, when before I felt like the worst one.

"What happened between you and Honor?" he asks. "Seems like there's a little animosity there."

I laugh. "A little?"

"Has it always been that way?"

I lose my smile and shake my head, looking down at Wolfgang. "No. We used to be really close." I think about all the times we refused to sleep unless we were in the same room. All the times we would switch clothes and try to trick our father. All the times we would talk about how lucky we were to be twins. "Do you have any brothers or sisters?" I look back up at him just in time to see him frown a bit, but the frown dissipates.

"Yeah. A little sister."

"How old is she?"

"Seven." His expression is stoic, which makes me wonder if he misses her and doesn't like talking about her.

"Do you get to see her very often?"

This must be where the point of contention comes in with his family because he just inhales and leans back on his hands. "I've never met her, actually."

Oh. There must be a story there, but I can sense the sadness in his voice. And then he leans over and starts petting Wolfgang like the subject is closed. It's apparent he doesn't want to dive deeper into conversations about his family. It disappoints me because I want him to feel like he can talk to me but he obviously doesn't feel that way. I wonder if Honor has these kinds of conversations with him.

The weight of her name bears down on me. I drag a hand over my mouth and hold it there as my arm rests on my knee. "Do you ever wish you had a different family? One who communicates?" I ask him.

"You have no idea," he says.

"I really wish I had that kind of relationship with Honor and Utah. We aren't close at all. And sadly, once we all go off to college, I doubt we'll speak much. The only reason we even interact is because we live together."

"It's not too late to change that, you know."

I try to force a smile, but I don't have enough strength in my body to pretend he's right. My family will never be any different. "I don't know, Sagan. There's a lot of baggage in our family. I think sometimes you luck out and get a family you connect with. But sometimes . . ." I try to fight back an embarrassing and unexpected tear. "Sometimes you get stuck with family members that do nothing but make mistakes they never have to apologize or pay for."

When I'm sure I've fought the tear back successfully, I look at Sagan. He's staring back at me sympathetically. There's a quiet reassurance about him. Maybe it's the way he seems to listen without judging. He nods a little, like he understands what I'm trying to say. But then he shrugs. "Not every mistake deserves a consequence. Sometimes the only thing it deserves is forgiveness."

I immediately have to look away because that comment hits me like a punch in the gut. I wish I could apply that thinking to my family but I'm not sure I'm capable of that much forgiveness.

Sagan pulls his right leg up and rests his chin on his knee, wrapping his arms around his leg. He stares out over the backyard, focused on nothing. "Merit?"

I squeeze my eyes shut. I don't even want to look at him because I can tell in his voice that he's about to ask me something I don't want to answer. "What?" I whisper. It feels like my heart is swollen when I finally look at him. Or maybe bloated is a better term for this.

"What was going on today? In your room?"

I immediately break eye contact with him. Please don't let him be referring to what he saw from the hallway.

"Were you and Luck . . ."

That's exactly what he's referring to.

"Did you have sex with him?"

I'm shocked that he came straight out and asked it. I open my mouth and then clamp it shut because I'm too embarrassed to respond. And even a little bit angry. Why is it his business? He's having sex with his dying friend's girlfriend. It shouldn't be any of his concern who I'm having sex with.

I roll my eyes and push myself off the

207

ground. "That's such an inappropriate question. Especially coming from you."

He looks a little ashamed that he asked it, but he doesn't apologize. He just silently watches me as I walk back toward the house. I go straight to my bedroom and close the door. It's not until I lock it that I remember my food in the microwave. "Great," I mutter. I'm not about to walk back out of this room. I hate being hungry. It makes me angry, and when I'm already upset, it makes me really angry. I'm angry and starving and now that I've picked up my phone, I have to read through all these texts from Honor. I fall onto the bed and scroll to the top.

> **Honor:** Okay, so tomorrow night. I'm going to visit my friend, Colby. I have to drive to Dallas, so I won't be home until the middle of the night.
> **Honor:** I promised Sagan this morning I wouldn't go, so I really can't let him find out.
> **Honor:** Or Dad. He'll be just as angry if he knows.

It really annoys me how she thinks every sentence should be a separate text. Why can't she just write me one long paragraph?

Honor: Sagan works until after ten tomorrow night. I'm going to text him around nine and tell him I'm tired and I'm going to bed. So that won't be an issue.

Honor: But Dad might notice I'm missing tomorrow evening, so just tell him I wasn't feeling well and that I went to bed early. If he tries to check on me, tell him you already did and that I'm fine.

Honor: I'll lock my bedroom door just so no one can walk in and see that I'm not there.

Honor: Are you getting these texts?

Honor: Merit?

Honor: Will you please just agree to cover for me this once? I'll owe you one.

I laugh at that. What do I ever do that would warrant collecting on a favor?

Merit: Got it.

Honor: Thank you!

Merit: Quick question, though. Why are you doing this to Sagan?

Honor: Can you please withhold judgment just once in your life?

Merit: Fine. I'll hold off judging your indiscretions until the day after tomorrow.

Honor: Thank you.

I set down my phone. I turn off my lamp

209

and my room grows pitch black. With no windows and no lights on outside the room, I can't see a single thing. It's the first semblance of peace I've had all day.

I wonder if this is what death is like. Just . . . nothing.

CHAPTER NINE

"You should go see if Honor needs anything to eat before you go to bed," my father says.

Honor. The sick sister, holed up in her bedroom all night. Poor thing. "I took her some food earlier," I lie. I pull the plug out of the sink and let the water drain. It was Honor's night to do dishes, but she's not here to do them. That's another favor she owes me.

"Has she taken any medicine?" my father asks.

I nod. "Yeah, I took her some earlier. Right after she vomited all over the bathroom floor." If I'm going to lie for her, I'm going to make it worth my time. "Don't worry, I spent half an hour cleaning up after her. There was vomit everywhere. I even washed all the towels."

My father buys it. "That was nice of you."

"That's what sisters are for."

I should probably stop. It's becoming obvious just how full of shit I am.

"Hopefully it's not contagious," Victoria says. "The last thing I need right now is a virus. We're being audited by the state next week."

Glad to hear she's so concerned for my ill sister.

"Good night, Merit," my father says. He's looking at me with uncertainty in his eyes. He's still concerned I'm going to reveal his terrible secret.

I smile at him. "Good night, Daddy. Love you."

He doesn't smile. He knows I'm just being a bitch. Or brash, as Sagan referred to it yesterday.

I turn off all the lights in the kitchen and head to the shower. Right before I get in, I receive a text.

Honor: Is anyone suspicious?
Merit: Nope. Everyone's gone to bed.
Honor: Phew. Okay. I just texted Sagan to let him know I was going to sleep. Thank you. I owe you one.
Merit: You owe me two. Tonight was your night to do dishes. You're welcome.
Honor: I'll do your dishes for the next month after this.
Merit: I'm screenshotting this text.

I spend the entire shower replaying last night's conversation with Sagan in my head, over and over. I still can't believe he had the nerve to ask me about Luck. Or maybe I'm confusing nerve with courage. Either way, he was out of line. He's dating my sister. Not me. He needs to worry about who *she's* sleeping with.

When I get out of the shower, the emotions from last night have hit me again. I think I'm so angry because I liked that Sagan seemed a little jealous when he asked me about Luck. I don't want to feel that way. I don't want a guy to drive an even bigger wedge between me and Honor, even though Honor is off doing God knows what right now.

It's almost time for Sagan to get here and if I'm not hiding in my room by then, I'm going to be forced to lie to him. He'll ask me about Honor, how she's feeling, if she's eaten. He might even want to check on her, but I'll have to tell him she's fine.

It isn't fair to him. I know he isn't innocent in this, but at least he's being honest with Honor. Whereas she's off with his dying best friend, Colby.

She's just like my father. I guess she's also just like our mother.

I make my way to the laundry room to get

213

my pajamas out of the dryer. I pull the whole load out, but sift through them for mine. Honor's pajamas are mixed in with this load as well. I take both of our pajamas out and compare them.

This is why she's the prettier twin, even though we're identical. She wears sexier nightgowns and sexier bathing suits and sexier hair. She braids her hair almost every night when she gets out of the shower so it'll be wavy when she takes the braid out in the morning. I don't bother. It doesn't really make that much of a difference if you ask me. Or at least that's what I tell myself. It really does look better than mine, but I keep mine pulled up most of the time, so it doesn't really matter what I do to it at night.

I stare down at her nightgown again. I wonder what it would be like to dress like her. My pajamas are mismatched cotton shorts and a T-shirt. Her nightgown is silk and black and not at all revealing, but sexy nonetheless. Do people sleep better if they feel sexy when they fall asleep?

She's not here to know if I test that theory or not.

I make sure the door to the laundry room is closed and then I drop my towel and pull Honor's nightgown over my head. I look at my reflection in the window. I still don't feel as pretty as Honor looks when she wears it.

I take the towel off my head and finger through my hair until it's untangled enough to braid. I pull it over my right shoulder like Honor does and I braid it until I reach the tips of my hair. I don't have a rubber band, but there's one in the bathroom. Since Honor isn't here, I won't feel like I'm copying her if I sleep with my hair like this tonight.

I turn off the light in the laundry room and make my way back toward the bathroom to grab a hair tie.

"You feeling better?"

I freeze. Sagan is locking the front door. All the lights are off, except for the glow from the electronics in the kitchen.

Shit.

He thinks I'm Honor.

I can't admit that I'm not. How would I explain wearing her nightgown and having my hair braided like her? This is so embarrassing. Why is everything with him so embarrassing?

"Yep," I say, inflecting my voice a tad to sound more like Honor. More . . . pleasant.

I start walking toward the hallway, but freeze when I realize what a bind I've just put myself in. I can't walk to my room because Sagan will wonder why Honor is walking into my room. I can't walk into Honor's room because her bedroom door is locked and she has her key.

"David got fired from the studio tonight," Sagan says.

I have no idea who David is. Sagan is removing his jacket and I'm standing in the hallway, completely shell-shocked. "It's about time."

Sagan tilts his head and releases a confused laugh. "What?"

Oh. So David getting fired is a bad thing.

I don't even know where Sagan works. This is going to end so badly.

"That's not what I meant," I say. "I just meant you knew it was coming."

Did he? I hope so.

He nods. "I know it's his fault for rarely showing up, but I still feel bad. He has four kids." He walks to the refrigerator and opens the door. The light illuminates everything, including me. I'm nervous he'll notice something that will set me apart from Honor, so I walk away from the light and toward the couch. Sagan follows me into the living room. I sit down and he sits down right beside me, propping his feet up on the table. He reaches across me for the remote. I pull my legs up beneath me and try to lean away from him. What if he tries to kiss me? How am I going to get out of this?

I could pretend I have to vomit. I'll run to the bathroom and lock myself in. But he would follow me. And knowing Sagan, he'd wait outside the bathroom until I was finished.

Sagan flips on the TV and the light is even brighter than the refrigerator was. I curl into myself even more. I can feel my palms begin to sweat from the nerves. And then as if sitting next to him isn't bad enough, he goes and touches me. He lifts his hand to the side of my head and tucks my hair behind my ear like I don't actually need oxygen to survive.

"You okay?"

I nod with my swallow. My mouth is too dry to speak.

"Honor." He wants me to face him. Good God, he wants me to look him in the eye. As Honor. Not as me. Just tell him, already. I face him, prepared to explain the last five minutes, but the look on his face prevents me from speaking. He's looking at me like he looks at Honor. Or . . . he's looking at Honor like he looks at Honor. But I'm not Honor. I'm me, and now those eyes are staring at me like I mean the world to him.

"Are you still mad?"

I shake my head. "No." It's the truth. I'm not mad at him, but I have no idea if Honor is.

He nods, squeezing my hand. "You know how I feel about everything. But I don't want to tell you what to do."

Honor is terrible. She's a terrible human, doing this. Lying to him. Cheating on him. I want to tell him so bad, but knowing he's lying to his friend kind of justifies what Honor is doing in a way. And for some reason my loyalty is with her. I think. I don't know, I'm so confused.

I close my eyes because I'm beginning to not be able to function. He's so close and it makes me wonder if he would taste like mint ice cream again. I'd give anything to taste that again.

She wouldn't know.

She's not even here.

If it happened, it would be her fault. Not mine. This entire situation is all her fault. She's off kissing some other guy right now. Maybe this is her karma.

I do what I do best. I react without thinking.

I lean forward and press my lips to his. His hands meet my shoulders. I pull away long enough for him to say her name. "Honor."

I hate it.

I don't want him to say her name again. I just want him to kiss me.

I slide my leg over his lap until I'm straddling him. I keep my eyes closed as I slip my hands up his neck. I don't want him to notice I'm not wearing contacts. Honor wears them all the time and I never wear them.

I can feel his fingers digging into my waist and I wait for him to kiss me like he did the first time he kissed me, but he's hesitant.

I'm too impatient. I press my mouth to his again, but I'm met with resistance. It's nothing like our first kiss. His lips are hard and firm and closed. His hands leave my waist and slide up my arms until they're wrapped around my wrists. He pulls my hands off him.

"What are you doing?" he asks.

I open my eyes. His are full of confusion. I pull back just enough to give us both space to think, but it's not enough. His thumb slides across the Band-Aid on the underside of my wrist. His eyes fall to the Band-Aid. The one he gave me. The one I used to cover up the scratch on my wrist with last night. My wrist. Not Honor's.

I suck in a quick rush of air when I see realization swallow up the confusion on his face. He looks at the bandage on my wrist and then back at my face. "Merit?"

I don't move. I don't even make excuses. Here I am, dressed like Honor, straddling him. I don't even know how to come back from this. I've never prayed for a stroke before, but I'm praying with everything I have that God will strike me down dead right here and now.

I keep my eyes glued to his, waiting for him to push me off him in disgust. But he just keeps staring at me, his eyes fixed on mine. He finally lets go of my wrists, but instead of grabbing my shoulders to scoot me off of him, he grabs my face.

And then he kisses me. *Devours* me.

Me.

Not Honor.

I close my eyes and completely melt into him. I melt into his chest, his arms, his mouth. When his tongue finds mine I all but give up on trying to reciprocate. My mind isn't connecting with my limbs. It's like they're being controlled by some other force. My hands slide through his hair and his hands move to my waist, and then to my lower back. And it's nothing like the first time we kissed.

It's better.

It's real.

It's me.

Not Honor.

His mouth is like a cacophony of flavors right now, each fighting to overpower the other. Everything delicious, all at once. Sugar and sweet against salty and savory.

Is this the answer to my prayer? That Honor would treat him so terribly; he'd have no choice but to want to be with me?

I push the thought of her out of my head at the same moment Sagan pushes me back against the couch. He doesn't take his mouth off mine as he climbs on top of me, both of us equally as desperate to take in as much of each other as we can.

It feels so surreal, I want to smile, but it's all so serious, I want to cry. My emotions are everywhere. Just like his hands. Sliding down my thigh, roaming around my leg, grasping the back of my knee and pulling my leg up and around him. The position he just put us in makes us both gasp for air. He breaks the kiss, but moves his mouth to my neck. "Merit," he says between kisses.

I could listen to him breathe out my name like that for eternity.

"Merit," he says again, kissing up my jaw. "What is this?"

I shake my head, wanting him to stop questioning it. Don't stop. Just go. Green light all the way.

He somehow mistakes my green light for a yellow light, because he pauses. He presses his forehead to the side of my head and takes a moment between kisses to catch his breath. I do the same.

"Merit," he says again, pulling away to look down on me. His eyes roam over my face and then down to my chest, back up my face. "Why are you wearing this?" He puts most of his weight on his hands now, removing the pressure that was just all over me.

I want the pressure back. I try to pull him back to me, but he just pulls his face from my hands. He puts all of his weight onto one arm now as he moves his hand to the braid in my hair. He wraps his hand around the braid and slides his fingers down it, all the way to the end. His eyes are moving from my braid, to my face, to the night-gown, to my braid, to my face.

I don't like this.

He sits up, falling back onto his calves. He's kneeling on the couch in front of me. My legs are still on either side of him.

"Why are you wearing Honor's clothes?"

I push my hands into the couch and sit up, pulling my legs away from him. We're facing each other now, but he's so much taller than me, even kneeling. He's towering over me. Questioning me. I close my eyes.

I feel his hand on my chin. Gentle. "Hey." The word is a whisper. "Look at me."

I do, because I'd do anything he asked as long as it was done in that tone. Sweet and protective. He brushes my hair back and repeats himself.

"Why are you dressed like her?"

I can feel the tears as they begin to form in my eyes. I shake my head, hoping to stop the flow. "I was curious."

He releases my face and his hand falls to his lap. "About what?"

I shrug. "I just wanted to see what it felt like. Being her. But then you walked in the door."

His lips fold together. He pulls a hand through his hair and then sits back against the couch. He's no longer facing me.

"Why did you try to kiss me? Before I knew you weren't her?"

I blow out a steady breath, but the air around me is shaking. My whole body is shaking. I'm scared of the truth. I'm not as good at it as Sagan seems to want me to be. "I don't know. I guess I just wanted to kiss you again." I drag my hands down my face and fall against the couch next to him. As if one mortifying life moment isn't enough for one week.

I feel Sagan stand up. I hear him pace the floor a few times. When he pauses, I open my eyes and look up at him. His hands are on his hips and he's looking down at me. "Do you think Honor and I . . ." He tosses his hand at the couch. "Do you think I do things like this with her? Do you think we're together like that?"

My mouth falls open. I clamp it shut. His question is confusing me. "Aren't you?"

He doesn't say anything for a moment. He just stares at me in disbelief. And then . . .

"No."

There's so much truth in that word, but it has to be a lie. Of course they do stuff like this. Of course they kiss.

"Merit, Honor is my friend. She's seeing my best friend, I would never do that to him." He sighs. "It's complicated."

"But . . ." I shake my head, more con-fused than ever on how to respond. "Why do you both make it seem that way?"

He laughs incredulously. He tilts his face up and stares at the ceiling for a moment. "We don't. That's just how you choose to see it."

I think back on the last couple of weeks. All the times he's been referred to as her boyfriend were when I referred to him that way. He never called himself her boyfriend. Honor never said he was her boyfriend. And aside from a few hugs, I've never once seen him kiss her. I've only seen them hold hands at the pool.

But that doesn't explain why he kissed me the day he followed me out of the antiques store. He thought I was Honor then and he kissed me. And the fight they had the other night about Colby . . .

I cover my face with my hands again as I try to separate everything I'm feeling. Everything that's happening. "But your fight the other night. About her seeing Colby . . ."

"Colby is my friend," he interrupts. "But so is Honor. I don't like that she's so caught up in these unhealthy relationships. I get angry at her when she doesn't listen to me. We fight. It's what friends do."

"Oh."

Sagan begins pacing the floor again. He walks from one end of the couch to the other. He stops in front of me. "Why did you kiss me when I thought you were Honor?"

I'm pretty sure I already answered this question. "I already told you . . ." I look up at him and it's the first time he looks angry. I clamp my mouth shut again.

He inhales a slow, controlled breath. "Let me get this straight," he says. "You thought I was Honor's boyfriend so you pretended to be her and then you tried to kiss me?"

I try to shake my head, but my head doesn't move. "Sagan."

"What kind of person does that to her own sister, Merit?" He grimaces and turns away from me, gripping the back of his neck with his hands. He walks into the kitchen and grabs his hoodie off the back of a chair. I look completely pathetic as I stand up and take a few steps toward him.

He walks to the door and opens it, but he pauses before he exits. When he lifts his head to look at me, his eyes are full of disappointment. "You are such an asshole."

He closes the door.

I stumble back to the couch until I'm sitting on it again.

You are such an asshole.

I've been called a lot of things in my life, but no one has ever called me an asshole. It hurts so much worse than anything anyone else has ever said to me.

I guess I was wrong. I *am* the worst person out of the three of us.

Chapter Ten

I listen for a car to start, but it never does. Sagan left, but he didn't leave in a vehicle, which means he's either walking or just lingering outside until he cools off. I want to run after him and beg him to forgive me, but I'm not sure I want his forgiveness right now. I'm not sure I deserve it.

I'm hugging my knees, wondering how I've been so blind. I just assumed he was in love with Honor. They do so much together. They talk like they're a couple. And almost every time I've referred to him as her boyfriend, no one has corrected me. It's as if they wanted me to believe that.

Or maybe it was just Honor who wanted me to believe that.

I use the blanket on the back of the couch to wipe away my tears. Jesus is staring down at me, judging me. I roll my eyes. "Oh, shut up," I say to Him. "Aren't you up there so people like me can be forgiven for doing terrible things like this?"

I fall back on the couch and feel like I want to scream. I grab a pillow and cover my face and do just that. I'm frustrated, embarrassed, angry, disappointed. It's a far fall from what I was feeling while Sagan was kissing me just a few moments ago. It's like I plunged from the warmth of the tropics straight into the ice-cold waters of Antarctica.

I don't want to feel anything anymore. These past two days have supplied me enough emotional turmoil for a lifetime. I'm done. Done, done, done.

"Done, done, done," I reaffirm as I roll off the couch. I walk to the kitchen and grab a red Solo cup. I open the cabinet above the refrigerator and pull out a bottle of liquor. I don't even know what it is. I've never had alcohol before, but what better time to try it than in the same week I almost lose my virginity and piss off the one person I actually feel something for in this house?

I don't know how much it takes to get a person drunk, but I fill my glass halfway to the top. Or maybe it's halfway to the bottom. Am I an optimist or a pessimist? I glance down into the cup.

Pessimist.

I down as much as I can before I feel like

I'm gagging on a fireball. I sputter and cough and even spit a little bit of it into the sink.

"This is disgusting!" I wipe my mouth with a paper towel. I can feel the burn as it slides down my chest. I can also still feel the frustration, the anger, the sadness.

I somehow manage to get down the rest of what's in the cup. I take the bottle and the cup with me as I exit the kitchen. I don't want to be in here when Sagan gets back from his walk. I open the door to my bedroom, but it's lonely. Empty. Depressing. It reminds me of me. I set the bottle of alcohol on my dresser, but the cup falls to the floor. Whatever. It's empty.

The first thing I do is change out of Honor's nightgown and into my own pajamas. I also undo the braid and pull my hair up. I don't want to be her anymore. It's not as fun as I thought it would be. I also don't want to be alone right now. The only person who might feel bad and sympathize with me is Luck.

I'm not sure if he's asleep, so when I open his door I do it as quietly as possible. I slip inside and then face the door as I close it with both hands, not wanting to make a noise. When I turn around, I'm relieved to see there's a tiny sliver of light coming from my father's computer on the other side of the office. Enough light for me to be able to make it to the sofa bed.

I hear Luck groan as I tiptoe further into the room. The mattress squeaks and it sounds like he's rolling over.

"Luck?" The mattress squeaks again and it sounds like he's making room for me. "Are you awake?" I whisper, taking a seat on the edge of the bed.

All of a sudden, I hear the word, "Shit!" but it isn't out of Luck's mouth. It's not out of mine, either.

"Merit?" That's Luck's voice.

"Luck?"

"What the hell?!" That's Utah's voice.

Utah? I jump up.

"Shit!" Luck says. "Merit, get out!"

Something crashes to the floor. The lamp, maybe?

"Get out!" Utah yells.

"Shit!" Luck says again. There's so much commotion going on, it takes me several seconds to regain my bearings and turn around for the door. When I open it, I make the mistake of glancing back into the room. There's enough light now that I can see both of them as they struggle back into their clothes. Utah freezes when he locks eyes with me. Only one of his legs has made it

230

into his pants. He's not wearing any under-wear.

"Oh my God." I'm scarred for life. Luck is on the other side of the sofa bed, strug-gling to pull on his boxer shorts.

I slap my hand over my eyes when Utah yells, "Get the hell out, Merit!"

I slam the door shut.

Please be a nightmare.

I go to my room and grab the bottle of li-quor and don't even bother with the cup this time. I need these feelings to stop. I need to forget, forget, forget. What in the hell did I just see?

I squeeze my eyes shut. I can't be that oblivious. Then why were they naked? To-gether? In bed?

Luck almost had sex with me yesterday. He said he couldn't finish because I looked like Moby, but Utah looks more like Moby than any of us! Now he's having sex with my brother? If this isn't the ultimate form of rejection, I don't know what is.

What's wrong with me? Luck would rather have sex with my brother than me. Sagan called me an asshole right after we made out on the couch. Drew Waldrup broke up with me with his hand on my boob. WHY AM I SO REPULSIVE?

"Merit!"

Utah is knocking on my door as I pace my bedroom floor. What in the hell did I just interrupt?

I swing open the door and Utah pushes himself into my room and closes the door behind him. He looks angry and a little bit worried when he points at me. "Keep your mouth shut," he says. "What I do is none of your business."

I stop pacing and step closer to him. "Have I ever spilled your secrets before this?"

His anger fades with the mention of his past indiscretions.

"You think I forgot about that, Utah? Well, guess what? I didn't. And I never will."

He winces and I can see the guilt in his expression. I want to punch him, but I'm not a violent person. I don't think. I'm not sure, because my hand balls into a fist right before he slips out of my bedroom and shuts the door.

I hate him. And I hate myself for never telling anyone the truth about him.

I sit down on my bed and squeeze my eyes shut. I feel like I might puke and I'm not even sure why, exactly. I think it's everything. It's Luck, Sagan, Utah, Honor, my father, Victoria, my mother.

This family is just as terrible as everyone in this town believes it to be. Maybe even worse. I'm sick of it. I'm sick of the secrets and I'm sick of the lies. And I'm tired of being the one person in this house who has to hold on to all of them!

I have Utah's secret.

I have my father's secret.

My mother's secret.

Honor's secret.

Luck's secret.

I don't want any of them anymore!

Maybe if I let all the secrets out, they wouldn't make me feel like drowning anymore.

Yes. Maybe that would help. Maybe getting it all out will help me feel like I'm not about to implode.

I reach to my nightstand and grab a pen, then open the drawer and sift through it until I find a notebook with enough empty pages to hold all these secrets.

It still hurts. All of it. The entire past few days. I grab the bottle of . . . what the hell am I even drinking? I read the label. Tequila. I grab the bottle of tequila and slide to the floor because I'm starting to feel dizzy. I grab my pen and notebook and open to the first blank page I can find. I squeeze my eyes shut until my vision feels sturdier. I feel wobbly. My hand feels wobbly when I start writing.

Dear inhabitants of Dollar Voss. Every last one of you. Except Moby. He's the only one I like and still have respect for at this point.

I have so much anger building inside of me, and it has nothing to do with me. It's anger at almost every single person in this house. Anger due to all the secrets you've been keeping from each other, from the outside world. I refuse to hold on to any of it for one more second. Every day, there are more and more secrets and I'm tired of looking like the bad guy. You all hate me. You all think every argument in this house is my fault. You all wonder why I'm so damn BRASH all the time. IT'S BE-CAUSE OF ALL OF YOU!

Where do I even begin?

How about I begin with the oldest se-cret? Did you think I would forget, Utah? Did you think, because I was only twelve, that I wouldn't remember the night you forced me to kiss you?

It's hard to forget something like that, Utah. If you knew how much I worshipped you as my big brother, you would under-stand why it's so hard to forget when you did what you did.

"It's not a big deal, Merit."

That's what you said to me when I shoved you away. You tried to make it seem like I was overreacting to what had just happened. One minute I was in my brother's room watching a movie, the next minute my brother was trying to kiss me.

I ran out of your room that night and never looked back. Not once. I've never been to your bedroom since then. I've never allowed myself to be alone with you since then. And it's like you don't even care. You never even apologized. Do you even feel guilty?

Is that why you find it so difficult to look me in the eye? Because the few times you do look at me, you look at me with con-tempt and disgust. The same way I look at you.

All of you think I'm rude to Utah. You're all telling me, "Calm down, Merit." Think about how you would feel if your family tried to force you to be nice to the brother who stole your first kiss from you.

You disgust me, Utah. You disgust me and I'll never forget and I'll never forgive you.

But at least you have Honor. She worships you because she didn't endure the side of you I endured. She thinks you're sweet and innocent and the best thing to ever happen to her. She looks at me the same way you do, but only because she can't understand how I can treat you so terribly when you do nothing to deserve it.

I know you probably find all of this hard to believe, Dad. Yes, I'm speaking to you now, Barnaby Voss. I've said all I need to say to Utah.

You've set the perfect example for us on how to treat each other, haven't you? You created this beautiful family, but as soon as your wife became ill and couldn't satisfy your needs anymore, you slept with her nurse. You couldn't even be discreet about it. Couldn't you have slept with her and then pretended it never happened once Mom got better? No. You had to take it a step further on the selfish scale and screw Victoria without a condom. Now we're stuck with a woman who hates us. A woman who hates our mother.

I wonder how Victoria would react if she knew you were still sleeping with Mom?

Yeah, that sentence probably shocked ALL of you.

Sorry, Victoria, but it's true. I saw it with

my own two eyes. At least we have an explanation now for why our mother still dresses up every day. She lives in your basement, hoping her ex-husband will sneak down and pay her a visit, so she keeps her makeup pretty and her hair perfect and her legs nice and smooth.

Your husband is probably why our mother still lives here in the basement. He's doing so much damage to her mentally that she's under his complete control. He gets you in the bedroom and my mother in the basement. And you're both Victoria, so he doesn't even have to worry about screaming out the wrong name! He's living every man's fantasy. He doesn't even have to worry about the two of you overlapping because he's got my mother so doped on medication, she's too scared to even leave the basement.

And don't think you're getting off easy, Mother, simply because I feel sorry for you. I liked you more before I knew you were still sleeping with Dad. At least then I could excuse why you're still here, living in a dungeon, wasting away your life. I thought it was because of your social phobia, but now I know it's because you're playing some kind of sick game, trying to win Dad back. Well guess what, Mom?

He's not taking you back! Why would he? You open your legs to him any time he wants it.

You're probably more pathetic than he is. At least he's raising his children. At least he's working to put food on the table and a roof over our heads. He's damn shitty at the whole father thing, but he's a much better parent than you've ever been to us. So yeah, consider this my goodbye. I won't be visiting you in the basement anymore. If you care about any of us, you'll suck it up, get a job, move out, and get a life!

Who else?

Oh! Let's not forget the newest addition to Dollar Voss. Luck Finney! He seems great, doesn't he? Shows up this week, makes up with his sister and then almost fucks his step-niece.

Granted, it was my idea to lose my virginity to him. Not like it would have made a difference to him since he's had sex over three hundred times! But now that I know he's making his way through ALL the Voss siblings, I feel even cheaper than I felt after what I'm sure would have been the worst sexual experience in history . . . had he been able to go through with it.

Maybe he couldn't finish with me because he prefers dick. Utah's dick, at least.

Oh! Did no one know Utah was gay? Not that I have anything against anyone being gay. Love is love, right? But I just didn't know that about Utah. But yes, Utah is gay and he's sleeping with Luck. I know because I walked in on them. I can't get the image of them out of my head no matter how hard I try. It's embedded there, just like the image of Sagan when he called me an asshole.

He was right, though. I am an asshole. What kind of person betrays their own twin sister in the worst possible way? Of course, the fact that I pretended to be Honor so I could kiss Sagan wasn't really a betrayal, considering Honor and Sagan aren't even a thing. But how was I supposed to know that? Honor doesn't tell me anything! A sister should know who her own twin sister is dating! But I still somehow get stuck with everyone's secrets, and then you all beg me to keep them from everyone else!

Kind of like the one I'm keeping for Honor right now. She's off with some guy tonight, probably naked with him on his death bed.

Can we please address this?

239

Can we please discuss how disturbing it is that Honor is obsessed with the terminally ill?

Why is this okay?

Why have you not put her in therapy, Dad?

WHO IN THEIR RIGHT MIND SEEKS OUT LOVE FROM PEOPLE WHO ARE DYING?

Honor, from one sister to another, please get help. You need it. Desperately.

Who am I forgetting? Moby? I won't even go there. Just someone please save this kid from this family before it's too late.

Sagan, I really don't have anything negative to say about you. You're quite possibly the only sane one living in this house. I guess in a way that's your flaw. You actually have the option to leave, yet for some reason, you stay with the most screwed-up family in Texas. Your family must really suck. Is that why you've never met your own sibling? Because you were smart enough to get as far away as you could?

Well, that was fun. I think I feel better now that all your secrets are no longer my responsibility. In the future, keep your shit to yourself because I don't care.

I'll say it again in case none of you are getting it.

I.
Don't.
Care.

Sincerely,

Merit

I slap the pen to the page.

That felt good. Too good. I feel like a weight has been lifted and it's now evenly disbursed among every person in this family. Or at least it will be once I make copies for everyone.

If it felt that good just writing it, I can't imagine how good it will feel delivering it. I tear the pages out and stand up, but I have to grab my dresser to steady myself. I laugh because I think I finally drank enough to make all my feelings go away. Or maybe it was the letter I just wrote. Either way, I think I like tequila. I feel freaking great. I like it so much; I drink the rest of it before I head to my father's office to make copies.

I don't bother knocking. I heard Utah's door slam earlier, so I know he's not in here with Luck anymore. When I open the door, Luck is messing with his phone. He doesn't look happy to see me. "What do you want?"

"Not you," I say, walking to the other side of the room. "I need to use the copier."

Luck sighs and leans against the back of

the sofa bed. I place the first page on the copier and hit the number 7. There are nine people in this house, but Moby can't read and I've got the original. I press the Copy button and then turn to face Luck.

"So," I say. "Is there anyone you won't have sex with on this earth besides me?"

"Are you drunk?"

I open the copier and put the second page facedown. I hit the copy button again. "Yes. It's the only way I can deal with this family, Luck. The family you chose to move in with." I turn around and look at him again, this time with confusion. "Why would you willingly choose to live here?"

Luck doesn't answer me. He looks back down at his phone and starts texting again. "Are you almost done?"

I put the final page on the copier. "Yep. Nearly there." I glance to the other side of the copier and see Luck's worn notebook with all his conquests in it. I glance back at him and he isn't looking at me. I flip to the last page and sure enough, he has my name written down. It says, 332.5 M.V., her bed, DNF.

I got DNF'd. A big, fat DID NOT FIN-ISH.

"Do I at least get a participation trophy for this?" Luck sees the notebook in my hands. He jumps off the sofa bed and snatches it out of my hands. He walks back to the bed. I chuck a pen at him. "Here. Don't forget to write Utah's initials down. Lucky 333."

When the copier is finished, I gather all the pages and take the original off the copier.

"Go to bed, already," he says, agitated.

I grab the stapler. I shake it at him as I walk out of his room. "I liked you better before I met you."

I close the door and make my way back to my room. I lay all the pages out on the floor but I'm forced to take a moment for my vision to settle before I can put them in the right piles. All the pages are starting to run together. I have almost all of them stapled when someone knocks on my door.

"Go away!" I crawl to the door and lock it before whoever it is can open it.

"Merit."

It's Sagan. The sound of his voice makes me wince. There wasn't enough tequila to dull this feeling, apparently.

"I'm sleeping," I call out.

"Your light is on."

"*Your* light is on!"

He doesn't respond to that. I'm glad, because I'm not even sure what it meant. A few seconds later I hear the door to his bedroom close.

I squeeze my eyes shut to keep the room from spinning. I lay my head down on the floor. I'm too dizzy to keep sitting up like this. As soon as I close my eyes, I hear a text message come through on my phone. I reach my hand to my bed and search around until I find it.

Honor: What happened?

So much has happened in the last two hours, I don't even know which part she's referring to.

Merit: What do you mean?
Honor: Sagan just texted me and told me to be careful coming home. WHY does he know I'm not home?
Merit: Well . . . he's very hard to lie to. Besides, what's it matter? He's not even your boyfriend.
Honor: It matters because I lied to him and thanks to you, he's now aware of that. Remind me not to ask you to cover for me in the future!
Merit: Okay. Don't ask me to cover for you in the future.

Is it normal for a person to hate their own

family this much?

I find the bottle of tequila but it's still empty. That doesn't help me much because I still feel things. I stumble my way into the kitchen and open every single cabinet, but I can't find more alcohol. I open the refrigerator and the only thing that might help me numb what's happening in my chest right now are three beers. I grab all of the cans and take them to my bedroom. I slide back to the floor and pop open one of the beers. I stare at the letter I wrote.

Should I give it to them?

Probably not. It would only give them more reason to hate me. They wouldn't feel sorry for me after reading it, they'd be mad at me for telling all their secrets.

I down the first beer and my stomach already hurts, but it still doesn't help the pressure in my chest. You know what this feels like? It feels just like the day I decided to stop going to school. I was walking into the cafeteria when Melissa Cassidy grabbed my arm and said, "Honor, come here. You won't believe what I found out!" She dragged me about five feet to her table, where Honor was already sitting. She glanced back at me and then at Honor and she said, "Oh. Sorry. I thought you were Honor." She let go of my arm and walked back to the table and started whispering in Honor's ear.

I just stood there, staring at Honor. Everyone liked her, despite the fact that she was a Voss. Everyone wanted to hang out with her and be her friend and I was simply a by-product. The identical twin sister with less to offer. There wasn't a single girl at that table who would rather be friends with me than Honor.

Nothing terrible happened that made me want to drop out that day. I was never bullied at school, despite everyone having their unsavory opinions about our family. I was just . . . there. When I kept to myself, everyone was okay with that. No one bothered me. When I decided to join in on conversations with Honor and her friends, everyone was okay with that, too. I was Honor's twin sister, they weren't going to be rude to me. What they were was indifferent. And I think their indifference bothered me more than if they would have hated me.

It was like seventeen years of denial smacked me in the face right there in the cafeteria. The whole school would notice if Honor stopped showing up. But if I stopped showing up, life would go on. With or without Merit.

In fact, I've had two texts from friends in

my class, asking why I haven't been at school for two weeks.

Two.

That's it.

And that's another reason why I've stayed home. But for some reason I thought I would like staying at the house more than going to a school where I didn't matter, but I don't. I hate it here, too. I don't matter here, either. If I dropped out of life, just like I dropped out of school, everyone's lives would go on.

With or without Merit.

I down the second beer and as soon as it's empty, I toss the can at my bedroom door. "Without Merit," I whisper to no one. "That'll show 'em."

And then I do what I do best. I react without thinking. My spontaneity will be the only thing I miss about myself. I crawl to the closet and grab the black boot. I pull out the bottle of stolen pills and I open the lid. I reach for the third beer and my hands are shaking so bad, it takes me three tries to pop it open.

I look down at the beer in my left hand and the bottle of pills in my right. I don't even give it a second thought. I pour some of the pills in my mouth and then try to swallow. I pour a few too many so I end up spitting them back out in my hand. I relax my throat and then try it again. They go down this time, so I pour a few more and then swallow. I can't get but about three or four down at a time, so it takes me the entire beer to wash them all down.

I toss the empty beer can aside and then grab all seven stacks of pages. I grab a pen and go through each stack and add the word *Without* to my name. Sincerely, *Without* Merit. That's more like it. I start with Sagan's room, since his is closest. I slide one set of the stapled pages beneath his door. Then I continue down the hallway until Utah, Luck, and Honor have been covered. I don't even bother sliding the pages beneath the basement door. I open the door and throw my mother's stack down the stairs. If they stayed at the top of the stairs, she'd never see them. I make my way to Quarter Three and shove the last set of pages beneath my father and Victoria's bedroom door.

On my way back through Quarter One, I notice a sheet of paper on the couch that wasn't there earlier. Between pretending to be Honor and kissing Sagan, I would have noticed I was sitting on a sheet of paper.

It's upside down but I can already tell it's a sketch. I snatch it up and walk to my bedroom. I close the door and sit down on my bed. I don't know what he drew, but on the bottom of the back page he wrote,

"Heart < Carcass."

I cover my mouth as I flip over the sketch. My fingers are trembling against my lips as I work up the courage to look at what he's drawn.

I shudder when I see it. I wrap my arm tightly around my stomach. Two hearts on either end of a couch. One of them whole, one of them cut in half.

Which one is mine?

I feel sick. I drop the drawing and watch it float to my bedroom floor. It lands on top of the empty bottle of pills. I stare at the word *carcass.*

Carcass. Death. *Dead.*

I roll over and bring my knees to my chest and hug them. I squeeze my eyes shut and try not to let it all sink in.

Don't let it sink in.

The tears begin to slip out of my eyes, no matter how tightly I have them closed. My bottom lip begins to tremble worse than my hands.

I don't want to die.

I grip myself even tighter.

I don't know what happens next. What if it's worse than this?

My fearful cry turns into a sob. I clamp my hand over my mouth.

"No, no, no, no, no." My voice is full of panic when the reality of what I've done begins to hit. If I lie here one second longer, I might not be able to do anything about it. I pull myself up into a sitting position. I grip my mattress and try to stop the room from spinning long enough to make it to my bedroom door.

What have I done?

I fall to my knees as soon as my bedroom door is open. I'm not sure I can stand up again, so I crawl. I crawl to the bathroom. I reach up and open the door and I crawl to the toilet. I shove my fingers down my throat.

Nothing.

I don't know that I've ever cried this hard. I can't make a sound, I can't scream, I can't breathe, I can't breathe, I can't breathe. I try to make myself vomit again, but it doesn't work. Every time I reach the back of my throat, my fingers recoil and it won't work, it won't work, it won't work!

"Help."

It's pathetic. My voice is pathetic through my tears and this is how I'm going to die. On my bathroom floor, leaving behind what is about to become the most despicable suicide letter anyone has ever written.

This is not happening. This is a dream. I'm dreaming. Please let me wake up. "Please, God," I whisper. "I'll never drink again, I'll never steal again, I'll never even write another letter again, just please, please, please." I've managed to crawl to the bathroom door. Utah's room is the closest. I try to open his door but it's locked. I start beating on it. "Utah!" I beat on it again. I know my voice isn't loud enough, but I'm hoping he can hear me knocking. I'm on my hands and knees now, too dizzy to make it to someone else's door. I don't know how long it takes for pills to dissolve, but it hasn't been that long since I took them. Five minutes?

Utah's door swings open. He's standing on the letter I wrote. He doesn't even notice it because he bends down and says, "Merit?" He's on his knees now, grabbing my jaw, lifting my face up to his. I can feel the tears and snot and slobber all over my face, but he doesn't care about any of that because he reaches for the hem of his shirt and wipes it away. "What's wrong? Are you sick?"

I shake my head and grab his arms, looking at him desperately. "Utah, I messed up."

"Are you drunk?"

"Her pills," I say, choking back more tears. "I took them, I wasn't thinking, Utah I wasn't thinking." I hear another door open and seconds later, Sagan is right next to Utah. I'm too scared to be mortified at this point.

"Whose pills?" Utah asks. "Merit, what are you saying?"

I fall back against the wall, panicking, shaking my hands out because they're numb. "Mom's! I took her pain pills!" Utah looks at Sagan and I know they're trying to figure out what's happening, but they aren't getting it! "I swallowed them!"

Sagan pushes Utah out of the way. "Go call 911!" He grabs the back of my neck and pushes me forward, then shoves two fingers in my mouth. My body tries to reject them but he doesn't care because he holds them there and now I'm vomiting. All over the floor, all over him. I can't keep my eyes open anymore. "How many pills, Merit?"

I shake my head. I don't know.

"How many did you swallow?" His voice is panicked, just like my pulse.

He keeps asking me how many pills I swallowed. I can't remember. How many did I have? I stole eight the other night. I added them to the twenty I had already stolen. "Twenty-eight," I whisper.

"Christ, Merit." His fingers are back in my mouth, assaulting the back of my throat. The pressure coming from within me lurches me forward and I vomit again. I can hear Utah yelling into the phone, Luck is now in the hallway, Moby is crying, my father is saying, "What's going on? What in the hell is going on?"

I open my eyes and Sagan is counting in a fast and frantic whisper. "Twenty-two, twenty-three, twenty-four . . ." He's focused on the floor, sifting through what just came out of me, his voice trembling. "Twenty-five, twenty-six, twenty-seven, TWENTY-EIGHT!" he yells.

And then he scoops me up after my dad says, "Take her to the couch."

I'm on the couch, still dizzy, still feeling like I want to throw up again.

"What did you take?" Utah asks. He's kneeling down in front of me, still on the phone. Victoria brings me a wet rag.

Sagan takes it from her and wipes my face. "Merit, they need to know what kind of pills you took."

"She took pills?" my father says. He's pacing back and forth behind them. Luck is behind him with his hand over his mouth.

"What were they?" Sagan asks. He's brushing back my hair and he looks just as panicked as my father. As Utah. As Victoria. As Luck. Even Moby looks panicked with his arms locked around Victoria's neck.

"What's going on?"

Everyone looks at the front door when it closes behind her. Honor's here.

"Where have you been?" My father is walking toward Honor. He stops and shakes his head. "I'll deal with you later," he says, changing his mind as he walks back toward me. "Merit, what did you take?" He's hov-

254

ering over me now. They're all hovering over me.

"She threw them all up." — Sagan.

"But what were they?" — My father.

"Probably aspirin." — Victoria.

"She said she stole them." — Utah.

"What's going on?" — Honor.

"Merit swallowed pills." — Luck.

"Did you see this, Barnaby?" — Victoria.

"Not right now, Victoria." — My father.

"What did you take, Merit?" — Sagan.

"You need to read this, Barnaby!" — Victoria.

"Victoria, please!" — My father.

"Merit, what were they?" — Utah.

"They were Mom's." — Me.

"You took your mother's pills?" My father is asking me this as he leans over the couch from behind my head. He's upside down and I'm looking up at him and I never noticed how much Moby looks like him. "Your mother's prescription pills?" he asks again. I nod. My father exhales. "It's fine," he says. "It's fine, they can't hurt her." He grabs the phone from Utah and walks into the kitchen to talk to the 911 operator. "Hello? Hey, hey, Marie. Yeah, it's Barnaby. Yeah, it's fine. She's fine."

It's fine. She's fine.

I'm fine.

How does he know if I'm fine? He doesn't even know which pills I took. I guess it doesn't matter at this point since they're sitting in a pile of vomit on the hallway floor.

"You feeling okay?" Sagan asks. I nod. "I'll get you some water."

I close my eyes. Everything is calming down now. My heart is calming down. The commotion is calming down. I blow out a steady breath. It's fine. She's fine.

I'm fine.

"Is this true?" It's Victoria's voice. I open my eyes and she's holding the pages I stapled together. She's looking down at them. Her expression is anything but fine.

It's not fine anymore.

I clench my stomach, feeling like I want to puke again.

"Merit. Did you write this?"

I nod. Maybe she'll be so embarrassed about my father cheating on her, she'll gather all the other letters before anyone else reads them. She takes a step toward me. But she doesn't look at all angry, even though I put in the letter that my father was cheating on her. She looks . . . sad.

She looks at Utah. "You did this to her?"

Utah looks at me and then back at Victoria. "Did I do what to who?"

Victoria walks toward Utah and slaps the

letter against his chest. She keeps walking past him until she's in the kitchen with my father. I look back at Utah and he's staring down at the first page of the letter. Sagan is back with the water. "Here, drink this." He helps me sit up and tries to get me to take a drink, but I can't take my eyes off Utah. I push the glass away and shake my head.

That's when I see it.

A tear.

Utah looks up from the first page of the letter, just as a tear rolls down his cheek. I can't help but wonder if it's a tear of guilt or a tear of fear over me finally spilling the truth. He drops the pages and runs his hands through his hair. Of course he's not making eye contact with me.

I hear sirens in the distance. My father says, "Thanks, Marie," into the phone. He ends the call and Victoria is right there, whispering something to him. She points at Utah. She points at me. She points at the pages that are now at Utah's feet. My father looks at Utah. He marches to the living room just as the ambulance pulls onto our road. He grabs the pages from the floor and begins reading. One minute. Two minutes. Utah is frozen in place. There's a knock on the door but my father ignores it.

"Dad," Utah whispers.

My father looks up from the letter. His eyes meet Utah's and then mine.

There's another knock at the door.

"Dad, please," Utah says. "I can explain."

Another knock.

A punch.

Honor screams.

Utah is on the floor now. My father is standing over him. He points to the door and says one word to him.

"Leave."

Honor is helping Utah up, glaring at our father. "What the hell is wrong with you!?"

Once Utah is standing, he turns and heads toward his bedroom. Honor and Luck follow him. Sagan opens the front door and lets in the paramedics.

"She's fine," my father says to them, pointing toward me. "Check her out, but they were only placebo pills."

Placebo pills.

Why were they placebo pills?

The next ten minutes go by in a blur as the paramedics bombard me with questions, check my blood pressure, my oxygen, my eyes, my mouth. "It probably wouldn't hurt to let us take her overnight," I hear one of the paramedics whisper to my father. "Otherwise, we'll have to let the social worker

258

know what happened. They'll have to follow up."

My father nods and walks over to me. He kneels down, but before he even says anything I force out an "I'm fine. I don't want to go to the hospital."

"Merit," he says. "I think you should . . ."

"I don't want to go," I say with finality. He nods. I don't hear what he says when he returns to the paramedic, but the guy squeezes my father's shoulder. They must know each other. Of course, they do. It's a small town. And since they know my father, they'll tell their wives and then their wives will tell their friends and then their friends will tell all their daughters and then the entire town will know I tried to kill myself.

With placebo pills.

Why is she taking placebo pills?

As soon as that thought crosses my mind, my mother appears at the top of the basement steps. The door is open and she's looking at me from across the room. "Are you okay?" She starts to take a step toward me, but she looks down at her foot as it meets the wood floor and she quickly returns to the top step of the basement.

"Everything is fine, Vicky," my father says to my mother. I glance over at Victoria and she's walking toward her bedroom with

Moby. She can't even be in the same room with her. I wonder if she's even read the entire letter yet. Does she know they're still sleeping together?

"What happened?" my mother asks.

I'd give anything for her to walk over here and hug me. Anything. She knows something bad has happened or she wouldn't have opened the basement door. Yet she's more concerned about not leaving the basement than she is about me. I look down at my hands. I'm shaking, and I feel like I'm about to be sick again.

"I'll explain everything in a little while," my father says to her. "Try to get some sleep, okay?" I hear the basement door close. I don't get a hug from my mother.

"Dad," I whisper, looking up at him pleadingly. "I threw a letter in the basement. Can you please go get it before she reads it?"

He nods and heads to the basement without question.

"Merit!" Honor yells. I look up just in time to see her marching down the hallway, letter in hand. She crosses Quarter One and looks like she's ready to attack me, but Sagan steps in front of her and grabs her arms. She struggles to get out of his grip, but when she realizes he won't let her past, she just chucks the pages at me. "You're a liar!"

She's crying and I suddenly realize we're not at all attractive when we cry. I hate that I've been doing it for the past two hours.

I feel like I'm watching a movie. I don't feel like I'm in it, living it, taking the brunt of her anger right now. I don't even respond to her anger because I feel so disconnected from it.

"Not now, Honor," Sagan says, walking her away from me.

"It's not true!" Honor yells. "Tell them it's not true! Utah would never do something like that!"

I watch everything unfold as I remain curled up on the couch, wrapped in a blanket. Victoria is back, but Moby isn't with her anymore. Honor runs up to her and my father. "You can't make him leave, she's lying!"

Victoria looks at my father. "You can't let this slide, Barnaby."

"Mind your own business!" — Honor.

"Honor," — My father.

"Oh, shut up!" — Honor.

"Go to your room!" — My father. "Everyone! To your rooms!" — Still my father.

"What about me? Can I go back to my room?" — Utah.

"No. You leave. Everyone else to their rooms." — My father.

"If he's going, I'm going." — Honor.

"No. You're staying." — My father.

"I'll go with Utah." — Luck.

"You aren't going with him, either." — Victoria.

"You're seriously going to tell me what I can do? I'm twenty!" — Luck.

"Everyone just stay. It's fine. I'm fine. I'll go." — Utah.

"Why are you leaving? You didn't do anything!" — Honor.

And here it is. The moment of truth. The climax.

Utah's shoulders rise with his heavy intake of breath. Then they fall, like all great empires eventually do. He looks across the room at me. He stares at me, but doesn't use the opportunity to admit his guilt. Or even apologize. Instead, Utah walks to the door after it's clear my dad isn't going to relent. The slam the front door makes when it closes makes me jump.

Sagan slowly takes a seat on the couch next to me. He's popping his knuckles like he's angry, but I have no idea which person in this family he's angry at. More than likely me. Everyone is quiet until my father says, "It's late. We'll discuss everything tomorrow. Everyone go to bed." He looks at Luck and points at him. "You stay in your room.

If I see you anywhere near my daughters, you're gone." He must have read the rest of the letter.

Luck nods and retreats to his room. Honor is staring at my father, her hands in fists at her sides. "This is your fault," she says to him. "You and your pathetic choices and your pathetic parenting. You're the reason this family is so screwed up!" Honor walks to her room and slams the door.

It's just me and Sagan now. And my father. A moment passes as my father gathers himself. He finally walks toward me, squatting down in front of me so that we're eye to eye. "You okay?"

I nod, even though this feels far from okay.

He looks at Sagan. "Do you mind keeping an eye on her tonight?"

"Not at all."

"I don't need a babysitter."

"I'm not so sure of that," my father says. "I need to go deal with Victoria."

He stands up, but before he's able to walk away, I say, "Why is Mom taking placebo pills?"

He stares down at me, the imprints of all his secrets gathering in the corners of his eyes. "I'm just thankful that's all they were, Merit."

He turns and makes his way into the

kitchen, toward his bedroom. But when he passes by the kitchen table, he pauses. He grips the back of one of the chairs and drops his head between his shoulders. He stays like this for about ten seconds, but then he lifts the chair off the floor and throws it against the wall, smashing it to pieces. When he makes it to his bedroom, he slams the door.

Sagan releases a breath at the same time I do. He runs his hands down his face and we're both quiet. Speechless. An entire minute goes by and we're just staring at the floor until he says, "Take a shower. You'll feel better."

I nod. When I stand up, Sagan stands up with me. I think he can tell I'm still dizzy, because he grabs my arm and helps me to the bathroom. Once we're inside, he pulls back the shower curtain and picks up the razor. He slides it into his back pocket.

"Really, Sagan? You think I'll nick my wrist to pieces with a disposable BIC?"

He doesn't say anything. But he also doesn't give me back the razor. "I'll clean up in the hallway while you're in the shower. You want to stay in my room tonight or yours?"

I think about that for a moment. I'm not so sure I want him in my room, on my bed, where I tried to end my life. "Yours," I whisper.

He closes the door and leaves me alone to shower. But then he opens the door and walks back inside. He swings open the medicine cabinet and takes the two bottles of medicine off the shelves.

"Seriously? What could I even do with any of that? Swallow eighty gummy vitamins?"

He leaves without responding.

I spend at least thirty minutes in the shower. I don't do anything other than stare at the wall while the hot water beats down on my neck. I think I'm in shock. I still feel disconnected to everything that happened tonight. I feel like it happened to someone else.

Sagan has checked on me twice in the last thirty minutes. I don't know how long it's going to take me to convince him that tonight was a fluke. I'm not suicidal — I was drunk. I did a really stupid thing and now he thinks I'm in this shower trying to plot ways to off myself.

I don't want to die. If I wanted to die, I wouldn't have gone to Utah for help. What teenager doesn't think about what it would be like to die every now and then? The only problem when I thought of it was that my thought was coupled with my spontaneity. And alcohol. Most people think things like this through. Not me. I just do them.

I'm going to need a really big trophy after tonight. Maybe I can find an unwanted Academy Award statuette on eBay.

"Merit?" Sagan's voice is muffled from the other side of the bathroom door.

I roll my eyes and turn off the water. "I'm alive," I mutter. I grab a towel and dry off. Once I'm dressed in my pajamas, I enter his bedroom. The door is open, so I shut it. I want to block myself off from the outside world.

Sagan is making a pallet on the floor.

"You can take the bed," he says.

I look at the bed and notice he brought my pillows in here. I sigh with relief. I don't think I've ever wanted to go to sleep more than I do right now. I glance at his clock and it's after three in the morning. "Do you have to be up early?" I ask him. I feel bad. It's so late and everyone still has to wake up and go to work and school in a few hours. And I don't even know where Sagan goes every day, whether it's work or school. I know very little about the guy who has been put in charge of my life tonight. Thanks for that, Dad.

He shakes his head. "I'm off tomorrow."

I wonder if that's true or if he's just too scared to leave me alone. As bad as I feel for making him worry like he is, it feels kind of nice to be worried about.

I lie down on the bed and pull the covers up over me. His pallet is on the floor on the other side of the bed. I want to be as far away from him as possible tonight. I know myself all too well and as soon as those lights go out, I'm going to be trying to muffle my tears. The more distance between us, the better.

"You need anything before I turn off the light?" He's standing by the door with his hand on the switch. I shake my head, and right before the lights go out, my eyes catch a glimpse of the letter I wrote. It's sitting on his dresser, flipped to the back page.

He read the whole thing. I close my eyes as he walks back to his pallet on the floor. I wonder if anyone else read it. I pull the covers up tighter over my mouth. Of course they read it. I pull my knees up and curl into the fetal position. Why did I write it? I can't even remember everything I wrote.

It slowly comes back to me, paragraph by paragraph. By the time my mind recollects every single page, the tears are falling. I wad the blanket up and bite it, trying to stifle my sobs.

I still don't even know what I'm feeling, or if I even regret writing it. But this feels like regret. Maybe I regret swallowing the pills, but not writing the letter.

Maybe I regret everything.

The only feeling I'm certain about is that I am completely and utterly mortified. Which should be a feeling I'm growing accustomed to, but it isn't. I don't think it's something anyone could get used to.

I can't believe I did what I did tonight. Or even yesterday. I wish I could go back and not drop out of school and none of this would have happened. Hell, I wish I could go back several years and never have that moment with Utah. Or maybe I should have gone back ten years ago to the day Wolfgang showed up in our backyard. If I'd have just killed that damn dog, then we never would have moved into this church. Dad would have never met Victoria. Mom would have never gone crazy and felt the need to hide in the basement.

I bury my face in the pillow and try as hard as I can to prevent Sagan from hearing how sad I am.

But it doesn't work. I feel him lift the covers and slide into the bed beside me. He wraps his arm around me and pulls my back against his chest. He finds my hands still

268

knotted in the covers and he squeezes them. And then he curls himself around me until his legs are wrapped over mine and his chin is pressed to the top of my head. His whole body is hugging mine and I can't even remember the last time someone in this house hugged me. Moby's hugs don't count because he's only four. My father hasn't hugged me in years. I can't remember the last time Utah hugged me. Honor and I haven't hugged since we were kids. My mother doesn't like physical contact, so a hug from her has been out of the question since her phobia reached its peak several years ago. Acknowledging that this is the first hug I've had in years makes me cry even harder.

I feel his lips press against the top of my head. "You want me to tell you a story?" he whispers.

I somehow laugh between my pitiful tears. "Your stories are too morbid for a moment like this."

He moves his head a little until his cheek is pressed against mine. It feels nice. I close my eyes and he says, "Okay, then. I'll sing you to sleep."

I laugh again, but I stop laughing when he actually starts to sing. Or . . . rap, rather.

"Y'all know me, still the same OG . . ."

"Sagan," I say, laughing.

"But I been low key . . ."

"Stop."

He doesn't stop. He spends the next few minutes rapping every single line to "Forgot About Dre." By the time I fall asleep, the tears have dried on my cheeks.

CHAPTER ELEVEN

Imagine the chaos a normal family must experience in the morning after one of its members attempts suicide. The phone calls to therapists, the tears, the apologies, the constant hovering and smothering and chaotic mess of everyone thinking, "How did this happen?" and "How did we not see the signs?"

I stare at Sagan's bedroom ceiling, painfully aware that everyone in the house other than Sagan left a few minutes ago. Or else, I'm assuming because I heard the door slam several times and no one bothered to check on me. I wonder what that must be like — to live in a normal family. A family where people actually give a shit. Not a family like ours, where everyone goes on with their day like I didn't just try to kill myself a few hours ago. A family like ours, where my father still wakes up and goes straight to work. A family where my mother still refuses to leave the basement. My twin sister leaves for school. My step-uncle leaves for his new job. And no one who shares any sort of blood relation to me sticks around to make sure I'm okay.

I get it. They're all pissed at me. I said some really hateful things in that letter and by this point, everyone has read it more than once, I'm sure. But the fact that Sagan is the only one here right now proves that nothing I said in that letter got through to them. Everyone is still blaming me.

I sit up in the bed as soon as Sagan's bedroom doorknob begins to turn with a knock. I'm disappointed — yet somehow relieved — to see my father peek his head in. "You awake?"

I nod and pull my knees up, hugging them. He closes the door behind him and walks over to the bed, taking an unsure seat on it.

"I, um . . ." He squeezes his jaw like he always does when he doesn't know what to say.

"Let me guess," I say. "You want to know if I'm okay? If I'm still suicidal?"

"Are you?"

"No, Dad," I say, frustrated. "I'm a girl who found out her parents were having an affair, so I took my anger out on a few ille-

272

gal substances. It doesn't make me suicidal, it makes me a teenager."

My father sighs heavily, turning to face me full-on. "Either way, I think it's a good idea for you to see Dr. Criss. I made you an appointment for next Monday."

Oh my God.

"Are you kidding me? Out of all the people in this family, you're forcing *me* to go see a psychiatrist?" I fall back against the headboard in defeat. "What about your ex-wife who hasn't seen the sun in two years? Or your daughter who's one heartbeat away from being a necrophiliac! Or your son who thinks it's okay to molest his sister!"

"Merit, stop!" he says, frustrated. He stands up and paces the floor before coming to a pause. "I'm doing the best I can, okay? I'm not the perfect father. I know that. If I were, you would have never gotten to a point where you would rather be dead than live with me." He turns for the door, but then he pauses and faces me again. He hesitates a moment and then lifts his eyes to mine. His expression is full of disappointment, and his voice is much quieter when he says, "I'm doing the best I can, Merit."

He shuts the door and I fall back onto the bed. "Yeah, well. Try harder, Dad."

I wait for the sound of the front door closing before going across the hall to my bedroom. I change, brush my teeth in the bathroom, and then make my grand entrance to Quarter One. No one is there to greet me or tell me how happy they are that they were only placebo pills.

I walk to the kitchen and take a seat at the table. I stare at the marquee outside. It's the first morning it hasn't been updated since we moved in all those years ago. The same message Utah put up yesterday is still there.

IF THE ENTIRE HISTORY OF THE EARTH WERE COMPRESSED INTO A SINGLE CALENDAR YEAR, HUMANS WOULDN'T EVEN APPEAR UNTIL DECEMBER 31ST AT 11:00 P.M.

I have to read it a few times for it to actually sink in. Are humans really that insignificant? We've only existed for one hour out of an entire year?

Sagan walks into the kitchen from the backyard. He's holding a water pitcher. "Morning," he says, his voice cautious. I stare at him a moment and then look back out at the marquee.

"Do you think that's true?"

"Do I think what's true?" he asks. He walks over to the table and takes a seat with his sketch pad.

I nudge my head to the window. "What Utah put on the marquee yesterday."

Sagan looks out the window and stares at the marquee in thought. "I'm probably not the right person to ask. I believed in Santa until I was thirteen."

I laugh, but it's a pathetic, forced laugh. And then I'm frowning because laughter is only a fleeting cure for melancholy, which seems to be my constant state of mind here lately.

Sagan puts down his pencil and leans back in his chair. He stares at me thoughtfully. "What do you think happens when we die?"

I glance back at the marquee. "I have no idea. But if that marquee is true and humans really are that insignificant to the earth's history, it makes me question why a God would go through all the trouble to revolve an entire universe around us."

Sagan picks up his pencil and puts the end of it in his mouth. He chews on it for a moment before saying, "Humans are romantic creatures. It's reassuring to believe this all-knowing being who has the power to create anything and everything still loves the human race more than any of it."

"You call that romantic? I call it narcissistic and ethnocentric."

He smiles. "Depends on the perspective

you look at it from, I guess."

He resumes sketching like he's done with the conversation. But I'm stuck on that word. *Perspective.* It makes me wonder if I look at things from only one point of view. I tend to think a lot of people are wrong a lot of the time.

"Do you think I only see things from one perspective?"

He doesn't look up at me when he says, "I think you know less about people than you think you do."

I can feel myself instantly wanting to disagree with him. But I don't, because my head hurts and I might be a little hungover from last night. I also don't want to argue with him because he's the only one still speaking to me at this point. I don't want to ruin that. Not to mention that he seems wise beyond his years and I'm not about to compete with him intellectually. Even though I have no idea how old he actually is.

"How old are you?"

"Nineteen," he says.

"Have you always lived in Texas?"

"I've spent the past few years with my grandmother, here in Texas. She died a year and a half ago."

"I'm sorry." He doesn't say anything in

response. "Where are your parents now?"

Sagan leans back in his chair and looks at me. He taps his pencil against his notebook and then drops it on the table. "Come on," he says, scooting his chair back. "I need out of this house."

He looks at me expectantly, so I stand up and follow him to the front door. I don't know where we're going, but I have a feeling it's not this house he wants to get away from. It's the questions.

An hour later, we're standing in the antiques store, staring at the trophy I couldn't afford to buy a few weeks ago.

"No, Sagan."

"Yes." He pulls the trophy from the shelf and I try to take it out of his hands.

"You aren't paying eighty-five dollars for this just because you feel sorry for me!" I stalk after him like a tantrum-ridden toddler.

"I'm not buying it because I feel sorry for you." He sets the trophy on the register and pulls out his wallet. I try to grab the trophy but he moves so that he's standing in my way.

I huff and cross my arms over my chest. "I don't want it if you buy it. I only want it when I can afford to buy it myself."

He grins like I'm amusing him. "Well then, you can pay me back someday."

"It's not the same."

He hands the guy behind the register a hundred-dollar bill. "You need a sack?" the guy says.

Sagan says, "No, thanks," and picks up the trophy and heads to the exit. Once we're outside he turns around and hides the trophy behind his back like I didn't just watch him buy it for me. "I have a surprise for you."

I roll my eyes. "You're so annoying."

He laughs and hands me the trophy. I take it and then mutter, "Thank you." I really am excited to have it, but I hate that he paid this much money for it. It makes me feel uncomfortable. I'm not used to getting gifts.

"You're welcome," he says. He throws his arm over my shoulders and says, "You hungry?"

I shrug. "I don't really feel like eating. But I'll sit with you if you're hungry."

He pulls me into a sandwich shop a few doors down from the antiques store. We walk to the register and he says, "I'll take the lunch special. And two sugar cookies, please." He looks at me. "What do you want to drink?"

"Water's fine."

"Two waters," he says to the woman behind the register. He asks for them to go and then we take them across the street and sit at one of the tables next to the water fountain where we first kissed. It makes me wonder if he brought me here on purpose. I doubt he did.

The same question has crossed my mind many times, though. If he doesn't see Honor as more than a friend, why did he kiss me at this fountain when he thought I was Honor? Because he definitely thought I was Honor. Not even the best actor in the world could have faked the confusion and shock when she called him on his cell phone.

I don't ask him about it, though. Our conversation hasn't veered in that direction and I'm not sure I can handle his answer right now. I'm too exhausted from the last twenty-four hours to add more heaviness to our conversation.

"Have you ever had one of their sugar cookies?" Sagan asks.

"Nope." I take a sip of my water.

"It'll change your life." He hands me the cookie and I take a bite. And then another. It really is the best cookie I've ever eaten, but he exaggerated.

"When is the life change supposed to happen, exactly? Do I have to eat the whole cookie to get the results?"

Sagan narrows his eyes at me. "Smartass," he says playfully.

I finish the cookie and watch as he takes a bite of his sandwich. My eyes are drawn to a new tattoo on his arm. It looks like GPS coordinates. I point to it. "Is that one new?"

He looks at his arm and nods. "Yeah, I did it last week."

"What do you mean *you* did it?"

"I do my own tattoos."

I tilt my head and inspect a couple more of his tattoos. "You did all of these?" I suddenly find them much more fascinating than I did prior to this knowledge. I want to know the meaning of all of them. Like why he has a tiny toaster on his wrist with one slice of bread. Or what "Your turn, Doctor" means. Or what the flag stands for. I point to the toaster. "What's this one mean?"

He shrugs. "It's just a toaster. It doesn't mean anything."

"What about this one?" I ask, pointing to the flag.

"It's the Syrian Opposition flag."

"What does that mean?"

He runs his thumb over the flag tattoo. "My father is from Syria. I guess I did it as a tribute to our heritage."

"Is your father still alive?"

That question changes something in him. He shrugs and takes a drink, looking off to the right. It's like a wall raises behind his eyelids when he doesn't want to elaborate. Which is pretty much all the time. I respect his need for privacy about his family and I grab his arm and turn it over to look at the rest of the tattoos. "So some of them have meaning and some are just random?"

"Some of them are random. Most of them have meaning."

I run my finger over the GPS coordinates. "This one has meaning. Is it where you were born?"

He grins and lifts his eyes, meeting mine. "Close to it." The way he looks at me when he says that makes me too flustered to ask another question. I continue to inspect every tattoo on his arm, but I do it quietly. I even lift his shirt sleeve so I can look at the ones on his shoulder. He doesn't seem to mind as long as I'm not asking invading questions about why he got each of them. "Are you right-handed? Is that why they're only on your left arm?"

"Yeah. I'd rather practice on myself than someone else."

"You can practice on me."

"When you turn eighteen."

I shove him in the shoulder. "Come on. That's seven months away!"

"Tattoos are permanent. You need to give it more thought."

"Says the guy with a toaster on his arm."

He arches an eyebrow and it makes me laugh.

I immediately recognize how weird it feels to laugh after last night. I almost feel guilty — like it's too soon. But I like that he forced me out of the house today. I feel a lot better than I would if I were holed up in my room all day and night like I'd planned to be.

He shakes his head. "I'm not giving you a tattoo. I'm only an apprentice right now."

"What's that mean?"

"On the days I don't have school or work, I sometimes go to the local tattoo shop. They're letting me learn the ropes."

"Do you go to college in Commerce?"

He nods. "Yeah, three days a week. I work the days I'm not in school, and then I try to fit in the tattoo shop one or two nights a week."

"Do you want to do tattoos as a career?"

He shrugs. "Nah. I have other plans for my future, but I enjoy it as a hobby."

"What's your major?"

"Double majoring in political science and Arabic."

"Whoa. That sounds serious."

He nods, tight-lipped. "Well, there are some serious things going on in the world right now. I kind of want to be a part of that." The wall goes up again. It's invisible, but somehow I see it every time.

I have so many questions. Like, Why is he majoring in Arabic? And political science? Does he want to work for the government? What serious things going on in the world does he want to be a part of? That's the last thing I'd want to be a part of. This just proves how different he is from me. He's already working toward his future, which sounds quite serious, and I still don't even know if I'm going to return to high school next week.

I feel like such a . . . *child.*

Sagan finishes his cookie and then picks up my trophy and inspects it. "Why do you collect these?"

I shrug. "I don't have any talents. Since I can't win them on my own, I just collect other people's awards when I have a shitty day."

He runs his thumb over the small plaque on the front of the trophy. "Seventh place is hardly an award."

I take the trophy from him and admire it. "I didn't want this one for the title. I only wanted it because it was ridiculously expensive."

Sagan smiles and grabs my free hand, pulling me up. "Come on. Let's go to the bookstore."

"There's a bookstore here?"

He shoots me a crooked grin. "You know very little about the town you live in."

"Technically, I don't live in this town. I live fifteen miles from here."

"You live in this county. It's all the same."

We walk down Main Street until we get to a small bookstore. When we walk inside, we're greeted by a woman standing at a register, but she's the only one in the store. It's quiet, other than a soothing Lumineers song playing in the background. I'm shocked at how modern it looks on the inside. It didn't have this much promise from the outside. The walls are purple, which is my favorite color. There are several bookshelves lining the wall full of books. The rest of the bookshelves are full of candles and merchandise.

"There aren't that many books here," I say, taking in the small space and the limited number of shelves.

"It's a specialty bookstore. For charity. They only sell books signed and donated by the authors."

I pick up one of the books from the shelf

and open it to see if he's telling the truth. Sure enough, it's signed. "That's kind of cool."

He chuckles, but he continues to walk and browse the shelves like he might find something he likes. I pick up a few of the titles and inspect them but already know I won't be getting one. I don't have any money and I'm not about to let him buy me something else. We browse quietly until we get to a row toward the back of the store. Sagan stands in front of the books, fingering them, plucking a few out to read the backs of them. I just watch him. After a moment, his phone rings and of course he acts as though the whole world has to stop. He fishes the phone out of his pocket and looks at the caller ID. He sighs, disappointed, but answers the call anyway.

"Hey."

He grips the back of his neck while the person on the other end talks. He glances at me briefly and then looks away when he says, "Yeah, yeah. Everything is fine."

Everything is fine.

I'm curious who he's talking to and if he's referring to me and my situation when he says everything is fine.

He motions to the door to let me know he's going to take the call outside. I nod and watch as he slips out the door to the bookstore. I walk over to a couch by the window and take a seat as I watch him on the phone.

"Can I help you find anything?" The woman behind the register is staring at me. It's a little unnerving. She looks to be in her late thirties and her frizzy hair is piled into a knot on top of her head. She's sitting behind a laptop, looking across the room at me, waiting on me to answer her.

"I'm good."

She nods, but then she says, "Are you okay?"

I nod again, a little annoyed that this woman is asking me if I'm okay. That seems a little intrusive. I glance out the window again and Sagan is pacing back and forth, doing very little talking. He's mostly listening to whoever is on the other end. He squeezes his forehead at one point, which makes me sad for him. He seems stressed and I can't help but feel a little guilty about that.

"Is he your boyfriend?" the woman asks as she makes her way over to me. I try to keep my eyes from rolling, but I'm pretty sure it's obvious that I'm not in the mood to make small talk.

"No."

"Brother?" she asks, taking a seat on the couch across from me.

"No."

She gets comfortable and looks out the window at him. "He's cute. How do you know him?"

If I stare hard enough, I wonder if Sagan will look inside and see how desperate I am for him to come save me. Until that happens, though, I have no choice but to answer this woman's questions. I try and answer them all at once so it'll leave her no room to ask me more.

"He's a family friend." I point down Main Street toward the courthouse. "He kissed me for the first time over there. But he mistook me for my twin, which is the only reason he kissed me, so it was an accidental kiss. I've tried avoiding him for the past few weeks because I thought he was dating my sister. But last night I dressed up as her and kissed him again, only to find out he's not even dating my sister. We got into an argument and he left, so I went to my stepuncle's room and he was having sex with my brother. So I got drunk, swallowed a bunch of pills and almost killed myself. Sagan," I point outside at him. "That's his name. Sagan thought a sugar cookie and a bookstore would make me feel better, so that's why we're here."

The woman's eyes are wide, but she doesn't look shocked. Just a little overwhelmed by the info dump. She eventually leans forward and says, "Well, he sounds like a keeper. There really isn't anything better than sugar cookies and bookstores." She stands up. "You thirsty? I have soda in the fridge."

Anything to get her away for a minute. "Sure."

She walks toward the back of the bookstore, just as Sagan ends his call and walks inside. He glances around the bookstore before spotting me on the couch. I stand up when he makes his way over. "Everything okay?" I ask.

"Yeah."

I nod. "Was it my Dad? He checking up on me?"

Sagan doesn't answer me. Instead, he just slides his phone in his pocket and says, "You want to go home?"

Home.

I laugh halfheartedly. I'm not even sure home is a word that can be used to describe where I live. It's just a house filled with people who are counting down the days until they don't have to live with each other anymore.

I try to say, "Okay," but I have to choke it out because it's so quiet and there are tears mixed in with the word. Sagan doesn't even ask me why I'm suddenly emotional. He just wraps his arms around me and pulls me to him.

I press my face against his chest and hug him back because it feels good and as strong as I'm pretending to be today, I'm still sad. I'm full of regret for writing that letter last night and sad that it caused so much drama and even sadder that it's all the truth. I don't want to be mad at Utah. I don't want to be annoyed with Honor. I don't want my father to be cheating on Victoria — even if it is with my mother. And I don't want Honor to be obsessing over unhealthy relationships anymore. I want us all to be normal. It can't be that hard.

"Why can't we be a normal family?" My voice is muffled against Sagan's chest.

"I don't think such a thing exists, Merit," he says, pulling back to look down at me. "Let's go. I can tell by the look in your eyes that you're exhausted."

I nod and he wraps an arm around me. We turn to head toward the door, but we both stop suddenly because the lady from the bookstore is standing in our way, uncomfortably close, holding up a soda.

"Don't forget your Diet Pepsi," she says.

Sagan takes a step back and hesitantly reaches out for the can of soda. "Um. Thanks?"

The woman nods and then steps aside to let us pass. Right before we walk out, she says, "Don't even think about stealing one of my gnomes! Teenagers are always stealing the gnomes!"

I glance back at her and give her a reassuring wave. When we get outside, Sagan laughs. "That was odd."

I don't disagree.

But I like odd, so I'll probably come back.

CHAPTER TWELVE

Utah: Are you home?
Utah: Mer, I really want to talk to you.

I stare at his texts with disdain. He hasn't called me Mer since we were kids. I lock my phone and slide it back into my pocket. I pick up my fork and take another bite of enchiladas.

Sagan and I got back right before everyone started to return from school and work. I stayed in my room until dinner was ready. When I came out, no one spoke to me other than my father and Sagan. My father asked how I was feeling. I said fine. Sagan asked me what I wanted to drink. I said fine. I didn't even catch it until I saw him smile and hand me a glass of soda.

Now we've been sitting in complete silence and we're halfway through dinner. The tension is so thick, I'm not sure I'd be able to speak through it even if I tried.

Honor is the first to attempt it. She receives a text shortly after the two texts from Utah that went ignored by me.

"Utah wants to talk to you, Dad," she says, looking down at her phone. "Can he come by tonight?"

My father is patient with his answer. He finishes the bite he just took. He swallows. He takes a sip of his drink and places the glass back down on the table. Then he says, "Not tonight."

Honor glares at him. "Dad."

"I said not tonight. I'll reach out to him when I'm ready to discuss it with him."

Honor laughs halfheartedly. "You? Discuss something important? He'll be waiting his whole life for that."

"Honor." Victoria says Honor's name like it's a warning.

Honor doesn't like that. She looks like she's about to explode when my father senses it, too. He cuts her off before she has a chance to respond.

"Enough, Honor."

Honor stands up with so much force, her chair falls over behind her. She leaves her plate on the table and marches off to her room. Victoria sighs and pushes back from the table with less anger than she usually does when she gets fed up. "I'm not feeling well," she says. She lays her napkin next to her plate and walks to her room. My father follows her.

I have no idea what has transpired between the two of them since I spilled everything in the letter. But Victoria doesn't seem very happy.

I look over at Moby just as he covers his mouth with his hand and leans in to me. "Can I go watch TV? I don't like my food."

I smile. "Sure, buddy." He slides off his chair and runs into the living room. It's just me, Luck and Sagan at the table now.

"I'm not sure this family has finished an entire meal since I got here," Luck says.

I don't laugh. It's kind of sad that we can't even get along long enough to finish a plate of food. Luck starts poking at the food on his plate. He eventually lays down his fork with a heavy sigh and looks up at me.

"Have you spoken to Utah at all?" Luck asks. "What if he wants to apologize?"

"He's had several years to apologize. The only reason he's willing to do it now is because it's out in the open. Doesn't feel very genuine at this point."

"Yeah. I guess." Luck takes a few more bites of food. I just scoot the food around on my plate. I don't have an appetite anymore, now that everyone seems to be upset with me over something Utah did. I know it was a long time ago and I know they hate finding out something terrible about Utah. But where is my sympathy? Am I that unlikable that they have absolutely no compassion for how much I was affected by that incident?

Sagan has started cleaning off the table and Luck finally walks to his bedroom.

"You finished?" Sagan asks. I nod, and he walks my plate to the sink and then returns to the table.

I slide my finger down the condensation on my glass. "Do you think I'm overreacting?"

He stares at me a moment and then finally gives me a small shake of his head. "Your anger is valid, Merit."

I want his words to make me feel better, but they don't. I don't want to be angry at Utah. I don't want everyone else to be angry at me. I just wish we could be content. "I hate this family sometimes," I whisper. "So much."

Sagan pulls his sketch pad in front of him. "Not an unprecedented feeling for a teenager." He slides the tip of his pencil down his page and I watch him sketch. It's relaxing. The sound the pencil makes against the paper. The way his whole arm moves with his hand. The intense concentration on his face.

"Will you draw me?"

Sagan lifts his eyes to mine and nods. "Sure."

A few minutes later we're in his bedroom. I notice he leaves the door propped open and I'm curious if he does that out of respect for Honor or fear of my father. He walks to his dresser and opens a box of charcoal pencils. "How do you want me to draw you? Realistically?"

I look down at what I'm wearing. Jeans and a T-shirt. It's all I ever wear. "Can I change?"

Sagan nods and I walk across the hallway to my closet. I thumb through my clothes until I get to the far right side of my closet and pull out the ridiculous bridesmaid dress I had to wear to my cousin's wedding last year. It's a taffeta gown in a bright yellow. The top of it is a strapless bustier and then it flares out at the waist and stops right before the knee. It's hideous, so of course I put it on. I slip on a pair of combat boots and pull my hair up into a high bun. When I walk back into Sagan's room, he laughs.

"Nice."

I curtsy. "Glad you like it." I walk over to an empty spot on the floor and sit cross-legged. "Draw me like this, but not on the floor. I want to be floating on a cloud."

Sagan takes a seat on his bed and flips to a blank page in his sketchbook. He looks at me and then the page. He does this three or four times, never pressing his pencil to the paper. I don't know what to do with my hands so I just rest them in my lap. He repositions himself on the bed twice, but nothing seems to help. Every time he begins to draw, he gets frustrated and crumples the paper.

At least ten minutes pass without either of us saying a word. I like watching his creative process, even though it doesn't seem to be going his way at the moment. He eventually leans back against his headboard and tosses his sketch pad to the side.

"I can't draw you."

I push out my bottom lip. "Why?"

His eyes remain locked with mine when he says, "I'm not that good of an artist. I don't think I could do you justice."

I can feel the heat rise to my cheeks, but I try not to take that in the way that I'm hoping he meant it. He might have just said that because he's self-deprecating. I sigh and then push myself off the floor. "Maybe another time." I walk over to his bed and fall backward onto it. My dress makes a lot of noise when I hit his mattress.

"You look like Big Bird."

I laugh and lift up on my elbow. "You should have seen the bridesmaid lineup at this wedding. We were all wearing a different primary color."

Sagan laughs. "No way."

"She's a preschool teacher. I don't know if she meant for that to be her theme or not, but it was a very bright wedding."

Sagan's gaze scrolls over my dress and then his eyes eventually meet mine. There's a lot of thought in his expression when he says, "You feel like going for a walk?"

I nod and stand up. "Let me go change out of this ridiculous dress first."

He smiles and says, "I dare you not to."

We don't even make it to the end of the driveway before my dress is already annoying both of us. Every time I take a step, it sounds like we're about to be whisked away by a tidal wave.

"Any way you can make it stop?" he says, laughing.

"Nope. It's the loudest dress ever invented."

"In more ways than one," he says with a laugh. "How about we just go sit on the swing?" He slides his hands into his back pockets and then walks across the yard to the outdoor swing my father set up for Victoria. She wanted a place under a shade tree where she could read, so he bought her an oversized swing that could double as an outdoor bed. But I've only seen her use it twice. She works a lot and Moby doesn't really give her time to read. I've probably used it more than she has.

Sagan knocks a few of the throw pillows to the ground to make room for us. He pats the spot next to him. The skirt of my bridesmaid dress makes it difficult to sit down and by the time I find a way to sit down without it smothering either of us, we're both laughing.

"You could just take it off," he suggests.

I shove him in the arm, but he takes advantage and grabs my hand, pulling me against him. Not in a sensual way, but in a comforting way. His arm wraps around me and I scoot into him and stare out over the front yard. Our white picket fence runs down both sides of the front yard until it reaches the road.

"Was that yours?" Sagan asks, pointing up at a tree house.

"No, my father built it for Moby. Honor and I used to have a tree house, but it's in a tree at our old house in the back. Pretty sure it rotted."

"I like that it's purple," Sagan says. "Is that Moby's favorite color?"

"No, it's mine. Moby picked it because he wanted me to love it so I would go up there and play in it with him."

"Do you?"

I nod. "Sometimes. Not as much as I probably should, though."

Sagan sighs, and it makes me feel bad, remembering he told me he has a little sister he's never met. He pulls one of his legs up onto the swing. His left arm is resting in his lap, so I touch one of his tattoos and begin to trace it. He really is talented. Each tattoo is so small but the detail is incredible.

"You're really talented."

Sagan squeezes my shoulder and presses his lips into my hair. It's the sweetest thank you anyone has ever said to me. And he didn't even use words.

I look at him but he's staring out over the front yard. His forehead is wrinkled with worry. Eventually, he glances down at me and in a quiet voice, he asks, "Merit? Do you think you might be depressed?"

I sigh, frustrated by his question. "I'm fine. I just had a bad night and made a stupid mistake."

"Will you promise to talk to me first if

you ever feel like making a stupid mistake again?"

I nod, but it's as much of a promise as I can give him.

Sagan turns toward me on the swing, but he doesn't make eye contact with me. "Do you think maybe . . ." He seems nervous about this question. "Was it something I did?"

I sit up straight. "You think I tried to kill myself because of you?"

"No. No, I'm not saying that. At least I hope that's not what I'm saying." He runs a hand down his face. "I don't know, Merit. I called you an asshole and then the next thing I know I'm forcing you to puke up pills you swallowed. I can't help but feel like I had a hand in whatever was happening. Like maybe I was the catalyst."

I shake my head. "Sagan, it wasn't you. I swear. It was my stupidity and my family and everything just sort of snowballed." I close my eyes and slump my shoulders. "To be honest, I don't really feel like talking about it."

He lifts a hand to my cheek and brushes his thumb across my chin. "Okay," he whispers. "We won't talk about it right now." He pulls me against him again and I appreciate the silence he gives me. At least fifteen minutes pass as we both stare quietly ahead. There's a full moon tonight and it's casting a glow over the yard. Even the white picket fence is glimmering.

"So many people dream of living in a house with a white picket fence. Little do they know, there's no such thing as a perfect family, no matter how white the picket fence is."

He laughs. "Let's make a pact. Whenever we get our own houses someday, our picket fences won't be white."

"Hell no, they won't be white. I'd paint mine purple."

"Just like the tree house," he says. There's a moment's pause and then, "Do you have any leftover purple paint?"

I glance up at the tree house and then look back at Sagan. "I think so. In the garage."

Neither of us moves for a moment, but then it's like someone shoots us out of the swing at the same time. We're both laughing and running toward the garage in search of purple paint.

Luckily, we find two cans. Enough to do the front yard fence, at least. We spend the next two hours painting. We talk about everything but the most important stuff. Sagan tells me about the apprenticeship he's been doing over at Highwaymen Ink. I tell him stories from our childhood — back when our family was less screwed up. We talk about ex-girlfriends and ex-boyfriends and favorite movies. By the time the entire right side of the fence is painted, it's after midnight and my yellow taffeta dress is covered in purple paint splatters. "I don't think I can ever wear this again," I say, looking down at it.

"Damn shame," Sagan says.

I look at the left side of the fence — the one that hasn't been painted purple yet. "Are we gonna do that side, too?"

Sagan nods but motions for me to come sit down. "Yeah, but let's take a break first."

I sit down next to him and it's becoming so natural for him to just pull me to him when we're close. It makes me wonder if he's ever going to try to kiss me again. I know our last two kisses haven't been great so I wouldn't blame him for not wanting to try it again.

Maybe he hasn't kissed me because of Honor. That's a subject I haven't been able to bring up to him yet, but I'm so tired at this point, I don't really have a filter.

I blow a raspberry with my lips and then sit up and face him, sitting cross-legged on the swing. "I need to ask you a question." My dress poofs up around me as I try to get comfortable, so I have to flatten it down with my arms. I have so many things on my mind, really, so I pluck one out that's front and center. I force myself to ask him the one thing I haven't stopped wondering. "Do you . . . are you attracted to Honor?"

He doesn't even react to that question. He immediately shakes his head and says, "I think she's beautiful, obviously. You both are. But I'm not attracted to her."

I can feel my shoulders wanting to slump forward. I can feel my forehead wanting to meet my hand. Instead, I try to keep my composure like he always does. "If you aren't attracted to her, then that means . . ." I can't even say it out loud. "We're identical twins, so . . ."

He laughs silently again. I wish I could figure out rhyme or reason to what causes him to do that. If I figured out the trick to his quiet laugh, I'd do it all day every day.

"You're wondering if it's possible for someone to be attracted to you and not to your identical twin." He says it with such little effort.

I shrug. Then I nod.

"Yes. It's possible."

I try not to smile because that answer didn't mean he was attracted to me. But a girl can hope. "Why did you and Honor never take things beyond a friendship?"

"She's seeing my friend," he says. "I'd never do that to him. Besides, when I met her, sure, I thought she was beautiful. But after spending a couple of days with her, it just . . . I don't know. There was never a romantic connection. She didn't like my art. She didn't like my taste in music. She was constantly on the phone gossiping about people and that annoyed me. But there were other things that drew me to her in a different way. She's loyal and fun and I like hanging out with her."

I absorb everything he just said without responding. I want to believe it, but it's hard when I had the wrong impression of them for so long. "What about that day on the square? If you aren't attracted to her, why did you kiss me when you thought I was her?"

Sagan's expression grows serious. He releases a heavy breath and leans back against the swing, looking out over the yard. He pulls my leg across his lap and leaves his hand lingering on my knee. "It's complicated," he says. He runs his hand down his face and struggles with his words for a moment. "I saw Honor . . . *you* . . . browsing the antiques store that day. I watched her for a while. I was curious, because she was so different that day. Dressed down in a pair of jeans with a flannel shirt tied around her waist. She wasn't wearing makeup, which completely threw me off because Honor always wears makeup. And I knew Honor had a sister but I didn't know she had an identical twin sister, so the thought that Honor might have been you never even crossed my mind. I don't know . . . it's hard to explain because you're identical. But I was drawn to her that day in a way I had never been drawn to her before. I felt things I had never felt before when I was around her.

"I liked how she looked at everything with the curiosity of a child. I liked that she never once pulled her phone out. Honor is always on her phone and sometimes I just want her to put it away and enjoy the world around her. And I really liked it when she took the blame for that little boy when he broke that antique. And then when I walked up to her outside and looked at her up close, it was like I was seeing her for the first time. And even though I had never kissed her before and I felt guilty as hell for kissing her, knowing my friend liked her, I couldn't not kiss her that day. Something came over me in that moment and I couldn't stop myself."

His eyes meet mine. "But . . . then she

called and I finally put two and two to-gether . . . and it made sense why I felt like I'd die if I didn't kiss her, when I'd never once felt like that before. I wasn't attracted to Honor. I was attracted to you."

My heart couldn't beat any faster if I drank a 5-hour ENERGY and chased it with a Red Bull. Everything he just said is everything I've been wishing were the truth. I've fantasized that he saw something differ-ent in me that he didn't see in Honor, and now that I'm hearing his version of it, I half expect to wake up from a cruel dream. I wish I could go back to that day and en-grain every moment into my memory. Espe-cially the moment he bent down to kiss me and said, "You bury me." I didn't know what it meant then and I still don't, but I hear those three words every time I close my eyes.

"Why did you say *you bury me* right be-fore you kissed me? Is that something you say to Honor?"

Sagan looks down at his hand — the one that's caressing my knee — and he smiles. "No. It's the meaning of the Arabic word *tuqburni.*"

"*Tuqburni?* What's the English word for it?"

He leans his head against the back of the

swing and tilts it a little so that he's looking at me. "Not every word can be translated into every language. There isn't an English equivalent for the word."

"*You bury me* sounds a little morbid."

Sagan smiles. I can see a hint of embarrassment in his expression. "*Tuqburni* is used to describe the all-encompassing feeling of not being able to live without someone. Which is why the literal translation is, 'You bury me.'"

I take in what he just said and the fact that he said those words to me right before he kissed me that day. I love that he said that, but I hate that he didn't know he was saying it to me. At the time, he thought he was saying those words to Honor. And even though he admits he was attracted to her that day because it was actually me, it doesn't explain why he didn't just explain that to me right after it happened. It's been more than two weeks now.

I clear my throat and swallow my nerves until I can find the courage to ask him about it. "If you and Honor aren't a thing, and if you're attracted to me like you just said, why didn't you act on it? It happened weeks ago."

Hesitation marks his expression as he searches for an answer. He releases a quiet sigh and then strokes his thumb across my knee. "Do you want the honest truth?" He brings his eyes to mine and I nod. He folds his lips together for a moment and then says, "The more I got to know you . . . the less I liked you."

It takes a moment for his response to fully register. "You don't *like* me?"

He lets his head fall back against the swing with a regretful sigh. "I like you today."

I let out a halfhearted laugh. "Oh, well that's reassuring. You like me today, but you didn't like me yesterday?"

He looks at me pointedly. "I *especially* didn't like you yesterday."

I can't tell if I should be mad. I stare at him a little in shock. I feel like I should be mad, but at the same time, I get it. I didn't like me yesterday, either. And I really haven't been myself around him since he started showing up at the house. I'm closed off and rude and I've barely spoken to him up until the past twenty-four hours.

"I have no idea what to say to that, Sagan." I look down at my skirt and start picking at a splatter of dried purple paint. "I mean, I know I've been rude to you, but it was self-preservation. I thought you were my sister's boyfriend and I didn't like how I felt about you. You were the first thing of hers I wanted for myself."

Sagan doesn't respond right away. I continue to pick dried paint off my skirt because I'm feeling way too many things to make eye contact with him right now.

"Merit." He says my name like it's a plea for me to look at him. I eventually do and I immediately regret it because everything I see in his expression right now is everything I didn't want to see. Regret. Fear. A preview to rejection.

"Let me guess," I whisper. "You still don't like me enough to kiss me?"

He lifts a hand and touches my cheek. He shakes his head softly and says, "I like you enough to kiss you. Believe me. But I just wish you could like *yourself* as much as I like you."

I don't even know what to say to that. Does he think I don't like myself because of what I did last night? "I already told you last night was a drunken mistake. I like myself just fine."

"Do you?"

I roll my eyes. Of course I do. I think. "So I have moments of unhappiness. What teenager doesn't? Everyone sometimes wishes they were someone else. Someone better. With a better family."

He shakes his head. "I've never wished that."

I peg him with my stare, silently calling him on his bullshit. "You said yourself you've never even met your little sister. If you tell me you don't wish you had a different family, I won't believe you. Just like you don't believe me that last night meant nothing."

Sagan holds my stare, long enough for me to notice the slow roll of his throat. He releases me, then stands up. He slips his hands in his pockets as he looks down at the ground and kicks at the dirt. I have no idea what I just said that made him angry, but his temperament has changed completely.

"You keep downplaying what happened last night, and to be honest, it's kind of insulting," he says. "You don't get to decide what your life means to anyone else." He pulls his hands from his pockets and folds them over his chest. "You could have died, Merit. That's huge. And until you recognize that, I don't want to pursue anything with you. I think you have a lot that needs to be addressed and I don't want to cloud that with whatever is going on here." He motions between us with his hand. "This can wait."

My face grows warm with the embarrassment climbing over me. "You think I'm too unstable for you to date me?"

He lets out a frustrated sigh. "I didn't say that. I just think you need to work on yourself first. Take your father's suggestion and go to therapy. Make sure there's nothing more serious going on." He closes the gap between himself and the swing where I'm sitting. He kneels in front of me, gripping the swing to still it. "If I interfere and allow myself to start something up with you, your feelings for me might lead you to believe you're happier than you really are."

I can feel my fingers trembling, so I clench them into fists. I'm flabbergasted. He can word it however he wants, but he has the nerve to sit here and tell me he thinks I'm too depressed to date right now?

"Get over yourself," I mutter. I push off the swing and he stands up to move out of my way. I walk toward the house, but when he calls my name, I start running. My stupid, loud skirt adds a serious level of ridiculousness to my anger. By the time I make it to the house, I slam the door so hard I'm afraid I might have woken Moby.

Who does Sagan think he is? He won't pursue me because I might get "too happy" with him and that elation could mask my supposed depression? "Get over yourself," I say again as I shut my bedroom door. Just because I've been unhappy lately doesn't mean I'm depressed. I unbutton my stupid dress and let it fall to the floor. I barely have a T-shirt over my head when Sagan walks into my bedroom without knocking.

I spin and face him and he closes the door, walking toward me. Apparently he isn't finished with this conversation like I am. "You accuse everyone else in your family of not having the courage to be honest, but the second I'm honest with you, you get mad at me and walk away?"

"I'm not mad because you were honest, Sagan! I'm mad because you arrogantly assume I'll be so happy with you that I'll use my feelings for you as a mask for my apparent depression!" I roll my eyes, folding my arms over my chest. "You're giving yourself way too much credit. If you tried to kiss me at this point, I'd probably slap you." It's a ridiculous lie, but I'm already embarrassed by how angry I am at this whole conversation.

Not everyone likes themselves! That doesn't mean I'm suicidal or depressed or unable to differentiate feelings for a guy with feelings for my life.

Sagan looks at me apologetically, like my frustration actually means anything to him.

He slides his hands in his pockets and stares at the floor for a moment. When he looks up at me, he does it slowly. Starting at my feet, trailing up my bare legs. I can see the roll of his throat when his gaze meets the hem of my T-shirt, then crawls up my body until he's looking me in the eye. He doesn't even have to speak for me to know what he's thinking. He's looking at me like maybe I'm right — maybe a kiss wouldn't interfere. Maybe it would bring us both relief.

I quietly inhale because that one look makes it feel like I just sank to the bottom of his heart and there isn't a single air pocket to keep me alive. He could probably open his mouth and call me an asshole again and I'd still want to kiss the lips the insult came from. I can't even remember what we're arguing about because my head is swimming.

Apparently, neither can he because he stalks toward me and grabs hold of me, one arm around my waist, one splayed out against the side of my neck. I tilt my face up to his, hoping he's about to realize how wrong he was so he can just kiss me. I want it hard and frantic and fast, but he's painfully slow as he draws closer.

He lets out a quiet sigh and his mouth is so close to mine, I steal his sigh with a gasp.

And then his lips finally connect with mine. It's both unexpected and overdue. I moan with relief against his kiss and immediately reciprocate.

As soon as our tongues collide, it becomes so frantic, I lose my way around him. My hands get lost in his hair, my reservations get lost in his touch, my anger gets lost in his groan. His tongue strokes mine with delicacy, but his hands are making up for the patience of his mouth. His right arm slides down my back and down to my thigh where my T-shirt ends. He slides his hand up my bare thigh, over my panties and then up my back, this time skin to skin. He pulls me against him but walks me backward at the same time until my back meets the wall behind me.

"My God," he whispers against my lips. "Your mouth is amazing."

I think his is pretty amazing, too, but I don't respond because I'd rather give him back my tongue. He takes it, kissing me deeper, pressing himself against me and into the wall.

This kiss is everything I thought it would be and more. I'm amazed at how healing his mouth is. As soon as he pressed it against mine, it's like all the stress that's been swimming around in my head disappeared. All the angst, the frustration, the anger — it subsides with every stroke of his tongue.

This is exactly what I needed.

His hand is now sliding around to my waist, but before he goes any higher, he pauses to catch his breath. I gasp when I have air again, clasping my arms around him, trying to stop the room from spinning. I let my head fall back against the wall. Sagan drags his lips across my cheek and then kisses me on the mouth, soft and gentle, before pulling back to look down at me. He runs a hand down my hair, stopping at the nape of my neck. "That was fucking dazing," he whispers.

I merely smile because he summed it up perfectly with a phrase I'm not sure I've ever used. Fucking *dazing*.

He kisses the corner of my mouth and then brushes his nose across my cheek. He pulls back, gently taking my face in both hands. With a small smile that completely melts me, he says, "It's incredible how much better a kiss can make you feel, right?"

I nod. "So incredible."

His thumb brushes my cheek, and then his satisfied grin falls into a pointed stare. "That's exactly why I won't do it again, Merit. You need to fall in love with yourself first." He watches me for a moment, his eyes searching mine.

I have no reaction.

I'm too shocked to move. Or too hurt?

Did he seriously only kiss me to prove his point?

What?

I'm flat against the wall, unable to move. When I say nothing in return, he releases me and calmly walks out of my room.

I'm too shocked to cry. Too angry to run after him. Too embarrassed to acknowledge that part of what he's saying might actually have some truth in it. That kiss took away everything I've been feeling and replaced it with a momentary sense of euphoria. I'd give anything to have that feeling back. Which is exactly what Sagan was trying to tell me. My feelings for him will cloud all the other stuff that's going on in my head.

Just because I finally understand what he's trying to say doesn't mean I'm over my anger. If anything, I'm even more pissed at him.

CHAPTER THIRTEEN

"Merit?"

I reluctantly open my eyes and Luck is standing in the doorway of my bedroom. I try to process what time it is, what day it is.

"Can I come in?"

It's afternoon, I think. I nod and sit up. "Yeah. I didn't mean to fall asleep. What time is it?"

"Almost time for dinna."

I smile at his random accent slip. It hasn't been happening as much as it did at the beginning of the week. He pulls my blanket over his lap and leans back against my headboard. "You've had a busy couple of days," he says. "You probably needed the nap."

I laugh halfheartedly. "In that case, I think we all needed a nap." But as it stands, this wasn't a nap. I'm just now waking up for the day, considering I stayed up most of the night last night pissed off at Sagan for what he said. I couldn't sleep. I tossed and turned all night, throwing around all the excuses for why he's wrong. I don't even want to think about it again. I glance at Luck. He's wearing his Starbucks uniform. He looks so strange in normal clothes.

"How do you like your new job?" I ask him.

"Great. Pretty sure any job I have from here on out will beat working on a cruise ship, though." He pulls at a string on my blanket until it comes loose in his fingers. He puts the string in his mouth and eats it.

"Do you suffer from pica?"

"What's that?"

"Never mind," I say, shaking my head.

He pats my leg, and the room grows awkwardly quiet. I sigh. "Are you here to talk about why I swallowed twenty-eight pills?"

Luck shrugs and then says, "Actually, I was going to ask you if you want any beef jerky yet. I still have half a tub in my room."

I laugh. "No, thanks. I'm good."

"But since you brought it up . . . are you okay?"

I roll my eyes and drop my head against the headboard. "Yes," I say, slightly annoyed. Not annoyed that he's checking on me, but annoyed that my behavior this week is embarrassing and I just want to forget it but I have a feeling no one is going to allow that. Especially my father and Sagan.

"Why'd you do it?"

I shake my head. "I don't know. I was just exhausted and over it. And drunk."

He starts unraveling another thread and then spins it between his fingers. "I tried to kill myself once," he says nonchalant. "Jumped off the deck of a cruise ship into the water. I thought it was high up enough that I would hit the water and it would knock me out and I'd drown peacefully."

"Did you drown peacefully?"

He laughs.

I don't know why I'm making light of what he's telling me. I've never been good with serious conversations.

"I sprained my ankle and got fired. But a few weeks later I had a new fake ID and a job with a different cruise line, so the firing didn't really teach me a lesson."

"Why did you do it? Did you hate your life that much?"

Luck shrugs. "Not really. I was mostly in-different. I worked eighteen-hour days. I was tired of the monotony. There wasn't re-ally anyone who would have missed me. So, one night I was standing on the deck, star-ing out over the water. I was thinking about what it would be like to jump and not have to get up and work the next morning. When the thought of death didn't put fear into me, I just decided to go for it." He pauses for a moment. "A friend of mine saw me do it and he reported it, so they threw me a life raft and had me back on the ship within the hour."

"You got lucky."

He nods and looks over at me. He's unusually serious. "So did you, Merit. I mean, I know they were only placebo pills, but you didn't know that at the time. And I don't know many people who would stick their hand down someone's throat and then sift through their vomit to count the number of pills they swallowed."

I divert my eyes and look back down at my lap. It occurs to me that I haven't once thanked Sagan for that. He saved my life, got covered in vomit, and then cleaned it up and watched over me all night. And I haven't even told him thank you. Now I'm not so sure I even want to speak to him again.

"I did learn something from jumping off that ship," Luck says. "I found out that depression doesn't necessarily mean a person is miserable or suicidal all the time. Indifference is also a sign of depression." He looks me in the eye. "That was a long time ago, but I still take medication for it every day."

I'm shocked. Luck seems like one of the happiest people I know. And while I do appreciate what he's trying to do, it's also annoying as hell. "Are you trying to turn this into an after school special?"

He shakes his head. "Not at all. It's just . . . I think we're a lot alike. And as much as you want to believe that it was a drunken mistake . . ."

"It was," I interrupt. "I never would have swallowed those pills if I hadn't gotten drunk."

He doesn't look convinced by my statement. "If you weren't intending to take them . . . why were you stealing them?"

His question silences me. I break eye contact with him. He's wrong. I'm not depressed. It was an accident.

"I really didn't come in here to say all that." He leans forward and rests his elbows on his knees. "I think maybe I had too much caffeine at work today. I'm not usually this . . . sappy."

"It's probably the whole gay thing you're experimenting with. It's making you sentimental."

He glances back at me and narrows his eyes. "You can't make gay jokes, Merit. You aren't gay."

"Does being gay make you the gay authority on who can or can't tell gay jokes?"

"I'm not gay, either," he says.

"Could have fooled me." I laugh. "If you don't think you're gay, you're sexually confused."

Luck rolls his head until his neck pops and then he leans back against the headboard again. "I'm not confused, either," he says. "I'm very comfortable with my sexuality. It seems like you're the one who's confused by it."

I nod, because I am definitely confused by it. "Are you bisexual?"

Luck laughs. "Labels were invented for people like you who can't grasp a reality outside of a defined gender role. I like what I like. Sometimes I like women, sometimes I like men. A few times I've liked girls who used to be guys. Once I liked a guy who used to be a girl." He pauses. "I liked him a lot, actually. But that's an after-school special for another day."

I laugh. "I think I might be more sheltered than I thought."

"I think you might be, too. Not just from the outside world, but you might even be sheltered from what's going on inside your own house. How did you not know Utah was gay? Have you not seen his wardrobe?"

"Who's making gay jokes now?" I say, shoving his shoulder. "That's such a terrible stereotype. And I didn't know he was gay because no one tells me anything around here."

"In all fairness, Merit. I've lived here less than a week and I can already tell you live in your own version of reality." He stands up before I can shove him again. "I need to go shower. I smell like coffee beans."

Speaking of showers. I could probably use one.

A few minutes later, I'm in the bathroom, trying to gather all the stuff I need to shower, but I still can't find a damn razor. I look in all the drawers, in the shower, under the sink. My God, they overreact!

I guess I'll just be hairy, then.

As soon as I pull my T-shirt over my head, a piece of paper is shoved beneath the door. I would assume it's from Sagan since this seems to be his method of delivering art, but the paper looks like an article. I bend to pick it up when Luck speaks to me from the other side of the door.

"Just read it. You can trash it if you want, but I wouldn't have a clear conscience if I didn't give it to you."

I roll my eyes and lean against the counter

and read the title. It's a Web page printed off the Internet.

Symptoms of Depression.

"Jesus Christ," I mutter.

Below it is a list, but I don't even read the first symptom. I fold the paper up and toss it on the sink because Luck is ridiculous. He really is a walking after-school special.

After I shower and change, I open the door to the bathroom. Before I walk out, I grab the paper and walk to my bedroom with it so no one sees it lying on the bathroom counter. I sit down on my bed and begin to open it, curious as to what symptoms Luck has if he's been diagnosed with depression.

When I examine the list, there are empty boxes next to each symptom, waiting to be checked off. It's a quiz. This might actually be what I need to prove to Sagan and Luck that I'm not clinically depressed.

I grab a pen and start with the first one. Do you ever feel sad, empty, or anxious?

Okay, that's a stupid question. *Check.* What teenager doesn't?

Do you ever feel hopeless?

Again. *Check.* They should just say "Are you a teenager?"

Are you irritable?

Um . . . yeah. *Check.* But anyone in this

household would be.

Do you have less interest in activities or school?

Okay. You got me there, Luck. *Check.*

Do you feel less energetic than usual?

If less energetic means sleeping at random hours of the day and night and sometimes not at all, then yeah. *Check.* My heart starts to beat faster, but I refuse to take this list too seriously. It came from the Internet.

Do you have trouble concentrating?

I've made it through this list, so I can answer no to this one. I don't check the box, but before I move on to the next question, I start to think about this question a little more. I haven't been able to focus on my crossword puzzles like I usually do. And one of the reasons I stopped going to school is because I was getting so antsy in class, it was hard to pay attention. I draw a check mark, but make it lighter than the rest. I'll count it as a no if I need to.

Have you noticed changes in your sleep patterns?

Well . . . I didn't used to sleep all day. *Check.* But I think that's just a side effect of skipping school.

Have you had a change in appetite?

If I have, I haven't noticed it. Finally! One I'm not checking.

Or . . . wait. I've been skipping meals lately. But that could also be a side effect of skipping school.

Do you ever feel indifferent?

Check.

Have you cried more than usual?

Check.

Have you ever had thoughts of suicide?

Does just once or twice count? *Check.*

Have you ever attempted suicide?

Check.

I stare at the list with a knot in my stomach. My hands are trembling as I look over the list and realize I've checked off every single box.

Fuck this stupid list. It's no different from any other online symptom checklist that leads people to falsely believe they're suffering from some terrible disease. *Have a headache?* You must have a brain tumor! *Have chest pain?* You're having a heart attack! *Trouble sleeping?* You're depressed!

I crumple it up into a ball and chuck it across the room. Five minutes pass as I stare motionless at the wad of paper on the floor. I eventually force myself to snap out of it.

I'll go check on Wolfgang. At least he won't torture me with conversation or questions.

"You want to help me feed Wolfgang?" I

ask Moby as I make my way through the living room. He's sitting on the couch, watching cartoons, but he jumps off the couch and beats me to the back door.

"Is he mean?"

"No, not at all." I fill the pitcher up with dog food and open the back door.

"Daddy said he's mean," Moby says. "He called him a bastard."

I laugh and follow him down the steps. I don't know why it's so cute when kids cuss. I'll probably be that mother who encourages her kids to say things like "shit" and "dammit."

When we make it to the doghouse, Wolfgang isn't inside it. "Where is he?" Moby asks.

I look around the yard. "I don't know." I walk around the doghouse, yelling his name. Moby spins in a circle with me as we scan the dark yard for him. "Let me go turn on the back porch light." I make my way back to the porch when Moby calls my name.

"Merit!" he says. "Is that him?"

He's pointing to the side of the house. I walk around the corner and Wolfgang is crawling out from under the house, right next to the window to the basement. I sigh, relieved. I don't know why I'm oddly attached to this dog, but I was about to start panicking. I walk back over to Wolfgang's bowl and fill it with dog food. He slowly makes his way to the bowl and begins eating. "Getting your appetite back, huh?" I pet him between the ears and Moby reaches out and does the same. Guess that means he's not depressed.

"How's he doing?"

I spin around to find Sagan making his way over to us. He's acting so casual, like nothing even happened last night. Two can play at that game. "He looks a little better."

Sagan kneels down next to me and runs his hand across Wolfgang's stomach. "Yeah, he does seem a little better." He moves his hand to pet Wolfgang on the head and his fingers brush against mine. It sends chills up my arms and I'm so glad it's almost dark. The last thing I need him to see is that he still flusters me.

"Can he sleep in my room with me tonight?" Moby asks.

Sagan laughs. "I don't think your dad would like that very much."

"We don't have to tell him," Moby says.

His comment makes me laugh. My father is going to have his work cut out with this one.

The headlights from my father's car scroll across the property as he pulls into the driveway. "Pizza's here!" Moby yells. It's so rare that Victoria allows him to have pizza, he forgets all about Wolfgang and runs back into the house. I don't want to be left alone too long in the awkwardness between me and Sagan.

"I'm starving." I grab the empty pitcher and Sagan follows me toward the back door. As soon as my hand is on the handle of the screen door, Sagan grabs my other hand and tugs on it, not wanting me to go inside yet. I close my eyes momentarily and sigh. When I turn around, I'm a step higher than him, so we're eye to eye.

"Merit," he says quietly. "I'm sorry about last night. I was up all night thinking about it."

He sounds sincere. I open my mouth, but then I clamp it shut again because I lost his attention to the ring of his phone. He's digging in his pocket, stepping back down onto the grass, bringing his phone to his ear.

"Wow," I whisper. I shouldn't be shocked that I misread his apology as sincere. He couldn't even silence his phone long enough for me to respond?

I leave him to his urgent phone call and let the screen door slam shut behind me.

I walk into the kitchen just as my father and Victoria are walking through the front door with the pizza. "Moby, they didn't have gluten free," Victoria says. "You can have regular pizza tonight, but don't get used to it."

Moby's eyes light up and he climbs onto a bar stool and pulls a box toward him before Victoria even has a chance to set it on the counter.

"That's not how being gluten intolerant works," I say to Victoria. "You can either have it or you can't."

Luck covers my mouth with his hand. "Merit. Let the mother allow her child some gluten tonight."

I pull my head away from Luck's hand and mutter, "I'm just making a point."

. Honor is next to me, pulling a stack of paper plates out of the cabinet when Sagan walks into the kitchen. "You need any help?" he asks her.

She shakes her head. "Nope."

That wasn't a friendly nope. I'm curious if she's mad at him, too. He scoots around her and grabs some cups. Moments later, we're all seated at the table, sans Utah.

Honestly, it's strange not having him here. I can't help but wonder where he is right now and where he spent the last two nights. Or how long my father is going to be mad

330

at him before he allows him to come back here.

Honor is staring at the empty spot where Utah usually eats. "It wasn't enough that you kicked him out? You went and got rid of his chair, too?"

My father glances at the empty spot. "The chair broke," he says, failing to mention that he's the one who broke it when he smashed it against the wall.

The next few minutes are quiet. Even from Moby. I think he can sense that things have been a little off lately. I watch Victoria for a moment, wondering how she's still here, sitting at this table with my father two nights in a row, knowing what he's been doing behind her back.

"Did anyone take pizza down to your mother?" my father asks.

I shake my head. "I won't be doing that anymore. If she wants to eat, she can come up and make her own plate."

My father narrows his eyes at me, like the dinner table is no place for honesty.

"Why don't you take her some pizza, Dad?" Honor says with a hint of condescension in her voice. "I'm sure she'd love to see you."

And this is where Victoria draws the line, I guess. She doesn't even yell this time. She just drops her pizza on her plate and pushes back her chair. The screech it makes against the floor is deafening. No one says anything until her bedroom door slams shut.

"We almost made it to the end," Luck says, reaffirming the fact that we can't even make it through a single meal. That's when my father drops his pizza onto his plate with the same frustration Victoria did. He stands up and heads to his bedroom, but he hesitates and then comes back to the table and points at us. At Honor and me. He opens his mouth to lecture us, but nothing comes out. Just fumes of frustration. He shakes his head and follows after Victoria.

I look down at Moby to make sure he's okay, but he's working a slice of pepperoni into his mouth like nothing matters but pizza. He's got the right attitude if you ask me.

Luck is the first to break up the awkwardness. "You guys want to go swimming at the hotel tonight?"

We all answer simultaneously.

"No." — Me.

"No." — Honor.

"Yeah." — Sagan.

Sagan glances at Honor and she's glaring at him. "I mean . . . no?" he says, trying his best to get that frown off her face. I feel bad for him, even though I'm still angry at him. Is she mad because he's paid attention to me for the last two days? Does she have to be the center of everyone's attention?

"It's not a competition, Honor," I say. "He can be friends with more than one person."

She laughs and takes a drink of her soda. "Friends?" she says, placing the can back down on the table. "Is that what you call it?"

"Honor," Sagan says. "We talked about this."

They did?

Why? What did they talk about?

Honor shakes her head. "Just because you make out with her doesn't mean you know her like I do."

I can feel my anger smash against my chest with nowhere to go but out. I want to scream at her but I try to keep my composure in front of Moby.

"What's 'make out'?" Moby asks.

"Hey," Luck says, standing up. "Let's go to your room, Moby." Thankfully he grabs Moby's hand and pulls him out of the kitchen, but not before Moby grabs his plate and takes it with them.

Honor is still glaring at me from across the table.

"Where is all this hostility coming from?"

I ask, frustrated. "I assumed you'd be a little more sympathetic."

"Oh, please," she says, scooting her chair back. She stands up. "If it was the truth you would have said something when it happened. Why would Utah do something like that to you and not to me?"

My jaw is tight and my teeth are grinding together as I hold back everything I want to say to her right now. "I can't believe you're taking Utah's side right now."

"You're calling him out when you admitted to the whole family that you tried to lose your virginity to our uncle?"

"Stop!" Sagan says, standing up. His chair falls back and crashes against the floor. "Both of you! Just stop it!"

Too late for mediation, Sagan.

I grab my glass of water and splash it in Honor's face. She gasps, wide-eyed and angry. Before I can escape, she's across the table with a handful of my hair in her fist. I scream and try to pry her hand loose, but it's useless. I grab her ponytail and yank it. Sagan's hands are around my waist and he's trying to pull me away, but I'm halfway across the table now and I refuse to let go until she does. Her other hand grips my T-shirt so I pull at the front of her shirt.

Several of the buttons pop off and Sagan

is still trying to break us up when someone yells, "Hey!"

That sounds like Utah's voice, but I'm not really in a position to turn around and look. I don't have to, because Utah jumps on the table and tries to climb between us. He's prying Honor's hands off me and Sagan is trying to do the same to Honor. "Stop!" Utah yells.

We don't stop. I'm pretty sure a good chunk of Honor's hair is now wrapped around my fingers, but I just grab hold of more.

"Cover her mouth!" Utah yells at Sagan. Utah says this just as he clamps his hand over my mouth and nose, smothering me. Sagan is behind Honor now, covering her mouth and nose with his hand.

What the hell are they doing? Trying to kill us?

I can't breathe!

Honor's eyes grow wide after several seconds and we're both trying to struggle out of their grips while still refusing to let go of each other.

I can't take it another second.

I can't breathe.

I release Honor's hair and grip Utah's hand that's covering my mouth. Honor does the same, pulling Sagan's hand away from her mouth. We're both gasping for breath when they release us.

"What the hell!?" Honor says, shoving Sagan. "Are you trying to kill me?"

Sagan looks at Utah and gives him a thumbs-up, then he puts his hands on his knees and bends over, catching his breath. "Quick thinking," Sagan says to Utah.

I fall into my chair again, trying to catch my own breath. I pull strands of Honor's hair from my fingers.

"What's going on?"

My father is back. He's standing next to the table, which is now a chaotic mess of pizza parts. Honor's shirt is ripped and both of us look a wild mess. But he isn't looking at any of that. He's addressing Utah, who is wiping pizza off his jeans.

"What are you doing here?" my father asks.

"I'm calling a family meeting," Utah says.

My father shakes his head. "Now's not a good time."

Utah laughs under his breath and says, "If you want me to wait for the perfect time to discuss kissing my little sister, we'll be waiting for an eternity. We're having a family meeting. Tonight." Utah walks past my father and heads toward his bedroom. He slams the door so hard, I jump in my seat.

My father grips the back of one of the chairs and shoves it at the table so hard, I jump again.

"Great," Honor mutters. She goes to her room and slams her door, too.

It's just me and Sagan now. He's standing on the other side of the table, staring at me. I think he's expecting me to cry or get angry or have some sort of normal reaction to everything that just happened. I scoot my chair toward the table and reach to the only box of pizza that isn't ruined. It's ham and pineapple. Figures.

"Next time Honor and I fight on the kitchen table, try to salvage a box of pepperoni, will ya?"

Sagan does that quiet laugh of his and shakes his head. He sits down across from me and pulls the box of ham and pineapple toward him. He pulls out a slice and takes a bite, then with a mouthful he says, "You're kind of a badass, Merit."

It makes me smile.

I don't want to be smiling at him, so I grab a slice of pizza and walk to my room with it, then close the door.

An hour later, Moby is asleep, I've washed the pizza off myself and almost everyone in the family is seated in the living room together for the first time in years. Utah is pacing the floor, waiting on my father to join us. I'm on the couch between Sagan and Luck. I mostly scoot toward Luck so that not too many parts of me are touching Sagan. Honor and Victoria have taken both the recliners.

When my father finally does walk into the room, he doesn't sit down. He leans against the wall near Jesus Christ and folds his arms over his chest.

Utah inhales a deep breath, like he's nervous.

He can't be as nervous as I am. I know I'm trying to play it cool, but my stomach has been in knots since he walked through the door an hour ago. I don't want to talk about this, and I especially don't want to talk about it in front of the entire family. I guess that's what happens when you lay everything out in the open with a letter, though.

Utah wrings his hands together and then shakes them out, still pacing the living room. Now that we're all here, he finally comes to a pause. Right in front of me.

I don't look up at him. I just want him to hurry up and say his lame apology so we can all move on and continue to pretend that it didn't happen.

"I feel like I owe everyone an explanation," he says. He begins pacing again, but I stare at my hands, clasped in front of me. I still have black nail polish on my thumb nails, left over from last month, so I pick at it.

"I was thirteen," he says. "Merit was twelve. And it's true . . . everything she said. But that's not who I am. I was a kid, and it was stupid, and I've regretted doing it since the moment it happened."

"Then why did you do it?" I snap. I'm shocked at the anger in my voice as I continue chipping away at the polish on my thumb.

"I was confused," he says. "My friends would come to school every day and talk about girls. We were all hitting puberty and our hormones were crazy, but I didn't care about the girls. All I could think about were the boys. I thought something was wrong with me."

He pauses in front of me again, and I know he's looking down at me, wanting me to make eye contact with him. I can't. He eventually begins pacing again.

"I thought maybe if I kissed a girl it would fix me. But I was a kid, and I didn't know the first thing about kissing or girls. All I knew was that there was one person I wanted to kiss, and according to society, I wasn't supposed to want to kiss Logan."

I finally lift my eyes to watch Utah speak for a moment. He isn't looking at me. He's still pacing.

"I had written Logan a letter that day, telling him I liked him. He showed everyone at his lunch table and then called me a queer when we were walking out of the cafeteria. I was so upset after that. I didn't want to be queer, I didn't want to like Logan. I just wanted to be what I thought was normal. So that night, I didn't even think about the consequences of what I was doing. I was desperate to fix myself, so I made Merit kiss me, hoping it would . . . I don't know. *Cure* me."

I squeeze my eyes shut. I don't want to hear anymore. I don't want to go back to that moment, and I don't want to hear his excuses.

"As soon as it happened, I knew I had done something terrible. She ran out of my bedroom, and I ran to the bathroom and threw up. I was disgusted with myself. Disgusted by what I did to Merit. And I've spent every day since then regretting it. Trying to make up for it."

I shake my head, trying to hold back my tears. "You're a liar," I say, finally looking up at him. "You haven't done a damn thing to make up for it! You never explained yourself and you've never *once* apologized to me!"

The tears have made an appearance, so I swipe at them angrily.

"Merit," Utah says.

I suck in air through my nose and then force it back out. It's an angry sound.

"Please look at me."

I fall back against the couch and look up at him. He actually looks remorseful, but he *has* had an entire day to practice this speech. He squeezes the back of his neck and then squats down in front of me so that we're at eye level. I fold my arms over my chest and hug myself.

"I am *so* sorry," he says. "Every day, every hour, every second since then I've regretted that moment. And I've never apologized because . . ." He looks down at the floor for a moment. When he lifts his eyes back to mine, there are tears in them. "I was hoping you forgot. *Praying* you forgot. If I had known how much it affected you I would have done everything I could to make up for it and I *mean* that, Merit. The fact that you remember and you've been angry at me all these years . . . I can't even tell you how much regret I have."

A tear slides down my chin and lands on my arm. I wipe it away with the sleeve of my shirt.

"Merit, *please,*" he says, his voice desperate. "Please tell them I have never done anything even remotely inappropriate since that day." He looks over at Honor and stands up. "You, too, Honor. Tell them," he says, waving toward my father.

Honor nods and looks at my father. "He's telling the truth, Dad. He's never touched me."

My father looks at me and I nod, too, but I can't speak yet. Too many emotions are caught in my throat. But I can tell by the look on my father's face that he wants to make sure I'm okay with Utah moving back in.

Everyone is looking at me now, even Utah.

I nod and manage to choke out a quiet "I believe him."

The room is quiet for a moment. Victoria eventually stands up. "Okay, then." She begins walking toward the kitchen, when she turns around and says, "I'd appreciate it if you all would clean up this damn mess you made."

Luck laughs under his breath. Utah faces me and mouths "Thank you."

I look away from him, because I don't

want him to think I'm doing him any favors. I can't just let go of years of anger simply because he finally apologized.

"Meeting adjourned," my father says, clapping his hands together. "You heard your stepmother. Clean up your mess."

The meeting may be adjourned, but this is just one of many issues that needs addressing in this family.

We spend the next fifteen minutes cleaning the kitchen in silence. I don't think any of us really know what to say. It was a very sobering family meeting. The Vosses aren't used to so much honesty in one day.

"How did pizza sauce end up on the window?" Luck asks, wiping the glass with a wet rag. "Looks like I missed a good fight."

I close the dishwasher once it's loaded and hit the Start button. Honor washes her hands in the sink next to me. "I've got pizza sauce in my bra," she says. "I'm gonna go shower."

Utah walks to the pantry and grabs his box of letters. Pretty sure this will be the first time he's ever changed the marquee at night. He walks toward the door and pauses, then turns around and looks at me. "You want to help?"

My eyes dart around the room until I find

343

Sagan. I don't know why I look to him for reassurance. I just honestly don't think I've been alone with Utah in several years and this all seems so strange. Sagan gives me a small nod, silently telling me I should go with Utah. It isn't lost on me that I just looked to Sagan for advice. I dry my hands on a towel and walk toward the front door.

When we're outside and the front door is closed, Utah smiles at me, but neither of us says anything. We just both walk in silence until we reach the marquee. He sets the box of letters down on the ground and starts removing the letters that are already on the marquee. I walk over to the marquee and start pulling down a few of the letters.

"You have a quote you want to put on the marquee?" he asks.

I think about it for a moment and then say, "Yeah. Yeah, I do."

He points down to the box. "They're in alphabetical order if you want to go ahead and pull them out."

I bend down and start pulling the letters I'll need out of the box while he continues to remove the words from the marquee. "Did you really not know I was gay?"

I laugh. "I don't know what I thought."

He bends down and puts the last of the letters in the box. "Does it bother you?"

I shake my head. "Not at all."

He nods, but he doesn't look convinced. And then I remember that he's probably still thinking about the letter I wrote and all the hateful things I said to him. "Utah, I'm serious. I don't care that you're gay. I know I said some mean things in that letter, but I was upset. I really am sorry for that. We were kids. I know that . . . I've just spent years building up a lot of animosity toward you."

I pull out the last letter and place it on the ground. When I stand up, Utah stands up, too. He holds eye contact with me for a moment, and then he says. "I'm sorry, too. Really, Merit. I mean it."

The sincerity in his voice makes me feel things and my God, I'm so sick of crying. But I do it anyway. Stupid tears start running down my cheeks, but I can't help it. I've needed to hear him say that for so long.

Utah reaches for my hand and pulls me into a tight hug. My face presses against his chest and he hugs me like a brother should hug his sister and that makes me cry even harder. I wrap my arms around him and as soon as I do, I can feel all the anger I've ever felt for him evaporate with every tear I shed.

"I'll be a better sibling," he says. "I prom-ise."

I nod against his chest. "Me too."

He releases me and then says, "Let's fin-ish this and go inside." We finish up the marquee and walk toward the front door. As soon as we open it, we see Luck at the kitchen table, looking down at a piece of paper in his hands.

"You're a dick!" he yells.

Utah and I close the door. "What now?" Utah asks, walking the box of letters back to the pantry. Sagan is seated across from Luck, who looks extremely pissed off.

"I don't look like this!"

Sagan laughs. "Don't ask me to draw you if you're going to argue with me about how I perceive you."

Luck pushes back his chair and tosses the sketch at Sagan. "If this is how you see me, you suck as an artist." He walks to the re-frigerator and Sagan is laughing quietly. I walk over to him and grab the sketch that pissed off Luck. I flip it over and immedi-ately start to laugh.

"Let me see," Utah says. I hand him the sketch of Luck and Utah bursts out in laughter. "Wow," he says, handing the sketch back to Sagan. "You holding a grudge or something?"

Sagan grins and slips the sketch into the back of his sketchbook.

"Actually, let me keep that," Utah says. "For blackmail."

Luck walks around the bar and tries to snatch it from Utah, but Utah holds it up in the air. Luck tries to grab it again but Utah runs down the hallway with Luck close on his heels.

"I like the marquee," Sagan says, pulling my attention back to him. I glance out the window at the quote I had Utah put up.

NOT EVERY MISTAKE DESERVES A CON-SEQUENCE. SOMETIMES THE ONLY THING

IT DESERVES IS FORGIVENESS.

I shrug. "I heard it from some guy."

It's hard for me to look at him right now because so much of me still likes so much of him. And for some reason, the way he's looking at me right now is the hardest to accept. Like he's proud of me.

Luckily, he gets one of his urgent phone calls again. At least this time he holds up a finger and says, "One second," while pulling out his phone.

I don't give him his second. I just give him privacy as I make my way to my room. I've had enough for one day, and even though I slept through most of it, I'm already ready to sleep through the rest of it.

When I get to my room, I realize just how literal Sagan was being when he said, "One second." He's knocking on my door almost immediately after I close it. When I open it, he's sliding his phone back into his pocket.

I don't ask him why he's at my door or what he wants to talk about. I just start with the question that's been bothering me the most. "Why do you get so many phone calls?" He's always answering his phone, no matter what he's in the middle of. It's actually kind of rude.

"It's never who I want it to be," he says, walking into my room uninvited.

"Come in, I guess."

Sagan walks around my room, looking at everything. He pauses in front of my trophy shelf. "When did you start collecting these?"

I walk to my bed and take a seat. "I stole the first one from my first boyfriend. He broke up with me in the middle of a make-out session and it made me mad."

Sagan laughs and then picks a few up and inspects them. "I don't know why I like this about you as much as I do."

I bite my cheek to hide my smile.

Sagan sets the trophy down on the dresser and faces me. "You want a tattoo?"

My heart skips at the thought. "Right now?"

He nods. "If you swear you won't tell anyone."

"I swear." I try not to smile, but I'm way too excited.

Sagan nods his head toward his room and I follow him across the hall. He pulls the desk chair close to the bed and motions for me to sit in it. He starts messing with a box of tattoo equipment that he pulls from the closet.

"What do you want?"

"I don't care. You pick."

He looks at me and arches an eyebrow. "You want me to pick the tattoo that's going to be permanently etched into your skin for the rest of your life?"

I nod. "Is that weird?"

He laughs quietly. "Everything you do is weird," he says. But before I can reflect too much on that comment, he says, "It's my favorite thing about you." He pulls out a piece of transfer paper and a pen, then places it on his dresser and begins drawing something. "You have five minutes to change your mind."

I watch him sketch my tattoo for the next five minutes, but I can't see what it is from where he's positioned. When he's done, I still haven't changed my mind. He walks to the bedroom door and locks it. "If anyone sees this, you better lie and say you got it from someone else."

I try to peek at it when he walks near me, but he hides it. "You can't see it yet."

My mouth falls open. "I didn't say I'd let you tattoo something on me before it gets my approval."

He grins and says, "I promise you won't hate it." He has me pull my arm through my sleeve. "Can I do it right here?" he asks, touching the top right area of my back. "I'll make it small."

I nod and then close my eyes, waiting anxiously for him to begin. He's sitting on the bed with all the tattoo equipment set up beside him. I'm facing the other direction, which is actually a relief. I don't really want to have to watch him the whole time. I might be too transparent in my thoughts.

He transfers the tattoo onto my skin first, then hands me a pillow to hug over the back of my chair right before he starts. The initial sting is painful, but I squeeze my eyes shut and try to focus on breathing. It's actually not as painful as I thought it would be, but it certainly doesn't feel good. I try to focus on something else, so I decide to make conversation with him.

"What does the tattoo on your arm mean? The one that says, 'Your turn, Doctor.' "

I can feel a rush of warm air meet my neck when he sighs. Sagan pauses a moment until my chills subside, then he begins the tattooing process again.

"It's a long story," he says, trying to dismiss it again.

"Good thing all we have is time."

He's quiet for so long as he continues tattooing me that I assume he's not going to elaborate, like always. But then he says, "Remember when I told you the flag on my arm was a Syrian Opposition flag?"

I nod. "Yes. You said your father was born there."

351

"Yeah, he was. But my mother is American. From Kansas, actually. I was born there." He pauses talking for a moment while he concentrates on the tattoo, but then he continues. "Do you know anything about the Syrian refugee crisis?"

I shake my head, grateful he's finally in a talkative mood. This tattoo hurts a little more than I imagined and I need a distraction. "I've heard of it. But I don't really know much about it." *Much* meaning *nothing.*

Sagan says, "Yeah, they don't really teach about it in schools here."

He's quiet for a few more painful seconds, but then he moves to a different spot of my shoulder and I feel some relief. He begins talking again. I do nothing but listen.

"Syria has been ruled by a dictatorship for a long time now. It's why my father moved to America for medical school. A lot of other countries around Syria are also ruled by dictators. Well, several years ago, something called the Arab Spring began. A lot of citizens in these countries began to hold protests and demonstrations to try and overthrow the dictators. The people wanted their countries to be less corrupt. They wanted them to run like more of a democracy, with checks and balances. The protests were successful in Tunisia and Egypt and the leaders stepped down. A new form of government was put in place. After that, the people of Syria and other countries were hopeful that it could happen in their countries, too."

"So the tattoo is somehow related to Syria?"

"Yeah," he says. "It's what many believe started the revolution. The Syrian ruler, Bashar al-Assad, studied to be an ophthalmologist before his father died and he took over as the new leader of Syria. Bashar's nickname is Doctor. Well . . . a group of school kids spray-painted graffiti on a wall at their school with the words, 'Your turn, Doctor.' They were essentially saying what many in Syria had been quietly hoping. That the Doctor would step down, just as the leaders of Egypt and Tunisia had, in order to allow for a democracy in Syria."

I hold up my hand to pause him. I'm soaking all of this in but I have so many questions. "At the risk of sounding stupid, what year did this happen?"

"Two thousand eleven."

"Did the Doctor step down after that?"

Sagan wipes at my tattoo again and then presses the needle against my skin. I wince when he says, "He did the opposite, actually. He had the children responsible for the graffiti imprisoned and tortured."

I start to turn around, but he puts a firm hand on my shoulder. "He had them arrested?" I ask.

"He wanted to make a point to the people of Syria that there would be no tolerance for opposition. He didn't care that they were just kids. When the parents started demanding the release of their children, the government didn't listen. In fact, one of the officers in command said to the parents of the children, 'Forget your children. Just make more children. And if you don't know how to make more, I'll send someone to show you.' "

"Oh my God," I whisper.

"I didn't say it would be a good story," he says, continuing. "Once the Doctor imprisoned the kids involved, people in the city of Daraa took to the streets. Protests and demonstrations started happening, but instead of being met with compromise, the government used deadly force against them. A lot of people died. This sparked nationwide protests. People demanded the Doctor step down. But he refused, and instead, he used military force to crack down even harder on the protestors. The violence escalated and soon turned into a civil war. Which is now why there's a refugee crisis. Almost half a million people have died so far and millions more have had to flee the country to save their lives."

I can't speak. I don't know what to say to him. I can't reassure him because there isn't anything reassuring about that story. And honestly, I'm embarrassed I didn't know any of that. I see the headlines online and in the paper but I never understand any of it. It's never directly affected me so I've never thought to even look into it.

He stopped tattooing but I don't know if he's finished, so I don't move. "We moved to Syria when I was ten," he says, his voice quieter. "My father is a surgeon and he and my mother opened a medical clinic there. But after living there for a year, when things started to get bad, my parents sent me back here to live with my grandparents until my father could get his visa to return home. My mother was due to give birth to my little sister so she couldn't fly at the time. They told me it would just be three months. But right before they were due to fly home . . ."

His voice trails off. Since he's no longer tattooing me, I spin the chair around to look at him. He's sitting with his hands clasped between his knees, looking down. When he looks up at me, his eyes are red, but he's holding his composure.

"Before they came home, communication just stopped. They went from calling me every day to complete silence. I haven't heard from them in seven years."

I cover my mouth in shock.

Sagan is sitting stoically, staring at his hands again. Both of my hands are pressed against my mouth in disbelief. I can't believe this is his life.

This is why he answers the phone with such urgency, because he's always hoping it will be news about his family. I can't imagine suffering through seven years of not knowing.

"I feel like such an asshole," I whisper. "My problems are nothing compared to what you've been going through . . ."

He looks up at me with completely dry eyes. I think that makes me the saddest, to know that he's so used to his life that it doesn't make him cry every second of the day.

He puts his hand on my chair and says, "You aren't an asshole, Mer." He turns me around. "Hold still. I'm almost finished."

We sit in silence as he finishes up my tattoo. I can't stop thinking about everything that's happening with him. It has my stomach in knots. And I really do feel like an asshole. He read a letter I wrote, complaining about my entire family and our trivial issues. And he doesn't even know if his family is alive.

"Done," he whispers. He cleans it with something cold and then he begins to bandage it up.

"Wait," I say, turning around. "I want to see it first."

He shakes his head. "Not yet. I want you to keep the bandage on until Saturday."

"Saturday? It's only Thursday."

"I want you to anticipate it a little longer," he says with a smile. I like that he's smiling after the heaviness of the conversation. Even if it is forced. "I'll apply lotion every few hours until then."

I like the idea of that, so I reluctantly agree. "At least tell me what it is."

"You'll see what it is on Saturday." He starts cleaning up his mess. I stand up and roll the chair back to the desk. He walks his box of supplies to his closet.

As I watch him, I'm overcome by an overwhelming sense of compassion for him. For what he's going through. I walk to him and slip my arms around his waist, pressing my face against his chest.

I just need to hug him after hearing all of that. And based on the way he wraps himself around me and accepts the hug without question, he must have needed it, too. We stand like this for an entire minute before he presses a kiss to the top of my head. "Thanks for that," he says, releasing me.

I nod. "Good night."

He smiles appreciatively. "Good night, Merit."

CHAPTER FOURTEEN

"Are you excited about today?"

"Yes!" Moby yells from the hallway.

"How excited?"

"So excited!"

"How excited?" Utah says.

"The most excited!" Moby yells back.

Normally, that exchange would make me roll my eyes this early in the morning. But that was before last night, when I started to like Utah as a brother again.

My father still doesn't know I dropped out of school, so I force myself out of bed. I brush my teeth, fix my hair, put on clothes and go through the same routine I go through almost every other morning. I would just tell him the truth, but I'm not so sure I want to deal with the aftermath right now. It feels like a lifetime has been crammed into the last few days.

I'll give it another week before I tell him. Maybe two.

Or better yet, I'll tell him I dropped out when he finally explains why my mother is taking placebo pills.

When I walk into the kitchen, Honor and Sagan are sitting next to each other at the table. She's laughing at something he just said, which makes me a little relieved to see her smiling. Maybe she'll stop being so mad at me now that I've made up with Utah.

Or maybe not.

As soon as she sees me, her smile disappears. She refocuses her attention on the smoothie in front of her, moving her straw around.

At least Sagan smiles at me. I smile back and feel ridiculously cheesy when I do.

"Merit, taste this," Utah says. He shoves one of his smoothies in my face and tries to stick the straw in my mouth.

"Gross," I say, swiping his arm and the smoothie away. "I'm not tasting that crap."

"It's good." He holds it out for me again. "I promise, just taste it."

I take the smoothie and taste the damn thing. Sure enough, it tastes like someone took a bunch of vegetables, blended them together and threw tasteless vitamins in the mix. I wince and hand it back to him. "Disgusting."

"Sucker," Sagan says.

The back door opens and my father walks in. "Something is wrong with that dog," he says, washing dirt off his hands. He dries them on a towel. "Has he been that lethargic since he showed up?"

I shrug. "He looked better yesterday." I walk past him and out the back door. I can hear Sagan following me. The three of us make it to Wolfgang's doghouse, and I kneel down and touch him on the top of his head. "Hey, buddy."

He looks up at me with the same lack of enthusiasm he's had since he showed up Sunday night. His tail twitches again, but he makes no effort to stand up. Or lick me.

"Has he been acting like that all week?" my dad asks.

I nod, just as my dad squats down. He runs his hand down Wolfgang's back and it's honestly a sight I never thought I'd see. My father and this dog . . . together again.

"I thought he was just depressed," I say. I feel bad for not making more of a fuss about his temperament, but I don't know anything about dogs.

"I called the vet yesterday," Sagan says. "They said they could squeeze him in tomorrow but I don't think he can wait that long."

"Which vet?" my father asks.

"The one out on 30, near the Goodwill."

"That's close to work," my father says. He slips his hands beneath Wolfgang. "I'll drop him off on my way in, see if they can check him out sooner." My father nudges his head toward the gate on the side of the house. "Merit, go open that gate so I can get him to my truck."

I run and open the gate, then I run and open the passenger door to my father's truck. He places Wolfgang in the passenger seat. Wolfgang doesn't even seem to care that he's been moved. "You think he'll be okay?"

"I don't know," my Dad says. "I'll let you know what they say." He walks around to the driver's side and climbs in. He begins to back out, but he stops the truck and calls me over to his window. "I forgot to give this to you the other night when you asked for it," he says, handing me a sack. I take it from him and watch as he continues backing out of the driveway.

Once he's gone, I look down and open the sack. Inside is a trophy. I had forgotten all about asking him for one. I pull out the trophy and it's a statue of a tennis player.

"What'd you win this time?" Sagan asks.

I read the small plaque on the bottom of

the trophy. " 'State Tennis champs, 2005.' "

He laughs. "You were a little child prodigy." He walks to his car and opens the door. "You need a ride to school today?"

I narrow my eyes at him. He knows I haven't been going to school lately. "Nice try."

He climbs in the car. "Worth a shot," he says, closing the door. He rolls down the window and says, "I'll text you if I get any updates about Wolfgang from your dad."

I nod, but then I tilt my head. "Why would he give *you* updates?"

"Because . . . I work for him?"

"You do?" Wow. I'm so out of the loop.

He laughs. "Did you really not know that?"

I shake my head. "I knew you had a job, but I've just never asked what it was."

"Your dad gave me a job and let me move in the first day I met him. That's why I like him so much, even though you can't stand him most of the time."

He looks over his shoulder and backs out of the driveway. Before he pulls onto the road, he gives me a small wave. I wave back and watch him drive off.

I don't know how long I stand in the driveway, watching the empty road. I just feel so . . . lost? I don't know. Nothing really makes sense this week.

I go back inside and spend the next several hours wasting time.

I mostly watch TV, but I can't stop checking my phone for updates. I still haven't heard from my father. I've only received one text and it was from my mother, asking if I'd come to the basement sometime this afternoon. I responded to her and told her I was busy. She replied with, "Okay. Maybe tomorrow."

I know I said I was never going to the basement again, but I only said that because I was angry. I'll visit her eventually, but right now I'm still upset with her. And my father. Still confused by how Victoria can choose to remain in such a strange marital environment.

And I still don't know what the hell the placebo pills are for.

I hate that I have any sort of resentment in me after hearing what Sagan's going through. But for some reason, his issues haven't negated mine at all and I hate that. I hate that I'm still emotionally affected by the poor choices of my parents when I should be lucky that I know they're alive. It makes me feel weak. And petty.

I kick my feet up on the kitchen table and text my father.

Me: Any word from the vet?

I wait to see if the text bubbles appear, but they don't. I set the phone down and pull my crossword puzzle in front of me. My phone rings, so I flip it over to check the caller ID. I smile when I see it's Sagan.
"Hello?"
"Hey." His voice is heavy, like he had to drag the word out.
"What's wrong?"
He sighs into the phone. "Your father wanted me to call you. He uh . . . Wolfgang . . . he died on the way to the vet."
I almost drop my phone. "What? How?"
"I don't know. I'm sure it was just old age."
I sigh and wipe away a surprising tear.
"You okay?"
"Yeah," I say, sighing again. "I just . . . is my dad okay?"
"I'm sure he is. He did mention we might go bury him later, though. Probably at Pastor Brian's church, so I'll be later than usual. I'll text you."
"Okay. Thanks for letting me know."
"See you tonight."

I end the call and stare at my phone for a full five minutes before I move. I'm surprised I'm sad. Other than living in the yard adjacent to the dog as a kid, I've really only interacted with him for a few days. But the last week of that poor dog's life was complete crap. His owner died and then he walked several miles in the rain in the middle of the night only to end up getting sick and dying in the midst of complete strangers. I'm glad they're going to bury him on Pastor Brian's property, though. I'm sure they'd both prefer it that way.

I don't hear from Sagan or my father for several hours. The mood in the house is awkward at best, so I stay in my room most of the evening. Victoria doesn't even cook, so we all eat separately.

I'm cleaning up the mess from my frozen dinner when Utah's phone rings. He's on the couch with Luck and Honor watching TV, but his phone is next to me on the bar.

"Who is it?" he asks from the living room.

I glance at the caller ID, but it's not a number he has saved. "I don't know. It's a local number, but there's no name."

"Will you answer it?"

I dry my hands on a towel and reach for his phone.

"Hello?"

"Honor?"

"No, it's Merit."

"Merit," my father says. "Where's Utah?"

"He's in the living room. What's up?"

He sighs. "Well . . . we need someone to pick us up."

I laugh. Is this some kind of joke? "You own like eighty cars. Why in the world do you need a ride?"

"We're uh . . . in jail."

I pull the phone away from my ear and put it on speaker. I motion for Utah to mute the TV. "What do you mean you're in jail? And who is we? Is Sagan in jail, too?"

"It's a long story. I'll tell you when you get here."

"Who's in jail?" Utah asks, walking into the kitchen. I motion for him to be quiet so I can hear my father.

"Do we need like . . . bail money? I've never picked anyone up from jail before."

"No, we just need a ride. We've been here two hours already waiting for them to let us make a phone call."

"Okay. We're on our way." I end the call.

"Why are they in jail?" Utah says.

I shrug. "I don't know. Should we tell Victoria?"

"Tell me what?" Victoria walks into the kitchen with impeccable timing.

"Dad's in jail," Utah says, turning to face her. "With Sagan."

She pauses. "What?"

"Don't know what he did, but I can't wait to find out," Utah says. Honor and Luck are now in the kitchen. We're all looking at each other like we don't know what to do. I guess we don't. It's not every day we have to go pick our father up from jail.

"Have him call me as soon as you pick him up," Victoria says. "I have to stay with Moby."

I nod and head to my room to find my shoes. What in the world did they do?

CHAPTER FIFTEEN

I don't know what I was expecting, but when my father and Sagan walk out of the doors of the jail, they look normal. We've been waiting in the parking lot for over an hour for them to process their paperwork. All they would tell us was that they were arrested for desecration. I don't even know what that means.

My first inclination is to rush up to Sagan and hug him, but I don't. Especially in front of anyone else. Instead, I wait until he reaches the car and I discreetly squeeze his hand.

"What'd you guys do?" Utah asks.

My father swings open the passenger door of the van. "We were trying to bury a damn dog, that's what we were doing." He sits down and slams his door shut. We all look at Sagan and he's got an exasperated expression on his face.

"I tried to tell him it was a bad idea," he says.

"Burying the dog?" Luck asks.

Sagan shakes his head. "I thought we were burying him at the church, but . . . your father had a different plan."

"He didn't," Honor says in disbelief.

"Didn't what?" Utah says.

"He wanted to bury him with Pastor Brian," Sagan says.

"In a cemetery?" Luck asks.

"You got arrested for desecrating a grave?" I ask.

Sagan nods. "I mean, technically we were just digging a hole near Pastor Brian, but when the police catch you in a cemetery with shovels, they don't really care what the explanation is."

"Holy shit," Utah says.

"Get in the van!" my father yells.

We all climb into the van. I end up in the backseat with Sagan, but I don't mind it. Utah cranks the van, but right before we pull out of the police station, a cruiser pulls in. My father rolls down the window.

"Oh, no," Sagan says.

"What?"

He nods toward the cops getting out of the car. "They're the ones who arrested us."

"Dad," I say, not wanting him to do anything stupid.

"What'd you do with the dog?" my father asks the officers.

The cop who was driving walks over to the window. "Buried him at Pastor Brian's church," he says. "Same place you probably should have buried him."

"Yeah, well . . . hindsight and all that shit," my dad says. He waves his hand to Utah. "Let's go."

Utah backs up and the cop taps the top of the hood before turning to walk toward the police station. I watch out the window as both the cops start laughing.

"Great. Another rumor to pin on the Voss family," Honor says from the seat in front of us.

"Technically, it's not a rumor," Sagan says. "We were digging in a cemetery without a permit. It's illegal."

Honor spins around. "I know that, but now the entire town is going to think Dad was trying to exhume Pastor Brian. Everyone knows he's an atheist, now there'll be rumors about him wanting to perform satanic rituals on his dead body."

"Won't be the worst thing people have said about us," my father says from the front seat.

Honor faces forward again. "I guess it

wouldn't be so bad if most of the rumors weren't true."

My father looks at her in the rearview mirror. "Are you saying you're ashamed to be a Voss?"

Honor sighs. "No. I'm just ashamed to be your daughter."

"Oh, shit," Luck says under his breath.

My father turns around. "And why is that, Honor?"

"Dad," Utah says. "Give it a rest. It's been a crazy week."

"Oh, I don't know," Honor says sarcastically. "Maybe because you don't know the first thing about being a decent husband or father?"

My father turns back around and unlocks his door. "Stop the van."

"What?" Utah says. "No."

"Stop the van!" my father yells.

"Just stop the van, Utah," I say. If my father is about to have a nervous breakdown, I'd rather he have it outside of the van than inside of it.

Utah pulls over, but before he even has the gear shift in park, my father is opening his door, climbing out of the van. We all watch, dumbfounded, as he starts kicking up gravel on the side of the road. I've never seen him this mad.

"Is he okay?" I ask Sagan.

Sagan shrugs. "He seemed fine after we were arrested. He even laughed about it."

Utah opens the driver's side door and walks around the car. Honor opens the side door to the van and everyone starts climbing out. Once we're all standing next to the van, my father pauses his assault on the gravel long enough to catch a breath. He waves a hand across all of us.

"You think just because I'm an adult I have it all figured out? You think I'm not allowed to make mistakes?" He's not yelling, but he certainly isn't talking with an inside voice. He begins to pace back and forth. "No matter how hard you try, things don't always turn out the way you wish they could."

Utah looks agitated. "Well when you make poor choices, things don't usually turn out to be sunshine and roses, Dad. Maybe you should have thought about that before you cheated on Mom."

My father takes several steps toward Utah. He rushes him fast enough that Utah walks backward until he's pressed against the van. "That's what I'm talking about! You all think you know everything!" My father spins and takes several steps away from us. He brings his hands up to the back of his head and inhales several deep breaths. When he finally turns around, he's looking directly at me. Sagan puts a reassuring hand against my lower back.

"Do you want to know why the pills you stole were placebo pills?"

I nod, because I've been dying to know since I found out.

"She isn't in pain," my father says. "Your mother isn't in pain, she isn't recovering from cancer. She never even *had* cancer." He walks closer to us. "Your mother never had cancer," he repeats. "Let that sink in."

I can see Utah's fists clench as he takes a sudden step toward our father. "You better elaborate because I am five seconds away from punching you."

My dad laughs halfheartedly and drags a frustrated hand down his face. His hands then fall to his hips. "Your mother . . . she has . . . issues. She's had issues since the day she was in that car wreck." He's not yelling anymore. Now he just looks defeated. "The brain injury . . . it changed her. She hasn't been the same, and I know you guys didn't know her before then but . . ." His face contorts and he looks up at the sky like he's trying to hold back tears. "She was amazing. She was perfect. She was . . . happy." He faces the other direction so none of us can see him cry. It's one of the saddest things I've ever seen.

I clasp my hand over my mouth and wait for him to gather himself. It's all I can do.

When he finally does turn around, he doesn't look any of us in the eye. He stares at the ground. "Watching her change from the woman I fell in love with to someone else entirely was the hardest thing I've ever been through. Harder than trying to take care of three kids under the age of two by myself when her episodes would hit and she'd lie in bed for weeks at a time. It was harder than when she started inventing these illnesses in her head, convincing herself she was dying. Harder than when I had to have her committed, and then lied to you all when I told you she was in the hospital for the cancer she was convinced she had." He looks up at me and then Honor. He finally rests his eyes on Utah. "She's not the woman I married. And yes, I know it was terrible of me to get involved with Victoria, but it happened and I can't take it back. And yes, it's terrible now when your mother has rare moments of clarity. Because when she does, she realizes what her life has become. What our marriage became. And it's devastating to both of us. And it's all I can do to hold her and reassure her that I still love her. That I'll always love her." He blows out a shaky breath and wipes his tears away. "Because I do love your mother. I always will. It's just . . . sometimes things don't turn out how you want them to. And even though I'm an atheist, there isn't a day that goes by that I don't thank God that I have a wife who understands that. Victoria has lived the past four and a half years in a house with a woman that I am still in love with. She doesn't question me when your mother needs me. Victoria doesn't correct any of you when you insult her and insinuate she's a homewrecker." He walks to the van and reaches inside for his jacket. "I've never told any of you the truth because I didn't want any of you to judge your mother. But I didn't cheat on your mother when she was dying of cancer. She was never dying. She's not dying now. She's sick, yes. But not in a way that any of us can help her." He puts on his jacket and zips it up. "I'm walking home."

He begins to head away from the van, toward our house that's still over three miles away. He pauses and faces us again. "All I've ever wanted was for you kids to have the opportunity to love a mother like you deserved. To think the world of her. That's all Victoria's ever wanted for you." He starts walking backward. "I just had no idea how much you would all hate me in the process."

He spins around again and starts walking in the direction of the house. I can hear Honor crying. I even hear Utah crying. I wipe away my own tears and try to inhale a breath that will sustain me for more than two seconds.

I think we're all in shock. It's several minutes before any of us move. My father is long out of sight by the time Utah regains his composure enough to speak.

"Get in the van," he says. He walks around to the driver's side and climbs in, but none of us move. He honks the horn and then hits the steering wheel. "Get in the damn van!"

Luck takes the front seat and the rest of us climb in the back. Before Sagan even has the door closed, Utah is peeling out, doing a U-turn.

"Where are we going?" Honor asks him.

"We're going to bury that damn dog with Pastor Brian."

CHAPTER SIXTEEN

Pastor Brian's newer church is much bigger than his old one — the one we live in. I don't feel so bad that my dad bought it all those years ago. Pastor Brian seems to have upgraded.

Well . . . until he died.

"Hurry up," Honor says. Sagan is digging the fresh dirt off Wolfgang's grave. Utah is at the end of the driveway keeping watch. Luck is . . . oh my, God.

"Are you picking your nose?"

Luck wipes his fingers on his shirt and shrugs.

"You're so gross," Honor says. She glances at me and mutters under her breath, "I can't believe you almost had sex with him."

I ignore her insult. I don't feel like getting into another fight with her when three out of the five of us are holding the brand-new shovels we bought on the way here. That wouldn't end well. I also don't argue with her because . . . well . . . I can't believe I almost had sex with him, either.

"Got it," Sagan says. He bends down and starts moving the dirt away from the sheet that Wolfgang is wrapped in. "Luck, give me a hand."

Luck shakes his head. "No way, man. There's got to be some bad karma attached to what you're doing. I want no part in it."

"Oh, for crying out loud." I bend down and help Sagan dig Wolfgang the rest of the way out of the dirt. Sagan is able to lift and carry him to the van on his own. I open the back door and he puts him inside the van.

"I need to put the dirt back on his grave so no one is suspicious," Sagan says.

"You're getting really good at this criminal life," I tease.

Sagan grins and closes the back door to the van. "Do you find hardened criminals attractive?" He raises his brow, and the obvious flirtation has my heart spinning in my chest.

I hear Honor groan as she passes us. "I hate this already."

Sagan rolls his eyes and then walks back to the side of the church to refill the grave. When we're all finally back inside the van, Honor says, "What's the purpose of this, anyway? Dad hated that dog. I don't think

379

he really cares where he's buried."

Sagan disagrees with a shake of his head. "No, he cares. I don't know why he was so adamant about burying the dog with Pastor Brian, but for whatever reason, he wants them together."

Utah pulls out of the church parking lot and flips on the headlights. "I think Dad has always felt a little guilty for buying Dollar Voss out from under Pastor Brian. Maybe this is his repentance."

"He's an atheist," Luck says. "I think remorse is a more fitting word."

Honor has her hand over her nose and mouth. "Someone please roll down a window. That dog smells so bad, I'm about to puke."

He really does smell. Utah rolls down both front windows but it doesn't help. I cover my nose with my shirt and keep it there until we make it to the cemetery.

"Which way is Pastor Brian's grave?" Utah asks. Sagan points to a grave not too far from the front gate. Utah follows the circle drive until the van is pointed toward the entryway of the cemetery. When he parks, he tells me and Honor to take the front seats and keep watch for them.

"I don't want to keep watch," I say as I close the side door to the van. "I want to help you guys bury him."

Honor walks around to the driver's seat. "I'll keep watch." Utah and Luck walk to the back of the van to get Wolfgang.

Sagan grabs my hand and squeezes it, looking down at me. "Stay in the van," he says. "It won't take long."

I shake my head. "I'm not staying alone in that van with Honor. She hates me."

Sagan looks at me pointedly. "That's exactly why you should stay in the van, Merit. You're the only one who can fix that."

I huff and fold my arms over my chest. "Fine," I say, agitated. "I'll talk to her but I'm not happy about it."

He mouths, "Thank you," right before he turns around. I watch the three of them walk across the cemetery to the freshly dug grave. And then I get in the damn van.

When I close the door, Honor turns up the radio, drowning out any possibility of her hearing me if I tried to speak to her. I lean forward and turn the radio back down.

She leans forward and turns it up.

I turn it down.

She turns it up.

I reach over and turn off the van. I pull the keys out and the radio cuts off for good.

"Bitch you," she mutters.

We both start laughing. *Bitch you* used to

be one of our favorite things to say to each other. She hasn't said it to me in years.

Utah used to have a friend named Douglas when we were kids. He lived about a mile down the road, so he used to come over all the time when we lived in our old house behind Dollar Voss. The last time Douglas ever came over was the day he accused me of cheating at hopscotch. Who cheats at hopscotch?

I remember Utah getting so mad at him for accusing me of cheating, he told Douglas to go home. Douglas shot back and yelled, "Bitch you!"

The insult might have been more damaging to Utah's ego had Douglas used the curse word correctly. I was only eight or nine, but even I knew that *bitch you* was funny enough to laugh at. That made Douglas even angrier, so he balled up his fists and threatened to hit me.

What Douglas didn't realize was that our father was standing right behind him.

"Douglas?" my father said, causing him to jump three feet off the ground. "I think it's best you go home now." Douglas didn't even turn around. He just started walking as fast as he could toward the road. When he was about fifteen feet away, my father called out, "And for future reference, it's *fuck you*! Not *bitch you*!"

Douglas never came back, but *bitch you* became our new favorite insult. It's been so long since I've heard it, I almost forgot it used to be our thing.

Honor slides both her hands down the stereo and sighs. "I heard what you said to Dad yesterday." She begins picking at the steering wheel with her fingernail, pulling tiny pieces of leather off.

"I said a lot of things to Dad yesterday. Which part are you referring to specifically?"

She leans back in her seat and stares out her window. "You told him I was one heartbeat away from being a necrophiliac."

I close my eyes and feel a pang of regret that's become all too familiar this week. I didn't know Honor was still there when I said that to my father yesterday.

"You make it sound like my entire life revolves around death, Merit. It's not an obsession. There have been two guys since Kirk died. Two."

"Are you counting Colby?"

Honor rolls her eyes. "No, he's still alive."

"And Kirk," I point out. "That's actually four. You've been averaging two dead boyfriends a year."

"Okay," she says, exasperated. "I get your

point. But it doesn't make you better than me."

"I never said it did."

"You don't have to. I see the way you look at me. You're always judging me."

I open my mouth to protest, but then I close it because she might be right. I have very strong opinions about my sister. Is that judging? I get so angry when people judge me, but maybe I'm no better.

I suddenly wish I hadn't turned off the radio. I'm not liking this conversation so far.

"Do you think you're in love with Sagan?" she asks.

"That's random."

"Just humor me. I have a point to make."

I look out the window and watch as Sagan digs up the same hole he dug up earlier today. "I barely know him," I say to Honor. "But there are things I love about him. I love the way he makes me feel. I love being around him. I love his quiet laugh and his morbid art and how he seems to think in a different way than most people our age. But I haven't known him long enough to be in love with him."

"Forget about time, Merit. Look at him and tell me you haven't fallen in love with him."

I sigh. Fallen is an understatement. It was

more like collapsed. Plummeted. Crumpled at his feet. Anything but fallen.

I pull my legs up and turn in my seat to face her. "I feel so stupid saying this because I barely know him, but I felt like I loved him the first moment I laid eyes on him. That's why I've been so cranky lately, because I thought you were dating him, so I did everything I could to stay away from both of you. And now, the more I get to know him, I care about him so much I can't stand it. He's all I think about. All I want to think about. It's so hard to breathe when he's near me, but it's also hard to breathe when he isn't. He makes me want to learn and change and grow and be everything he believes I can be."

I take a breath after that verbal vomit. Honor laughs and says, "Wow. Okay, then."

I close my eyes, embarrassed all of that just came out of me. When I open them, Honor is turned toward me in her seat. Her head is resting against the head rest and her eyes are downcast.

"That's exactly how I felt about Kirk," she says quietly. "I mean, I know I was a kid, but I felt those same things for him. I thought he was my soul mate. I thought we would be together for the rest of our lives." She lifts her eyes to mine. "And then . . . he died. But all the feelings I had for him were still there, with nowhere to go and no one to latch on to. And I worried about him constantly because I couldn't see him or touch him. And I thought maybe, wherever he was, he was just as devastated as me." There's a hint of embarrassment in her voice as she tells me all of this. She shrugs and says, "That's when I started talking to the guys in support groups online. Talking to other kids like Kirk who were dying. And I would tell them all about Kirk. I would make sure they knew how much I loved him so when they got to Heaven and they found him they could say to Kirk, 'Hey, I know your girlfriend. She sure does love you.' "

She falls back against her seat and kicks her feet up on the dash. "I don't think any of that anymore, but that's what started all this. A few months after Kirk died, Trevor, one of the guys from the Dallas support group, was put in a hospice. I didn't love him like I loved Kirk, but I cared about him. And I knew when Kirk was dying that my presence brought him peace. So when Trevor needed that, I gave it to him. And it was nice. It made me feel good to know that I made his death a little more bearable for him. And then after Trevor, there was Micha. And now . . . Colby. And I know you think it's this terrible thing, like I'm taking advantage of people, or I'm somehow oddly attracted to guys with terminal illnesses." She looks at me pointedly. "You're wrong, Merit. I do it because I know that in some small way, I help them through the hardest thing anyone should ever have to go through. That's all I'm doing. It makes me feel good to make them feel a little more at peace with their death. But you make it seem so terrible and you constantly talk about how I need therapy. It's . . . *mean.* You can be really mean sometimes."

I haven't said a single word the entire time she's been talking. I've just been listening . . . processing. I'm looking at my sister . . . my identical twin sister . . . and she's completely unrecognizable to me in this moment. For the first time in my life, I feel like I'm looking at a complete stranger. Like maybe all the opinions I've held about her all these years have actually been severe misjudgments.

I look away from her and glance out the window, watching the guys as they work to fill the grave with dirt. I try to imagine how I'd feel if something happened to Sagan. How would I feel if I had to sit by his side and watch him die?

Not once when Honor was grieving Kirk's

death did I ever empathize with that. I didn't understand that kind of love. We were so much younger then and I honestly thought she was being dramatic.

All these years I've hated Utah for not making an effort to be closer to me, and here I am treating my own twin sister the exact same way.

I turn and reach across the seat and pull her to me. As soon as I do, I feel her sigh, like all she's needed from me was a simple hug. For so long I've been resenting my family for not hugging me when maybe they've been resenting me for the same thing.

"I'm sorry, Honor." I sooth my hand over her hair and say the same thing to her that Utah said to me. "I'll be a better sibling. I promise."

She lets out a quiet sigh of relief, but she doesn't let go of me. We hug for a long time, and it makes me wonder why everyone in this family has been so opposed to honesty and hugging for the past several years. It's actually not so bad. I think we all just got to a point where we were waiting for someone else to initiate it, but no one ever did. Maybe that's the root of a lot of family issues. It isn't actually the issues people are hung up about for so long. It's that no one has the courage to take the first step in *talking* about the issues.

Honor eventually pulls away from me and flips the visor down. She wipes beneath her eyes with her fingers, clearing away her mascara. She falls back against her seat and reaches over for my hand. She squeezes it. "I'm really sorry about everything I said to you in the last couple of days. About what happened with Utah. I just . . . I think I was angry at you. For never telling me. Why wouldn't you tell me something like that, Merit? I'm your sister."

"I don't know. I was scared. And the more I kept it a secret, the more my fear eventually just turned into resentment. Especially seeing how close you and Utah were. I wanted that, too."

"We're both too stubborn for our own good."

I agree with her. We both inhale the silence while we stare out the window for a while. The guys are still working, but Sagan has pulled off his shirt. I can't tear my eyes away as he repeatedly bends over and refills the hole. "Is there *anything* wrong with him? He's so damn perfect."

"Meh," she says. "Too healthy for me. I like 'em a little more fragile."

389

"Oh, you can make jokes about it but I can't?"

She laughs and then her laughter turns into a smile. "He's really good, Merit," she says with a sigh. "Be good to him, okay?"

I would if he'd give me the chance. "I'm so glad I was wrong about you two. I don't know if we would have been able to make up as sisters if you were in love with him."

She laughs. "Bitch you."

I smile. God, I've missed that.

After a moment, she says, "Do you think he can tell us apart?"

I shrug.

Honor straightens in her seat. Her eyes are full of mischief. "Let's test him."

We both start grinning. We climb into the back of the van and start swapping clothes. I pull my hair out of my bun and hand her the hair tie. I smooth my fingers through my hair while she pulls hers up.

"I have to pee," she says, laughing. "Do you ever notice how being sneaky makes you have to pee?"

"I didn't until now."

As soon as our clothes are successfully swapped, we climb back up front, this time with me in the driver's seat and her in the passenger seat. Right when we get settled, the guys throw their shovels over their shoulders and start heading our way. My heart starts to beat wildly in my chest because now I'm nervous he won't notice. What would that mean? That everything he said about the first time he saw me was a lie? That he really can't tell a difference between us? He figured it out pretty quick on the couch the other night.

I'm starting to regret this prank.

Utah reaches the van first. "I'm driving," he says, motioning for me to get in the backseat. Honor and I climb to the back. I sit in the very backseat and Honor takes one of the middle seats. Sagan is talking to Luck when he climbs inside the van, so he doesn't even look at either of us. He takes the other middle seat and closes the door, just as Utah cranks the van. Sagan slaps the back of Utah's seat. "Hurry," he says, urging Utah on. "I don't want to be arrested twice for the same thing in one day."

Sagan falls back against his seat and looks over at Honor with a sweet smile. "You hungry?" He looks back at me and says, "What about you?" He faces forward. "Anyone hungry? I'm starving."

Honor nods, but she doesn't say anything. I don't either. I know we sound alike, but I'm sure if we start talking, it'll be easier for him to figure it out.

"Let's go to Taco Bell," Luck says.

"Honor hates Taco Bell," Utah says. "Let's do Arby's."

Good thing I'm pretending to be Honor because Taco Bell is my favorite. "Taco Bell sounds good, actually. I don't mind if we go there."

Honor turns around and glares at me.

"You know what?" Sagan says, turning in his seat to face Honor. He reaches out to her and grabs her hand. Oh, God. What if he finally decides to kiss me again and I'm not even her? He lifts his other hand and touches Honor's cheek. "You look really weird in Merit's clothes."

"Dammit," Honor mutters. "We thought we had you."

Oh, hallelujah.

He immediately releases Honor's face and turns around and climbs over the backseat. He sits next to me and wraps an arm around my shoulders. He presses a quick kiss to the side of my head and whispers, "Thank you."

I look up at him and he's smiling. I can see in that smile that he's glad Honor and I are pulling pranks on him. It means we made up, which is what he was hoping for.

"You smell like a dead dog," I say.

"No, I smell like a hardened criminal."

"No," Honor says. "All of you smell like death. Roll down the windows!"

The smell is overwhelming. I pull my shirt up over my mouth and keep my nose covered until we get to Taco Bell.

By the time we get back, it's after midnight. But despite the time, as soon as we walk in the front door, Honor, Utah, and I all get a group text from our mother. I guess she heard us walking in.

Can one of you please come down here? I hear something.

I look up from my phone and Utah and Honor are both looking at me.

"Whose turn is it?" Utah asks.

Honor shrugs. "Mine, I guess. I haven't been down in a couple of days."

"Neither have I," Utah says.

"Me, neither."

All three of us head toward the basement. We file down the stairs and our mother is standing on the other side of the room, below the basement window. It looks like she's been asleep. She's wearing pajamas and her hair is a mess. "Do you hear that?" she says, stepping toward us, wide-eyed. "I've been hearing it off and on all day."

Utah walks to the window, but he glances at Honor and me. We all try to hide what we're feeling, but things are different now. After knowing what our father has known all these years, I don't know that we will ever look at our mother the same way. I'm not sure that's a bad thing. It's good, actually. I feel more sympathetic toward her right now than I ever have. And there's zero resentment there, now that I'm fully aware of her situation.

There's suspicion, though. I'm already questioning whether or not she's actually hearing things now that I know what a big role her mental health has on her daily life. We've always known she has issues, but now that our father has finally enlightened us to just how deeply rooted those issues are, we're probably all going to be more suspicious of her erratic behavior. Utah stands beneath the basement window for a moment. We all remain quiet, but we don't hear anything.

"What is it you're hearing exactly?" Utah asks her.

She waves toward the window. "It sounds like something is wrong with that dog. It's been crying all day and night and I can't sleep."

Honor looks at me with a sad expression.

Our mother doesn't even realize that Wolfgang has died and has been buried. More than once, actually.

"Mom," I say. "The dog isn't here anymore." I try to say it in the sincerest way possible, but in my head I'm thinking, *You poor thing.*

"No, I'm telling you, there's something near that window." She's so adamant about it, she begins to pace.

Utah nods and walks toward the stairs. "I'll go check it out," he says, running up the steps.

Our mother walks over to her bed and sits on the edge of it. Honor sits down next to her and runs her hand soothingly down our mother's hair.

"Are you hungry?" Honor asks her.

As soon as she says it, I remember that none of us took her dinner tonight. We got the call that our father was arrested and we immediately left to go deal with that. I didn't even think to grab her anything at Taco Bell.

"No, Victoria brought me a plate of food. And you girls forget that I have my own refrigerator down here. I won't starve if I don't get a meal."

Honor and I both look at each other in surprise. "Victoria brought you food?"

My mother casually stands again like she didn't just throw out there that Victoria was in this basement. I didn't think Victoria had been in this basement since the day my mother moved down here.

But if I've learned anything this week, it's that I don't know people as well as I think I do.

There's a knock at the basement window. "Merit," Utah says, his voice muffled from behind the glass. "Come out here."

I run up the stairs and go outside, around to the basement window where Utah is kneeling on the ground. "You aren't going to believe this," he says. He lifts something up and motions for me to come closer.

"What is that?"

"A puppy," he says. "Two of them."

I immediately fall to my knees next to him. "You're kidding. Where in the world did they come from?" I grab one of the puppies from Utah. It's black and tiny and can't be more than a day or two old. I glance around. "Where do you think their mom is?"

Utah pulls the other puppy to his chest. "I suspect she's buried near Pastor Brian."

Wait.

Wait.

"Wolfgang was a girl?"

"Looks like it," Utah says, laughing.

"But . . ." I look down at the puppy in my hands. "They're probably starving. How are we supposed to keep them alive now?"

Utah hands me the other puppy and stands up. "I'll see if I can get in touch with an emergency vet. You take them down to Mom so she can see what's been keeping her awake."

I gather both the puppies in my arms and carry them inside the house and down to the basement.

"What the heck?" Honor says, immediately grabbing one from me. "Where did these come from?"

Surprisingly, my mother grabs the other puppy. "Oh, my goodness," she says. "So you're the culprit, huh?" She nuzzles the puppy with her nose. "Oh, you're so cute."

"Turns out Wolfgang was actually a girl. Utah is calling the vet to see what we can do for them."

"I want to keep one," my mother says. "Do you think I can keep one?"

I reach over and pet the puppy in her arms. "I don't know, Mom. It'll be kind of hard to raise a dog in a basement."

"Yeah," Honor says, giving me a knowing look before looking at Mom. "But I bet Utah would let you keep one if you moved back to the old house with him. It should be ready in a few weeks."

My mother doesn't say anything for a moment. She just stares down at the puppy while she smooths her hand down its back. "You think he would?" she says quietly.

Honor looks at me and smiles.

I have no idea if she'll actually move back to our old house, but this is the closest she's come to entertaining the idea of leaving the basement in a long time. That's progress.

Utah comes back down the stairs. "I found a vet who wants me to bring them in. He says there's a formula we can syringe feed them, but we'll have to do it every couple of hours for the first week."

"I can help," my mother says with eagerness. "Will you bring them back down here when you get back?"

Utah nods as he takes the puppies from her and Honor. "Sure. It might be a while, though. I'll wake you up when I get home."

"I'll go with you," Honor says, running up the stairs after him. Once they're gone, I look over at my mother. She's walking around her small basement apartment, tidying things up, preparing for the return of the puppies. It makes me smile, seeing her this excited about something.

"Did Utah say Wolfgang is their mother?

Is that the same dog your father used to hate so much?"

"One and only."

She laughs. "I don't know why, but that makes me like those puppies even more." She drops down onto her couch and yawns. I watch her for a moment, until she notices me staring. "What is it?"

I shrug. "Nothing."

"You look upset."

I sigh and then take a seat next to her. "Dad thinks I need to start therapy on Monday."

She pats my knee. An unusual gesture coming from her. "Your dad thinks a doctor can fix anything. But my doctor never fixed me." She glances at me. "You want me to talk to him?"

I think about that question for a moment. But I also think about the crumpled sheet of paper sitting on my bedroom floor. "Do you think maybe you just never had the right doctor?"

My mother regards me quietly for a moment. She starts fidgeting with her hands and I can see the anxiety starting to set in. She breaks eye contact and says, "It's late. I think I'm going to sleep."

Her words disappoint me, but not as much as they sadden me. "Okay," I say.

"Good night, Mom."

She's already off the couch and walking toward her bed. I head toward the stairs, but she calls my name.

"Yeah?" I say, pausing at the bottom.

She shrugs her left shoulder and says, "Let me know if you like the doctor."

I smile at her. *Another step closer.* Even if it's just a baby step.

When I make it upstairs, my father is staring out the window. I haven't seen him since he walked here earlier this evening. I hesitate a moment, wondering if I should just go to my room or if I should say something to him. I eventually walk to where he's standing and glance out the window. Utah, Honor, and Luck are walking toward the van. Honor is holding both of the puppies inside a box.

"He was a girl?" my dad asks, shaking his head. "That damn bastard dog was a girl," he repeats. We watch out the window as Honor takes a seat in the passenger seat of the van, but before Luck or Utah get inside, Utah grabs Luck's hand and they kiss briefly. It's kind of sweet if you can overlook the whole related-by-marriage thing.

My father groans after seeing their display of affection. "I hope that doesn't last."

I chuckle. "I'm pretty sure Utah will be

gay forever. It's not really something that fades."

My father turns away from the window, shaking his head. "I know that, Merit. I don't care if he's gay. I'm referring to whatever is happening between him and Luck. How am I supposed to explain to Moby that his uncle and his half brother are . . . a thing?"

"There are worse things he could find out about us."

"Like what?"

"You were arrested today for exhuming a corpse. That's pretty bad."

My dad laughs. "Moby would probably like that." He stares out the window again, long enough for them to pull out of the driveway.

I shove my hands in the back pockets of my jeans. "Dad?" I don't know what I plan to say to him. He's put up with so much in his life and I can't help but feel like I've been adding to that weight all these years, rather than trying to take some of the weight off his shoulders. Do I apologize? Tell him thank you?

My dad nods, just a little, and then he takes a step toward me and pulls me in for a hug. The first hug he's probably felt like I would allow him to give me in a very long time. "I know, Merit," he whispers, relieving me from the awkwardness of not knowing what to say to him. "Me too."

I pull my hands from my pockets and return the hug. My father presses his cheek to the top of my head and I can't help but smile because it's probably the best hug I've ever been given. It's the one hug I've needed the most. We stay like this for a while, almost as if he's making up for lost time. And maybe I am, too.

If someone had told me last week that we'd be having this moment tonight, I'd have laughed at them and said it would be a miracle.

Maybe it is.

I'm facing the living room with my head pressed against my father's chest. I look up at Jesus and wonder if maybe He answered my prayer, after all. It was just a few days ago that I got down on my knees in my bedroom and prayed for a new focus.

I'd say the events that transpired after that have definitely given me a new focus.

I loosen my grip on my father and look up at him. "Why don't you believe in God?"

He glances over at Jesus and contemplates my question for a moment. And then he says, "I'm just a pragmatic person." He smiles down at me and tugs at my hair as he releases me. "That doesn't mean you can't believe in Him, though. We aren't put on this earth to be carbon copies of our parents. Peace doesn't come to everyone in the same form."

He tells me good night and walks to his bedroom. I glance at the hallway and Sagan is leaning against the wall, watching me. There's a faint smile on his face.

"It's after midnight," he says.

I look up at the clock on the wall and it's almost one in the morning. Which means . . . it's Saturday. "It's Saturday! My tattoo!"

Sagan laughs. "Let's go to the bathroom so you can see it in the mirror."

I follow him to the bathroom, my heart pounding anxiously in my chest. I search for a handheld mirror so I can see it closer. "It better be pretty. If you gave me a poop emoji, I'll kill you."

He laughs quietly as he pulls down my shirt sleeve and works to remove the bandage. "You seriously haven't peeked at it?"

I shake my head. "I promised you I wouldn't."

He takes the mirror from me and holds it up behind me. "Okay. Open your eyes."

When I see it, I suck in a quiet rush of air. In small font are the words, "With Merit." I stare at it for several seconds before the meaning really hits me.

In the letter I wrote to everyone, I signed off, "Without Merit."

Sagan wrote the opposite.

"*With* Merit."

Tears immediately cloud my vision as I run my fingers over it. It almost feels like a badge of maturity.

"Sagan," I whisper. "It's perfect."

He smiles at me in the mirror. "I think it'll look cool as a watercolor tattoo. I'll add some colors to it once I get more experience." He touches it and my skin feels like it ignites. "I'm glad you like it."

"I love it," I whisper.

I turn around to face him. He's extremely close still, but he doesn't back away. He's looking down at me like he has something else to say. I wait with air stuck in my lungs, but he just clears his throat and takes a step back. My lungs deflate like balloons when he widens the gap between us.

"Good night, Merit." He walks out of the bathroom, and I sigh.

I walk to my bedroom and sit down on my bed. I reach behind me and touch my fingers to my tattoo again. *With Merit.* I should have asked Sagan why he chose this tattoo. Did he do it to make me feel better?

I've been wondering lately why he even seems interested in a friendship with me. Sure, we had an unusual connection the first time we met, but he thought I was Honor. And after that day, I was nothing but rude to him. He even said himself that the more he got to know me, the less he liked me. But despite all of that, he still invests in me. I don't know why I automatically assume he must have an ulterior motive. Maybe he actually does find something appealing about my personality.

I glance across the room at the wadded-up piece of paper still on my bedroom floor. I walk over and pick it up, unfolding the paper as I sit down on my bed. I look at all the check marks and it makes me wonder if this list is in any way accurate. I don't know a lot about mental health, but knowing that I might have inherited my mother's instability fills me with an unknown fear. Am I going to end up like her?

I shudder at the thought.

I fold the paper in half and set it aside, pulling my covers over me. I leave my lamp on and stare at Sagan's drawings for a while. I think about his family. I think about *my* family. I try to fall asleep despite all the thinking, but my mind has different plans. I lie wide-awake until I hear the front door open as everyone returns from the vet with the puppies.

I still can't believe Wolfgang was a girl.

At least another half hour goes by while I stare at the ceiling. The wall. I listen to showers running and doors closing. The house finally settles, but then I'm startled by a knock on my own door. I reach over and find the list Luck gave me and shove it under my blanket. "It's open."

Luck walks in and I shouldn't be surprised by his choice of clothing at this point, but I still laugh. He's wearing a pair of Victoria's pink scrubs.

"Do you need to go shopping?" I ask, scooting over on my bed.

He plops down next to me. "Nah. I keep finding plenty of stuff in the laundry room."

He only allowed an accent slip on the last word of that whole sentence. He's acclimating. I reach under the covers and grab the folded-up sheet of paper. I hand it to him. "So what does this mean?"

Luck opens the list and looks it over. I watch his expression carefully, but he gives none of his thoughts away. "It means you might be depressed," he says nonchalantly.

I groan and dramatically fall over on the bed. "Can't it just mean I've had a bad month?"

He lays the list on my chest and I grab it and wad it up again, sitting back up.

"It could," he says. "But you won't know until you talk to someone about it."

I roll my eyes. "What if I go to this dumb therapy session and find out I *am* depressed? What kind of life is that to look forward to, Luck? I don't want to spend the rest of my life like my mother."

Luck dips his head and looks at me pointedly. "I haven't met your mother yet and I'm no psychologist, but I think she suffers from a lot more than just depression. Agoraphobia being the main thing."

"Yeah, but she didn't even develop that until a few years ago. She gets worse with time. That's probably going to happen to me, too." The thought that there might be something severely wrong with me leaves a hollow feeling in the pit of my stomach. I don't want to think about it. I haven't wanted to think about it since Luck initially brought it up. "Why can't I just be normal?"

My question makes Luck laugh. I wasn't expecting that reaction. "Normal?" he says. "Describe normal to me, Merit."

"Honor is normal. So is Utah. And Sagan. Most people without a broken brain."

Luck rolls his head and stands up. He swings my bedroom door open. "Utah!

Honor! Sagan! Come here!" He stands by the door, holding it open. I bury my face in my hands. *What the hell is he doing?*

"Why are you yelling for them? It's the middle of the night!"

Despite it being as late as it is, Honor, Utah, and Sagan file into my room one by one. Luck motions to the bed. "Have a seat," he says to all of them. I look up and Sagan is watching me as he closes the bedroom door.

"Everything okay?" Sagan asks, looking directly at me. I shrug because I have no idea what Luck is up to.

"Sagan," Luck says. "What happens when you drink milk?"

Sagan releases an unsure laugh. "I don't drink milk. I'm lactose intolerant."

I didn't know he was lactose intolerant, but what does that have to do with anything?

"Do you take medication for it?" Luck asks.

Sagan nods. "Sometimes."

Luck turns his attention to Utah. "What happens if you go out in the sun for a long time without sunscreen?"

Utah rolls his eyes. "I burn. We aren't all blessed with skin that tans easily," he says, nodding toward Sagan.

408

"And you," he says to Honor. "Why do you wear contacts and Merit doesn't?"

"Probably because she has better vision than me, Einstein."

Luck looks back at me. "They aren't normal," he says. "Having depression is no more out of your control than Sagan's intolerance to milk, or Utah's pale skin, or Honor's bad vision. It's nothing to be embarrassed about. But it's not something you can ignore or correct on your own. And it doesn't make you abnormal. It makes you just as normal as these idiots," he says, waving toward everyone else.

I can feel my cheeks flush from a combination of the embarrassment and unwanted attention I'm getting right now. But I also can't stop from smiling because I really do appreciate my idiot step-uncle. I'm kind of glad he showed up when he did.

"I also have athlete's foot," Sagan says. I look up at him and he crinkles his nose. "It's really bad. Especially in the summer."

I laugh and Honor says, "Hey, speaking of things wrong with us. Remember when Dad was diagnosed with Tourette's?"

"No way," Luck says.

"Not the cussing kind," Utah clarifies. "That's mostly embellished on TV. He used to have these tics all the time and he'd make these noises with his throat. The doctor said they were brought on by stress, so he took medication for it for a couple of years. Not sure if he still does."

"See?" Luck says excitedly. "Your whole family suffers from all kinds of things. You shouldn't feel so special, Merit. We're all a degree of fucked-up."

I laugh, but I don't even know what to say. It feels nice to have their encouragement, no matter how strange it is.

"Merit," Honor says. She looks at me with a hint of guilt in her expression. "I'm really sorry. I feel like I should have . . ." She shrugs and looks down. "Seen the signs, I guess?"

I shake my head. "Honor, I'm the one who tried to kill myself and *I* didn't even know I was depressed."

Luck leans his head back against the wall. "Merit's right," he says. "A lot of people who suffer from depression don't even know they have it. It's a gradual change. Or at least it was for me. I used to feel like I was on top of the world. Then one day, I noticed that it felt like I was no longer on top of the world. I was just floating around inside of it. And then eventually, it felt like the world was on top of *me.*"

I soak in what Luck just said, because it's

like he summed up my entire past year in just a few sentences. I open my mouth to say something, but my voice is cut off by the sudden sound of my father's voice coming from the hallway. "Merit, you better not have . . ." As soon as the door swings open, my father clamps his mouth shut. I'm assuming he heard voices and thought something more sinister was going on. He looks around at all of us and it's obvious he wasn't prepared for this sight. It's been a long time since Honor, Utah, and I have hung out in the same room.

He hesitates, nods a little and then smiles before closing my bedroom door. We all start to laugh, but he swings it open again and says, "I'm glad you're all spending time together. But it's late. Go to bed."

"It's a weekend," Utah groans.

My father raises an eyebrow at Utah and that one look is enough to lift everyone off the bed. Sagan is the last to leave my room. Right before he closes the door, he smiles and says, "You were really easy to like today, Merit."

I sigh and lie back on my bed. What a night.

What a *week*.

I turn off my lamp again and try for a second time tonight to shut off my thoughts.

I'm finally almost asleep when I hear a soft knock on my door. It's pitch-black in my room, but when the door cracks open, the light breaks through. Sagan peeks his head through the door. "You asleep yet?" he whispers.

I sit up and reach over to the lamp. "Nope." My hands are already shaking at all the possibilities of why he's back. He closes the door and takes a seat on the bed next to me. He isn't wearing a shirt now. Only a pair of black sweat pants. I sit up, but keep the covers pulled up to my stomach. After everyone left my room earlier, I took off my pajama bottoms. Now I'm only wearing a T-shirt. Put us together, and we could make a whole naked person.

"I had something else to say but I didn't want to say it in front of all of them," he says.

"What is it?"

"You said something the other night about how you felt like an asshole after hearing my story."

I nod. "I did. And I still do."

He shakes his head. "It bothers me that you think that. You shouldn't compare your stress to mine. We all have different baselines."

I stare at him blankly. "What's that?"

He reaches to me and takes my hand, pulling it to his lap. He turns it palm-up and touches my wrist, drawing an imaginary line across it. "Let's pretend this is a normal stress level. Your baseline." He drags his finger up my palm until he reaches the tip of my middle finger. "And let's pretend this is your max stress level." He moves his fingers down and touches my wrist again. "Your baseline is where you are on a normal day. Not too much stress, everything is flowing smoothly. But say you break your leg." He runs his finger from the baseline at my wrist to the middle of my palm. "Your stress level would go up to like fifty percent because you've never broken your leg before."

He releases my hand and flips his own hand over. He looks up at me. "You know how many times I've broken a bone?"

I shrug. "Twice?"

"Six times," he says, smiling. "I was a rambunctious kid." He touches his wrist and makes an imaginary line across it. "So if I were to break my leg, it would be stressful, but I've been through it before. So it would only raise my stress level to like ten percent. Not fifty." He pauses. "You understand what I'm saying?"

I'm honestly not sure what point he's trying to make. "Are you saying you're tougher

413

than me?"

He laughs. "No, Merit. That was only an example. What I'm saying is, the same two things could happen to two people, but that doesn't mean they would experience the exact same stress over it. We all have different levels of stress that we're accustomed to. You probably felt the same amount of stress over your family situation as I sometimes do about mine, even though they're on completely different levels. But that doesn't make you weaker. It doesn't make you an asshole. We're just two different people with two different sets of experiences." He takes my hand again, but it's not to prove a point. He just threads his fingers through mine and holds my hand. "It annoys me when people try to convince other people that their anger or stress isn't warranted if someone else in the world is worse off than them. It's bullshit. Your emotions and reactions are valid, Merit. Don't let anyone tell you any different. You're the only one who feels them."

He squeezes my hand, and I'm not sure at which point during this conversation I fell for him, but it happened. I may look like I'm casually sitting on a bed next to him, but metaphorically, I've melted at his feet.

Between Luck and Sagan, the last couple

414

of hours have been eye-opening.

I don't even attempt to respond to all he just said to me. Instead, I rest my head on his shoulder as he wraps his arm around me. I think about what he said earlier when he told me I was really easy to like today. I find some comfort in that, because in the past twenty-four hours, he's probably seen the most authentic side of me he's ever seen. I close my eyes and readjust myself against him.

"You're easy to like *every* day," I whisper, right before I finally fall asleep.

CHAPTER SEVENTEEN

Even though it's Saturday — a day I finally don't have to pretend to wake up and go to school — I still wake up earlier than I want to. Sagan fell asleep in my room last night, so as soon as I open my eyes, I roll over to wake him up so my father won't catch him in here.

But he's not here anymore. On the pillow where he slept last night is a drawing. I smile and pick it up. On the back, Sagan has written, "I don't even know what this is, but I drew it while I watched you sleep. I thought you might like it."

I don't know what it is either, but I love it. It might even be my new favorite. I tack it to the wall.

I pull on some jeans and a tank top and then head to the kitchen, but I come to a halt when I look in Sagan's room. It's a mess. The drawers are open, his wall hangings are gone. My heart starts to beat wildly

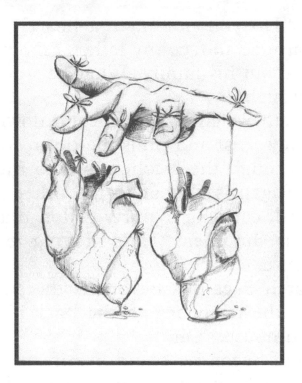

in my chest and I try to sustain the panic I feel coming. I turn to go to the kitchen and find out what happened, but I'm intercepted right outside Sagan's bedroom door by my father.

"Where's Sagan?"

"I kicked him out," my father says, matter-of-fact.

I bring my hands up to my head. "What?"

"He slept in your bed last night, Merit."

This is unbelievable. "So you kicked him out? Without even talking to me?" I spin around and look at the guest room again, hoping I'm dreaming. Almost everything is

417

gone. "Do you not have a heart?" I spin back around to face my father. "Do you not know about his family? What he's been going through?"

My father sighs. "Merit, calm down." He grabs my wrist and pulls me down the hallway, through the kitchen and to the back door. Sagan is almost to the other side of the yard, carrying a thirty-gallon trash bag over his shoulder. "He's moving into our old house."

I watch Sagan as he opens the gate and carries the trash bag to the back porch of our old house. "Oh."

"I told Sagan he could live in this house as long as he wasn't involved with either of you girls. He broke that rule."

"We aren't involved, Dad. We didn't even do anything last night. We just fell asleep talking."

My father raises an eyebrow. "Then why did he agree to move when I told him that was his only option if he wanted to date you?"

I press my lips together and look back out the door just in time to see Sagan disappear inside the house. "He agreed to move?" I ask quietly.

"Yep," my father says.

Oh. That somehow changes my whole attitude. "Can I go over there?"

"No. You're grounded."

I spin around again. "Why?"

"Let's see. For having a guy in your room. For stealing your mother's medicine. For painting my fence purple. For . . ."

I hold up my hand. "Okay. That's fair."

"For dropping out of school," he adds.

I scrunch up my nose and take a step back. "Oh. You know about that?"

"Your mother told me she's been getting phone calls from the school." My father walks into the kitchen and opens the dishwasher. He points at it, letting me know I'm getting all the chores while I'm grounded. He then turns to make himself a cup of coffee. I walk to the dishwasher and pull out a couple of plates.

"I met with your principal yesterday," my father says. "He's willing to work with you on catching up on missed assignments, but you can't miss another day of school for the rest of the year. I'll be taking you to school on Monday. And then I'll pick you up after and we'll go see Dr. Criss."

I reach for a pan and open another cabinet. "*We'll* go see Dr. Criss?" I say. "Does that mean you're also going to therapy?"

I'm half-kidding, so when he says, "We're *all* going to therapy," I'm shocked.

I turn and face him. "All of us?"

He nods. "Me, you, Honor, Utah, Victoria." He sets his coffee cup down. "I think it's a few years overdue."

I smile, because I'm relieved. *So* relieved. I've already decided I'd go to therapy, especially after that stupid crumpled-up piece of paper on my bedroom floor and the cheesy conversation it led to last night. But I really did think it was a little unfair that no one else in this family was being required to go. My father is right. This family is long overdue. "What about Mom? Will she be going to therapy?"

His face is sullen. "I'll try my best with her. I promise."

"You promise what?" Utah asks. He's walking through the back door with Honor.

My father stands up straight and clears his throat. "Clear your schedules after school Monday. We're going to family therapy."

Honor groans. "That sounds terrible."

"Is it too late to be emancipated from you?" Utah asks.

My father laughs. "You're eighteen, you're already an adult." He starts to walk out of the kitchen, but stops short and takes a step back. "Merit? What the hell is on your back?" I feel my father's fingers brush my back and I immediately freeze. Crap. I pulled on jeans and a tank top when I got out of bed, which doesn't fully cover my skin. *The tattoo.*

"Um . . ." I hear the screen door slam and look up to see Sagan standing there.

Honor leans around me and looks at the tattoo. "Uh . . . I drew it. It's only temporary."

"Yeah," I quickly agree. "It's . . . like henna."

"Honor doesn't draw that well," my father says.

I turn around and face him so he'll stop looking at it. "Dad, of course she does. Sagan's been teaching her." I look to Sagan for backup and he's immediately nodding his head.

"Yeah, Honor wants to be an artist. She's really good."

"I'm so good," Honor says.

My father watches all three of us, but then decides he can't tell who's lying. He gives up and walks away.

"Thank you," I mouth to Honor.

She winks at me and then says, "Feel like cooking breakfast?"

We're almost finished with the eggs when Victoria walks out of her bedroom.

"What's going on?" She's looking at us suspiciously.

Honor takes over the eggs while I start with the rest of the stuff. "Giving you a break," Honor says.

"Is this a trick?" Victoria asks.

"No trick." I pour water into the pancake batter. "Just making you breakfast."

Victoria doesn't stop with her suspicion. She walks slowly to an already made pot of coffee and pours herself a cup, never taking her eyes off us. "The eggs should be cooked last."

I smile. "We're learning. It's our first time."

Victoria takes a seat at the bar. "I'm enjoying this too much to stop watching."

I'm still stirring the pancake batter when I decide to lay things out in the open for Victoria. "Listen," I tell her. "I'm Moby's big sister. And sometimes big sisters do things like sneak donuts to their little brother. I'm not going to stop doing that because that's mine and Moby's thing. But . . ." I look up at her. "I'll cut it down to like once a week. If that's okay with you."

Victoria looks at me like I've been possessed. Then she nods. "I would appreciate that, Merit. Thank you."

And just like that, we come to an understanding that's been long overdue.

I turn around and pour the first pancake into the pan, just as Sagan walks in from another trip to the old house. He stops in his tracks and takes in the scene. Me and Honor cooking breakfast. Victoria standing by with a smile on her face. He soaks it up and then walks over to Honor and kisses her on her cheek. "Good morning, beautiful."

When he reaches me, he wraps his arms around me from behind in a much more intimate gesture than how he just said hello to Honor. He kisses the back of my head and then rests his chin on my shoulder as he looks down at the pancake I'm trying to make. "You win beauty pageants, bowling tournaments, track meets, and now I find out you're a chef? I think I might keep you, Merit."

"If I let you," I deadpan. *I would absolutely let him.*

"Sagan, look!" Moby says, barreling into the kitchen. Sagan picks him up and sets him down on the bar. Moby hands him a drawing.

"Oh. Wow," Sagan says, folding it in half. He immediately shoves it in his pocket.

"What is it?" Victoria asks.

Sagan shakes his head, obviously hiding

something. "Nothing. Nothing at all."

"I drew all the dead bodies the king shoved inside the mountain!" Moby says excitedly.

Victoria looks at Sagan. Sagan just laughs and pulls Moby off the bar. "Maybe we should practice drawing plants before we move on to dead bodies."

Utah intercepts Sagan and Moby and he grabs Moby and plops him into a chair at the table. "Are you excited about today, Moby?"

"Yes!"

"How excited?"

"So excited!" Moby giggles.

"How excited?"

"The most excited!"

Honor leans over me and looks down at the two pancakes I've managed to burn. "We're gonna need some practice. I think I just ruined the eggs."

Half an hour later, almost everything is done and I'm working on the last pancake when Luck walks into the kitchen. He's wearing his regulation Starbucks shirt . . . but he's paired it with his green kilt.

I hear Utah laugh from the table. "Are you trying to get fired?"

Luck grabs a cup from the cabinet. "If

they don't let me wear my kilt to work, I'll sue for religious discrimination."

I take the last pancake out and flip it onto the plate. Honor has just finished putting the rest of the food on the kitchen table when I set the pancakes down and take a seat between Sagan and Moby.

Moby takes a bite of a pancake and, with a mouthful, says, "Are you gay, Utah?"

We all immediately look at Moby. Utah spatters laughter.

Victoria clears her throat and says, "Where did you hear that word, Moby?"

Moby shrugs. "I heard it like ten years ago. Somebody said Utah is gay. Is that like a bastard?"

Utah laughs and says, "Being gay just means a guy might like to marry another guy instead of a girl."

Victoria adds, "Or a girl might marry a girl."

Luck nods. "And some people like guys *and* girls."

"I like Legos," Moby says.

"You can't marry a Lego," Victoria says to him.

Moby's face drops in disappointment. "Why not?"

My father points his fork at Moby. "It's not a living thing, son."

"So it has to be alive?" Moby asks my father. "Like the puppies you showed me last night?"

My father immediately shakes his head. "You have to stick with your own species. You have to marry a human."

Moby pouts. "That's not fair. I want to marry the puppies."

I laugh. "You're learning early that life isn't fair. Took me seventeen years."

Victoria forks another pancake onto her plate. "This is really good, girls."

"It is," my father agrees.

Everyone else kind of mutters the same with mouthfuls of food, but we're all distracted by a sudden banging on the front door. I look out the window and see a cop car in our driveway. "Oh, no."

My dad scans all of us. None of us look him in the eye. "Why do you all look guilty?" None of us speak. In fact, we all fork bites of food into our mouths at the same time, making us look even more suspicious. My father shakes his head and scoots back from the table.

No one else gets up when he opens the door. We all just listen quietly.

"Morning, Barnaby," the officer says.

"Morning. What's the problem?"

"Well . . . after we buried Pastor Brian's

426

dog at the church last night, his grave was tampered with. As was Pastor Brian's. Seems that someone moved the dog."

"Is that right?"

The officer sighs sharply. "Cut the shit, Barnaby. Did you dig up the dog again after we already arrested you for it?"

My father laughs and says, "Of course not. I came straight home and went to bed." The officer begins to speak again, but my father cuts him off. "With all due respect, you're wasting your time. The dog is dead and it sounds to me like she's right where Pastor Brian would want her to be. Don't you guys have more important things to focus on?"

The officer once again tries to get a word in, but my father says, "Do you have a warrant?"

"Well, no. We just came to speak with you about . . ."

"Good. You spoke to me about it. I'd like to get back to my breakfast now. Have a great day, crime fighter." Our father slams the door. I watch as he makes his way back to the table. It's hard to tell if he's angry or not. He scoots his chair forward and picks up his fork. He stabs at a couple of pieces of pancake and then looks up at all of us. "You're all a bunch of heathens."

CHAPTER EIGHTEEN

"What should we name them?" Moby asks. He's sitting with me in the backyard. Dad didn't say if I was grounded from the backyard or not.

"I don't know. Why don't you name one of them and I'll name the other one?"

"Okay," Moby says excitedly. He holds up the one in his hands and says, "I'm naming this one Dick."

I laugh. "I'm not sure your mom will go for that."

He frowns. "Why not? She named me Moby. I want to name my puppy Dick so we can be brothers."

"As long as you use that argument," I tell him. Sagan walks out the back door of his new house and heads toward us. He sits down in the grass next to me. I hold up the nameless puppy. "We get to name this one. Got any suggestions?"

Sagan doesn't even hesitate. "*Tuqburni*. We

428

could call him Tuck."

I smile. *You bury me.* I lift the puppy up to my face and kiss his nose. "I like that. Tuqburni." Moby stands up and grabs Tuck out of my hands. "Be careful with them, Moby."

"I will. I just wanna show Mom Tuck and Dick." He cradles both puppies in his arms and heads toward the back door.

Tuck and Dick? If I could be a fly on the wall when he tells her those names . . .

Moby disappears inside the house and Sagan looks at me. "Want to check out my new digs?"

I laugh and fall back onto the grass. "I can't. I'm grounded. And please don't ever refer to that place as your *digs* again."

"You're grounded? For how long?"

"He hasn't decided yet."

Sagan lies down beside me, and we're both staring up at the sky. "But didn't he leave earlier to go run errands? He's not even home."

I face him with a grin. I like this rebellious side of him. "You're right. Let's go check out your new digs." We push ourselves up off the ground and walk over to the old house. I haven't even been inside in over six months, since Utah started redoing the floors. It sat empty for so long, I kind of felt bad that Sagan was having to live in these conditions, but when I walk through the back door I'm pleasantly surprised. I mean, it needs a lot of work. But it's come a long way in six months.

"Wow. Utah has really put a lot of work into this place." The floors are almost complete. He just lacks the living room floors and then it looks like it'll be mostly finished. I follow Sagan down the hallway and he points to Utah's old bedroom.

"Utah is taking that room." He turns around and walks backward, pointing at Honor's old bedroom. "And if he can talk your mom into moving in over here, she'll take Honor's old room." He faces forward again and stops at my old bedroom door. "And your old room . . . is now my room." He opens the door and it's a complete mess. All of his stuff is still in trash bags and his mattress doesn't have sheets yet.

I walk over to the bed and fall down on the mattress. "It's terrible," I say with a smile.

He laughs. "I know. But it's free." He sits down next to me on the bed and his phone rings. Now knowing what each phone call could mean to him, I'm almost as anxious as he is when he retrieves it from his pocket. I can see the disappointment set in when he sees Utah's name. He answers it on speaker. "Yeah?"

"Did you take the roll of trash bags over there?"

"No, they're on the dresser in the guest room."

" 'K, thanks," Utah says before disconnecting the call. Sagan falls back onto the mattress and stares at his phone for a moment, then puts it back in his pocket.

I pull my legs up onto the bed and cross them, facing him. I want to ask him more about his family . . . what he thinks happened to them . . . if he thinks there's still any hope of ever finding out what happened to them. He must see the torn look on my face, because he reaches for my hand and laces his fingers through mine.

"I'm sure with time I'll get used to it never being them," he says. "But I still have hope."

I try to smile reassuringly, but I'm not sure it comes across that way. Because I can see in his eyes that he doesn't really have hope left for their situation. It makes me sad for him. I look at the arm attached to the hand that's holding mine. I touch the tattoo that says "Your turn, Doctor," and trace the letters.

He reaches up and presses a thumb to my forehead, right between my eyes. "Stop worrying about me," he whispers, smoothing out my furrowed brow. "I've had years to get used to it. I'm okay."

I nod, and then he pulls me down to the bed next to him. I press my cheek against his chest and we just lie quietly for a while.

I want to ask him about what my father said this morning — about how he chose to move here so he could be involved with me. But I also don't want him to know that I know.

Instead, I pull his arm closer and trace another one of his tattoos. I touch the numbered coordinates. "What's the location of these coordinates?"

"It's not that hard to figure out. All you have to do is type the coordinates into your phone."

Why didn't I think of that?

I reach for my phone and roll onto my back. I open Google Maps and type in the coordinates, 33°08'16.8"N, 95°36'04.4"W. When the location pops up on my phone, I stare at it. I zoom in. I stare at it some more. "But . . . I'm confused. The other day you said those coordinates are where you were born."

Sagan lifts up onto his elbow and takes my phone out of my hands, setting it on the bed beside my head. He's leaning over me when he says, "That's not what I said. You asked me if it was where I was born and I said, 'Close to it.' "

"You said you were born in Kansas. Those coordinates lead to our town square where you kissed me. In Texas. That's nowhere close to where you were born."

"Exactly," he says, brushing the hair from my forehead. "It's not where I was born. It's where you buried me."

I stare at him in quiet shock for a moment. I try to hide my smile, but it's hard when he's smiling right back at me. "That kiss was tattoo-worthy to you?"

He shakes his head. "I didn't get the tattoo because it was where I kissed you for the first time. I got it because it's where I met you." He slips a hand behind my neck and then slowly lowers his mouth to mine. "But the kiss was nice, wasn't it?" he whispers.

Our mouths connect, and it's soft and delicate. It's not accidental, like our first kiss, it's not deceiving, like our second, and it's not frantic, like our third. This kiss is the first genuine kiss we've shared, and I want to drag it out for as long as I can. His lips move over mine with patience, and I love the patience in this kiss more than anything else. It means we both know there will be many more that follow.

He rolls on top of me, and as soon as we get in the most perfect position I've ever been in while kissing him, my phone rings. Sagan laughs against my mouth and reluctantly pulls away. I pick up my phone and see that it's Honor. I debate not answering it, but I'm actually a little excited she's calling me. We never talk on the phone, so it's just more proof that maybe things really have changed between us.

"Hello?"

"Hey," she says. "Dad just got home. Better get your ass back over here."

I hang up and press a quick kiss to Sagan's mouth. "Dad's back, gotta go."

He wraps a tight arm around me and pulls me to him, giving me another quick kiss before he shoves me away. "See you at dinner, Mer."

I smile and run back home.

Home.

This is the first time I've ever referred to Dollar Voss as home.

If you would like more information on depression, please visit The Anxiety and Depression Association of America at https://www.adaa.org/.

ACKNOWLEDGMENTS

The thing I love most about writing is having the freedom to write what inspires me. Sometimes these stories are heavier than the actual books that contain them, and sometimes they're quirky and fun. But the one constant with every book I write is the support I receive from you, the readers. Thank you for allowing me the freedom to continue to love what I do, year after year.

A huge thank-you to CoHorts. 2017 has been my favorite year yet with you all. We laugh together, we cry together, we talk books together. I'm convinced we have the biggest online group with the fewest dickheads. I love that about us.

To my family. This deadline hit harder than most, but none of you complained. To my face, anyway. Thank you for that.

To my husband, who is my heart, my soul, my best friend. I can't do this without you. Literally. I cannot do anything without you.

Life, laundry, this career. Stick around for eternity, okay?

To Levi. You're my favorite child. I love you.

To the few who I dragged along during this particular writing experience. Brooke Howard, Joy Nichols, Kay Miles, and my mother. I LOVE ALL OF YOU!

To my editor, who would be dang near sane if it weren't for her favorite author. Seriously, Johanna Castillo, I will forever appreciate your immense patience with this book and with me.

To Beckham. You're my favorite child. I love you.

A huge thank-you to my agents at Dystel & Goderich. To my publishers at Atria Books. To my publicist, Ariele Fredman, for always rocking it, even through creating a new life.

To Cale. You're my favorite child. I love you.

And a HUGE thank-you to Brandon Adams for supplying Sagan's drawings and also for decorating The Bookworm Box with your talent. You are amazing and generous, and I'm happy to be able to call you a friend.

■ ■ ■ ■

READING GROUP GUIDE: WITHOUT MERIT

A NOVEL

■ ■ ■ ■

COLLEEN HOOVER

This reading group guide for *Without Merit* includes an introduction, discussion questions, and ideas for enhancing your book club. The suggested questions are intended to help your reading group find new and interesting angles and topics for your discussion. We hope that these ideas will enrich your conversation and increase your enjoyment of the book.

INTRODUCTION

The Voss family is quirky, flawed, and full of secrets. With everything going on at Dollar Voss, it's easy for Merit to feel pushed to the side or completely ignored. She starts to believe that it would be no great loss to her family if one day she were gone. But before she goes, Merit decides it's time to clear the air of her family's darkest secrets and force them to finally face the truth about one another. When she suddenly realizes that she doesn't want to leave after all, it's too late. Merit and the rest of the Voss clan are forced to deal with the layers of lies that have tied their family together, and the staggering power of love and truth.

TOPICS AND QUESTIONS
FOR DISCUSSION

1. Merit collects trophies she hasn't won, buying a new one whenever something goes terribly wrong in her life. Is there anything you like to collect? Why?

2. Honesty is a common theme and a big deal for Merit throughout the novel. How different would the Voss family's relationships be if they were more honest and open with one another?

3. Another prevalent theme is perspective. Luck tells Merit that after only a week he could tell that she lives in her own version of reality. How has Merit's perspective skewed the way she treats and passes judgment on herself and others?

4. Merit constantly compares herself to her twin sister, Honor; always painting herself

in a harsh, unforgiving light. How has this affected her sense of identity and self-worth? How has it affected her relationship with Honor?

5. While Merit's sense of identity is constantly in conflict with Honor's, Utah's identity is rooted firmly in what others think and believe of him. How did this lead to what he did to Merit? How did it inform his behavior afterward?

6. Merit keeps her feelings buried inside, like a lidded pot that's about to boil over, letting searing bits of truth spill out every so often until eventually pouring out every scalding secret into her letter. Why is it so easy for her to be candid about others' secrets yet so difficult for her to express her own truths?

7. "Not every mistake deserves a consequence. Sometimes the only thing it deserves is forgiveness." Consider the letter Merit wrote and all of the secrets and mistakes that were revealed in it and afterward. Do you agree with this? Why?

8. Sagan tells Merit, "*Tuqburni* is used to describe the all-encompassing feeling of

not being able to live without someone. Which is why the literal translation is 'You bury me.' " How does Merit interpret these words? What does it reveal about her self-perception?

9. Luck opens up about his own struggle with depression and attempt to take his own life. Compare his experience to Merit's. What led each of them to believe suicide was their only solution? Or that their absence would be met with indifference?

10. As Merit goes through the checklist of the Symptoms of Depression (pages 324–26), she confirms that she's experienced all of them. Think back on Merit's behavior throughout the novel and identify examples of each. Why are many of these symptoms so easily brushed aside by some as being normal teenage behavior? When do they become a sign of a deeper imbalance?

11. Despite efforts to raise awareness about mental illness, mental health and its treatment are extremely stigmatized. How does Luck try to help Merit see that suffering from mental illness and seeking treatment

doesn't make her any different from anyone else?

12. In the end, why is it so important that
Barnaby Voss decides it's time for the
whole family to go to therapy? What does
it mean to Merit and for Merit in particular?

ENHANCE YOUR BOOK CLUB

1. Have an open and honest discussion about mental health with members of your book club and/or at home with your family and friends.

2. Visit sites like the SuicidePreventionLife line.org, National Alliance on Mental Illness (NAMI.org), ProjectSemicolon.com, and To Write Love on Her Arms (twloha .com) to learn more and keep the conversation going.

3. To learn more about Colleen Hoover, check out her other books, and find her on tour, follow her on social media and visit her at http://www.colleenhoover.com/.

ABOUT THE AUTHOR

Colleen Hoover is the #1 *New York Times* bestselling author of *Slammed, Hopeless, Maybe Someday, Maybe Not, Ugly Love, Confess, November 9, It Ends with Us, Without Merit,* and *All Your Perfects.* She has won the Goodreads Choice Award for Best Romance three years in a row — for *Confess* (2015), *It Ends with Us* (2016), and *Without Merit* (2017). *Confess* was adapted into a seven-episode online series. In 2015, Colleen and her family founded The Bookworm Box, a bookstore and monthly subscription service offering signed novels donated by authors. All profits are given to various charities each month to help those in need. Colleen lives in Texas with her husband and their three boys. Visit ColleenHoover.com.

CORE

CPSIA information can be obtained
at www.ICGtesting.com
Printed in the USA
BVHW040030091222
653812BV00001B/4

9 781432 899806

PV 12/22